She had the Russians' attention now...

The gunman wasn't going to hold back forever. Knowing her chances of escape were diminishing by the second, Annja looked around until she found a baseball-size chunk of tombstone on the ground. She shifted her sword to her left hand and threw the stone in an underhanded pitch.

The rock streaked across the twenty feet separating her from the Russian as he tried to bring his assault rifle around. Too late. Annja had already sprinted across the distance. Whipping her sword in front of her in a fluid motion, she spun and slammed the hilt into the back of the man's head.

His eyes fluttered, rolled upward, and he dropped.

Annja turned toward the gates, but before she could take a step, she heard the helicopter rotors overhead. In the next instant, a spotlight picked her out of the darkness.

"Cape Cod Coast Guard! Stop right there!"

Frustrated, Annja did as she was told. Besides, she didn't have to run from law enforcement.

My producer is really going to hear about this.

Annja held her arms out and let the sword drop.

Titles in this series:

Destiny
Solomon's Jar
The Spider Stone
The Chosen
Forbidden City
The Lost Scrolls
God of Thunder
Secret of the Slaves
Warrior Spirit
Serpent's Kiss
Provenance
The Soul Stealer
Gabriel's Horn
The Golden Elephant
Swordsman's Legacy
Polar Quest
Eternal Journey
Sacrifice
Seeker's Curse
Footprints
Paradox
The Spirit Banner
Sacred Ground
The Bone Conjurer
Tribal Ways
The Dragon's Mark
Phantom Prospect
Restless Soul
False Horizon
The Other Crowd

Tear of the Gods
The Oracle's Message
Cradle of Solitude
Labyrinth
Fury's Goddess
Magic Lantern
Library of Gold
The Matador's Crown
City of Swords
The Third Caliph
Staff of Judea
The Vanishing Tribe
Clockwork Doomsday

ROGUE ANGEL

Alex Archer

CLOCKWORK DOOMSDAY

A GOLD EAGLE BOOK FROM

WORLDWIDE®

TORONTO • NEW YORK • LONDON
AMSTERDAM • PARIS • SYDNEY • HAMBURG
STOCKHOLM • ATHENS • TOKYO • MILAN
MADRID • WARSAW • BUDAPEST • AUCKLAND

Recycling programs
for this product may
not exist in your area.

First edition July 2013

ISBN-13: 978-0-373-62163-7

CLOCKWORK DOOMSDAY

Special thanks and acknowledgment to
Mel Odom for his contribution to this work.

Printed in U.S.A.

THE
LEGEND

...THE ENGLISH COMMANDER TOOK
JOAN'S SWORD AND RAISED IT HIGH.
The broadsword, plain and unadorned,
gleamed in the firelight. He put the tip against
the ground and his foot at the center of the blade.
The broadsword shattered, fragments falling
into the mud. The crowd surged forward,
peasant and soldier, and snatched the shards
from the trampled mud. The commander tossed
the hilt deep into the crowd.
Smoke almost obscured Joan, but she continued
praying till the end, until finally the flames climbed
her body and she sagged against the restraints.

Joan of Arc died that fateful day in France,
but her legend and sword are reborn....

PROLOGUE

Aegean Sea
48 BCE

"How far away is land?" Ceionius Gabinius held on to the ship's railing and silently prayed to Neptune to spare him and his men from the storm-tossed sea crashing around *Neptune's Concordia.* His stomach convulsed, but he had been sick for hours and there was nothing left for him to give up. He tilted back his head and gazed at the whirling dark gray clouds scudding across the sky.

Philemon, the ship's elderly captain, clapped Ceionius on the shoulder and smiled, revealing many missing teeth. "Are you nervous, then, Centurion?"

Ceionius shrugged off the man's hand and thought seriously of killing the captain where he stood. No one questioned Caesar's chosen army without paying a price. In his late thirties, a soldier in the military since he was a boy, Ceionius was thickset with muscle, a compact man capable of straightening horseshoes with his bare hands. His hair and beard were black as a raven's wing. The breastplate of his armor shone from hours of work on it. Rain trickled down from his helmet and the tall red plume that marked him as a commander. He carried his shield and spears over one shoulder, always ready to do battle.

"Give me a gladius, Captain Philemon, and a square yard of land, and I'll fight any man or beast." Ceionius waved toward the pounding waves. "But I cannot fight the sea."

"Then you are in luck, Centurion, for I have been fighting the sea all my life, with Neptune's good graces." Philemon gazed out at the storm clouds. "And I have won every battle I have fought. As to where land is, it lies that way." He indicated a few points to starboard off the bow. "We are now only a mile or so from the coastline. We should sail into port in short order."

Rain dripped from the brow piece of Ceionius's helmet. On other campaigns, that same helmet had dripped blood. In fact, the campaign he currently served, though in supposed secret, had earlier turned bloody. He had lost twenty-eight men and another nine were wounded, and his unit had never reached the full one hundred to begin with. Caesar was doing that to many of his units these days, shorting them to sixty. His surviving twenty-three were—as was Ceionius himself—bone tired and ready to return home to their families. Once they were in port, they would have a long journey ahead of them overland in the summer heat.

But at least Ceionius would once more have firm ground under his feet.

Philemon pulled at his beard and stared into the steadily darkening sky as if to read the portents there. "You have never said what took you to those islands, my friend."

Ceionius rankled at the casual use of the term *friend*. He did not take those assignations lightly. His friends were the men he served with, men who had trusted him and who had shed blood with him.

"No, I have not. Nor will I." Ceionius gave the captain a cold stare. The question brought up horrible memories of the caves and all of those traps that had claimed so many lives. Some of them had been left behind, but none of those could have survived the madness in those undersea chambers.

Gods, but he had thought they would go deeply enough to meet Pluto himself in the Underworld.

A cry came from the lookout astern. "Waterspout! *Waterspout!*"

Turning, Ceionius put his hand on the hilt of his gladius, as if that might somehow save him. He stared in horror at the funnel of wind and water that sped across the sea in their wake. It stood at least two hundred feet tall and contained several large fish in its embrace. A chill lanced through Ceionius as he realized the waterspout pursued them.

Neptune will not allow you to take this sacred beast from its home, Roman. The old man's dying words had haunted Ceionius's dreams since they had quit the island.

Ceionius didn't even know what the beast meant to Caesar. His orders had been only to retrieve it and bring it to Rome and to the general. The first sight of it had disturbed the centurion like nothing ever had before, and he had seen a great many things during his years campaigning.

Philemon slapped Ceionius on the arm. "Release your sword. Hold tight to the railing and the rigging if you would live." Then the old man raised his voice against the howling winds that were overtaking them. "Drop the sail! Hold the starboard oars! Pull the port oars! Double-time!"

At the hold, an officer relayed the orders to the drummer below. The tempo changed, and the slaves dipped their port oars into the water faster. The great ship angled in an effort to avoid the approaching waterspout.

Gripping the railing, Ceionius blinked against the saltwater spray that stung his eyes. Despite the crew's best efforts, the waterspout caught up with them and shattered the mast, tangling the rigging in broken yard arms as it came billowing down.

Hunkering down to avoid the maelstrom passing above them, Ceionius felt his stomach at the back of his throat as the ship twisted and turned. A great wall of water rose up from the sea and splashed down over them. Pushed by the towering wave, *Neptune's Concordia* almost laid over on its side. Screaming sailors shot across the deck as Ceionius clung to the railing.

Caught off guard, Philemon was one of the luckless men that got tossed overboard. Clawing for purchase, he fell into the white-capped waters.

Then, as quickly as it came, the waterspout was gone. The damage had been done, though. As the ship righted itself, even Ceionius knew something was wrong. The vessel felt sluggish now, though it still rocked precariously as it rode out the waves. It also no longer charted a course, flopping like a wounded animal seeking shelter.

A sailor climbed up from the hold and ran over to Ceionius. He was young and frightened, his face pale. "Where's the captain?"

"Overboard."

The sailor looked at the dark water and appeared on the verge of tears. "We are lost. The gods have forsaken us."

"What are you talking about?"

The sailor pointed to the rear of the ship. "We've lost the tiller, and the hold below has broken. We're taking on water. We're going to lose the ship."

Steeling himself, Ceionius looked for what was left of his men. Five remained on deck.

He called to them and pointed to one of the small boats lashed to the side. "Guard that boat with your lives, because they surely depend on it."

They nodded and made their way across the heaving boards, grabbing hold of the longboat and drawing their swords.

Although he feared what he was about to call on himself to do, Ceionius released the railing and ran to the hold. He clambered down the steps and arrived in the ship's waist where the slaves were chained to the oars. They called out as they pulled to the beat of the drum.

"You have to let us go!"

"You can't let us drown like rats!"

Overseers cursed the oarsmen and whipped them onward. Water sluiced across the floor, and more came crashing in as another wave smashed against the ship and flooded in through the oarlocks.

"If you're to have any chance at all, you have to *pull!*"

Ignoring them, Ceionius ran to the next hold that led even farther down to the cargo area. The rest of his men were there, the wounded as well as those guarding the thing they had brought back from the accursed island. He clambered down, boots slipping in the water.

The cargo hold was spacious, lit by lanterns whose flames fluttered like winged insects inside the glass. Amid the stores and provisions for the journey, and among the trade goods the captain had expected to profit from, the thing from the island sat wrapped in canvas sailcloth, ringed by the Roman soldiers.

Ceionius realized he was standing in water that reached his midcalf. Water in the hold wasn't unusual, but it usually wasn't any higher than the rocks carried as ballast to help keep the ship stable.

Ceionius clamped down on his fear and walked toward his men, holding one of the lanterns to illuminate his face so the soldiers would recognize him.

"Centurion." Fabius, Ceionius's second, stood ready as always.

"We've got to get the thing onto a boat." Under the canvas, it was ten feet long and six feet tall, twice as broad as a man's shoulders. Moving it was going to be difficult. His words barely carried above the rough pounding of the sea. Rolling thunder filled the cargo hold. "We're only a mile out from the shore. We can do this. Caesar needs us. We will not fail him. We will not fail Rome."

Ceionius didn't like standing next to it. None of them did. They didn't understand it, but it radiated power.

And it *clicked*.

Ceionius had thought that sometime during the ocean journey at least that hateful noise would stop. It hadn't. He heard the clicking, steady and measured. Grimly, he took up one of the lines that secured the canvas over it.

Before he could make another move, the ship lifted and tilted, and then the middle of the vessel ripped asunder. The cold sea poured in, rapidly filling the hold.

Ceionius fought to ascend, but the rushing water overtook him, lifted him from his feet and smashed him into the bulkhead. He flailed, trying to swim and divest himself of the armor that dragged him down at the same time.

Neptune's Concordia, split open like a gutted fish, sank like a rock.

Holding his breath, twisting this way and that with the current, Ceionius watched as the sea claimed the object they had given so much to recover. Somehow the ropes and canvas came free, and even underwater Ceionius was able to make the thing out.

Fashioned out of some metal, the minotaur's bull's head topped a giant's body. The horns spread wider than the thing's broad shoulders.

Trapped by his armor, unable to free himself, Ceionius

watched as the crates, the ballast and his men sank toward the ocean floor. He could still see clearly enough to watch as the minotaur reached the sea bottom first.

Struggling to hold his breath while his lungs were bursting, Ceionius knew he was about to die.

Still *clicking*—the sound carrying remarkably well through the water—the minotaur started walking.

Vision dimming, Ceionius thought he was imagining the creature come to life. Or maybe Neptune had called the minotaur home.

Then, unable to prevent himself, Ceionius breathed in the sea and his senses left him in a crushing rush.

1

Outside Salem, Massachusetts

"You should be here at Halloween."

Tramping across the marshy ground with her flashlight, searching for a firmer trail in the tall grass, Annja Creed glanced at her two companions. In the darkness of the Evergreen Harbor Cemetery, it was hard to tell them apart.

Twenty-year-old goth Colleen Digby was just shy of five and a half feet and wore all black, a skirt over skinny jeans and a hooded trench coat over that. She rustled every time she took a step, and the muddy ground sucked at her boots. Her cropped black hair had an electric-blue streak through it. Her dark makeup stood out against her pallid face.

In a black steampunk double-breasted jacket cut high in the front with a tail nearly down to his ankles, Victor Lambert's hair was cut only a little shorter than his girlfriend's, but he'd left it long in front so it dangled in his eyes. They walked so closely together that they looked, more often than not, Annja thought, like a two-headed creature.

Annja regretted wearing a dark turtleneck and cargo pants, because it smacked too much of the look her two guides favored. She wasn't even sure which one had spoken to her. Their voices sounded a lot alike. "Why Halloween?"

"The whole town loves Halloween." Colleen looked at her.

"They go all out." Victor watched the surrounding woods with his head ducked slightly, as if he thought he was going to be attacked at any moment. "Decorations. Parties. They've even talked about hanging a witch, just for old times' sake."

"He's kidding." Colleen rolled her eyes.

"Maybe I'm kidding. People go missing here, Colleen. For all you know some of the frat houses at the college grab women during Pledge Week and haul them up to Gallows Hill to string them up in the same place they killed all those suspected witches."

"They don't do that."

"How do you know? Remember when that woman went missing last year? The one who ran that herbal shop? I was told that was what happened to her."

Colleen looked at him. "Mrs. Entwhistle?"

Victor shook his hair out of his eyes. "Yeah. That was her. Weird name, Entwhistle. If you ask me, that sounds like a witch's name."

"The police found her."

"They did?"

"Yeah."

"Alive?"

"Yeah, alive."

"Nobody kidnapped her? Everybody was saying she was kidnapped."

"She's an old lady with Alzheimer's who got off her meds because she thought the herbs she was selling would work as a substitute. She got in her car and drove back to Boston." Colleen looked at Annja. "That's where the police found her. She went up to her old house and started yelling at the people who live there now, telling them to get out of her house. Totally wack, right? Old people should take their meds. There should be a law or something. You should see my grandma when she goes off hers."

Annja sighed. It was 3:00 a.m. and she was running out of steam. She'd been tramping through the woods with her "guides" since nine o'clock. "Maybe we could focus on finding the witch's ghost."

"Dude." Victor brushed his hair back with a hand. "You don't *find* the witch's ghost. The witch's ghost finds *you*. Kind of like Chuck Norris, you know?"

After listening to hours of inane conversation and now being addressed as *dude,* Annja was ready to shove Victor's face into the mud. At five feet ten, she had him by at least four inches and outweighed the scrawny guy, as well.

The late March air had enough of a chill to make Annja thankful for her wool beanie, thigh-length coat and gloves. She cinched her belt a little tighter, looking forward to her return to the hotel and a hot bath.

"We've been out here for hours and the witch's ghost hasn't found us yet." Some of her irritation came through in her voice, but she was past caring. Doug Morrell, her producer at *Chasing History's Monsters,* was going to get an earful in the morning.

Victor shrugged. "Sometimes she's like that. Fickle, you know?"

Annja couldn't believe it. "'Fickle?'"

"Yeah, you know. 'Likely to change.' Like the weather. Like the witch's ghost changes her mind, right? Gets you sometimes, doesn't get you others."

"And you know this to be true?"

"Sure. Even though she's dead, the witch's ghost is still a woman, right? Women are fickle."

Annja's grip tightened slightly on the five-cell flashlight she carried in her right hand that could have easily doubled as a truncheon. "I think that's a prejudicial over-generalization of women."

"Really? I don't." Victor nodded at his companion. "Take Colleen here. She's fickle. Aren't you, Colleen?"

Colleen nodded. "I am. It's part of my nature. I'm still struggling to integrate all my past lives."

"Your past lives?" The instant she asked, Annja wished she hadn't.

"Yeah. Four of them that Victor and I know of. Too bad you're not here about past lives."

Victor threw an arm around Colleen's thin shoulders and hugged her. "In one of those past lives Colleen was a witch who got hung on Gallows Hill. That's why she keeps breaking up with me."

"Colleen breaks up with you because in one of her past lives she was a witch?" Annja was struggling to keep up with the conversation and watch out for deep mud pits.

"No." Colleen rolled her eyes toward the dark clouds that obscured the stars. "Because I'm trying to integrate those past lives. Sometimes when I'm deep into one of them, I don't like Victor very much. Obviously, our relationship—the Colleen and Victor relationship—is solid. But some of the past lives that manifest don't care for him." She sighed. "It's just really hard being more than one person."

"I suppose it would be." Annja looked at Victor. "What about you? Got any extra lives in you?"

"None that we've found. I'm glad. It's sad enough being me." He studied Colleen. "Besides, I can't imagine how Colleen would feel if I broke up with her and went off with some other girl. It would probably kill her."

Colleen nodded. "Victor gets me, though. He knows that when I'm off with other guys, I'll be myself again soon and come back to him." She snuggled into him for a moment, and somehow they remained completely in step and didn't fall despite the sucking mud.

Annja played the flashlight beam around. The stone wall of the cemetery was a hundred yards off to her right, and the uneven coastline was eighty yards to her right. Small, white-capped waves smacked the beach.

An owl took off from one of the nearby trees. The *thump* of its wings in the wind caused Colleen and Victor to drop to their knees.

Victor cursed. "What was that?"

"Just an owl," Annja replied.

After a moment he helped Colleen to her feet. "What's it doing out here?"

"Probably hunting. They're nocturnal feeders."

Colleen glanced at the sky. "Do they travel in flocks? Was that some kind of scout?"

Annja couldn't believe college students could know so little. "Owls eat mice and rabbits and insects. A few of them eat fish. None of them eat humans."

Victor straightened. "I was a little worried there for a minute because I didn't know for sure. Glad we have an expert with us, you being an archaeologist and all."

Colleen hovered close to Victor.

Expert. Right. As usual, Doug Morrell's notes on the assignment had been spotty and incomplete. The information in the email had boiled down to: The witch's ghost is kind of like the love child of Casper the Friendly Ghost and Wendy the Good Little Witch. You know, if witches and ghosts could have a kid and she turned out evil. Find her. Get me video. This could set your star ablaze again.

Personally, Annja thought her star was doing fine. Ratings on the cable network show were better than ever, and a lot of that was because of the stories she'd brought in that weren't the half-baked, warmed-over wives' tales Doug gave her to run down. She preferred true archaeology, but the show's budget enabled her to travel.

And she liked doing the show. Having fans around the world was an unexpected pleasure.

"Tell me again," she said.

Victor walked between his girlfriend and Annja and did the honors. "There was this witch named Horrible Hannah back in the days of the Pilgrims, right?"

"Does Horrible Hannah have a last name?"

"I don't know. She might not have been married."

Annja made herself take deep breaths.

"Everybody said her father worked on a whaling ship. Back when it was still legal, I guess. Anyway, he wasn't well thought of by some of the crew. He was accused of stealing, so they hanged him and threw him overboard. But when his body dropped to the bottom of the ocean, this massive thing ate him."

Annja stopped in her tracks. "Wait. I don't remember that being in the story."

"Colleen doesn't tell it the way I do. Besides, you have to hear from all of Colleen's past lives. One of them tells the story just the way I do."

I cannot *get back to the hotel soon enough.* Annja folded her arms.

"Well, this thing felt sorry for Horrible Hannah's father because he really loved his daughter. So it agreed to give her the power to get revenge on the people that killed her father."

Evidently too much time had passed since Colleen had been the center of attention. "Because he didn't take their stuff. He was innocent."

Victor nodded. "The thing swam to shore—" he pointed "—and called Horrible Hannah to him. Except she was just Hannah then, but the horrible part is coming. The sea thing gave her witch powers and she went into Salem and destroyed that ship when it came into port. Smashed it to pieces by calling down a storm."

I'm getting a massage in the morning, Doug, and you're paying for it. Politely, Annja nodded.

"Some of the people in town saw it and decided to hang her for being a witch. And she's been haunting this place ever since." Victor smiled, satisfied with himself.

"Horrible Hannah could destroy a ship and its crew, but a group of townspeople easily captured her?"

Colleen and Victor exchanged a look. "I guess she was tired from, you know, destroying the ship and killing those sailors. That couldn't have been easy."

Annja tapped the flashlight against her thigh. "You're right. It probably wasn't easy." After tonight, there wasn't going to be another night in the cold if she could help it. She'd already searched for Horrible Hannah all she intended to.

Colleen suddenly stepped in front of Victor. "What if we go all shaky cam with this thing?"

"Shaky cam?"

"You know, run around with a camcorder and shake it and scream about seeing Horrible Hannah?"

"You mean *fake* the sighting?"

Colleen sneered. "Not fake the sighting. *Reenact* it. Victor and I have seen Horrible Hannah several times. We'll just do it over again. Simple."

Annja pinned the young woman with her gaze. "You're not serious."

Colleen thrust out her chin. "That Morrell guy is paying Victor and me minimum wage to guide you to Horrible Hannah. We agreed to do it because he also told us we'd be the stars of this story."

"There's no story, so nobody is a star." Annja held up

her hands. "Okay, that's it. I'm done. You two can wander around out here all you want, but I'm going back to the car."

"You can't just leave us here."

"If you're not at the car when I leave, I can." Annja turned and started walking through the brush back the way they'd come. She had marked the path, and the rental car wasn't more than a half mile away.

Behind her, Colleen and Victor started sniping at each other.

Annja kept walking. She would have sworn that some of the soupier parts of the marsh had migrated.

Then she heard a boat's motor in the harbor and spotted a speedboat powering toward the shore. One of the men standing behind the abbreviated windscreen held a familiar shape across his body.

Recognizing the cleanly efficient and brutal lines of an assault rifle, Annja switched off the flashlight and turned back to her guides. "Get down. *Now.*"

2

Neither Victor nor Colleen moved. They stood there and blinked owlishly as a spotlight aboard the speedboat flared to life and strafed the woods.

Grabbing hold of their jackets, Annja yanked the two forward, tripped them and dumped them in the mud behind a thicket of brush. She squatted beside them and watched the approaching watercraft.

"Hey!" Victor started to sit up and sling mud from his hands. "Why did you do—"

Annja grabbed him by the hair and shoved his face back in the mud. She put a knee in the middle of his back to hold him there while Colleen stared at her.

"I'm going to let you up in just a second, so you're not going to drown. There are guys with guns out there. Now…I'm letting you up. Don't yell. Don't even breathe loudly." Annja glanced over at Colleen. "And if you don't stay quiet, this life is going to be another past one, okay?"

Her hands clapped over her mouth, Colleen nodded.

Annja pulled Victor up but was ready to shove him down again if need be.

Wheezing, face rimed in dark mud, Victor wiped his eyes clear and glared at Annja. He looked like he was going to say something, then he started spitting and wiping his mouth with his coat sleeve.

Colleen scooted over closer to Annja and whispered, "What are we going to do?"

"We're going to stay here—quietly—and hope they go away without seeing us," she said as she watched the water through the brush.

Six men crewed the speedboat. In the shallows, two of them jumped out, grabbed the mooring lines and pulled the boat up onto the shore far enough to anchor it to a tree. They, too, carried assault rifles.

A tall man with bearded jowls took command of the group, waving them out to secure a perimeter while he remained on the boat. He spoke Russian in a gruff voice.

"Oh, my God." Colleen leaned over Annja's shoulder. "They're Russians. My mom's baker is Russian. I know the language when I hear it. They must be criminals."

Like the assault weapons, the late hour and the clandestine location didn't already give you a hint? Gently, Annja pushed the young woman back, then held up a hand, signaling her to be still.

Staring at the men, Colleen shook her head. "We can't just stay here."

"We can if you shut up. If they get on with their business without knowing we're here, we're going to be fine."

Once in position, the men remained where they were. The Russians seemed more concerned about the sea and the area to the east. Nobody was watching the forest to the west or Evergreen Harbor Cemetery. She turned to her guides.

"We have to get out of here."

Victor looked puzzled. "I thought you said we had to stay here."

"I changed my mind." Annja waited a beat to make sure they were both listening. "We're going back to the cemetery and taking a more circuitous route to the car. Then we'll get out of here and call the police." She had her satphone in her coat pocket but didn't want to use it at the moment in case the Russians could detect it. "Understand?"

Victor and Colleen nodded.

"Good. Now let's get started. Victor, you lead the way."

"Why me?" Victor complained unhappily.

Colleen raised her hand as if she was back in class. "I'll do it." She shot her boyfriend a look of disgust. "After all, in one of my past lives I was a Native American guide for the Pilgrims."

Annja couldn't resist. "I suppose that was *before* they hung you as a witch."

Colleen glanced over her shoulder. "I—"

"Keep going." Annja brought up the rear. Luck was with them. None of the lookouts saw them go.

THE LUCK ENDED in the graveyard.

Annja had been feeling somewhat relieved as they entered through the cemetery's back gate, where monuments and crypts were tall enough to provide cover from the Russians. She'd already used her satphone's GPS to log the exact coordinates of the speedboat. With any luck, the Salem Police Department or the Harbormaster's Division would be able to get here in minutes—as soon as she called them.

And then a "ghost" rose up from one of the nearby monuments. Moving swiftly and a little unsteadily, holding a bottle of Samuel Adams Boston lager in one hand, what appeared to be a drunk in a sheet intercepted Colleen, groaning.

Colleen stopped dead in her tracks and let loose a shrill scream that Annja figured hit an all-new decibel level.

Victor fainted, sprawling like a puppet with its strings cut.

The "ghost" clapped his hands over his ears spilling his

beer down the white sheet. "Stop screaming! Colleen, are you trying to wake the dead?"

Eight other "ghosts" staggered out into the open.

"Dude," said one of them, "I thought we were going to signal and do this all together."

Can this night get any worse?

The first ghost, now covered in beer, pointed at her. "It's the television chick. She *is* here!"

"Shut up, man. I told you she'd be here."

"Yeah, but she's not the one who takes her clothes off. I was hoping we'd meet that one."

That would be Kristie Chatham, the other host on *Chasing History's Monsters*. Glancing back, Annja saw the shadowy figures of men closing on the cemetery. "You guys need to run."

"We're not leaving. We've been out here for hours waiting on these—"

A fusillade of bullets from a silenced weapon chopped a cherub into bits and muzzle flashes briefly lit up the shooter.

Colleen slapped Victor's face and roused her boyfriend from his faint.

Thinking quickly as another burst of gunfire cut down a madonna, Annja shouted, "Five-Oh! It's a bust!"

"Oh, crap," one of the ghosts muttered.

They turned en masse and ran for the front gate, white sheets flapping in the wind. Colleen and Victor weren't far behind them.

A blind marksman could have taken them all out guided by the noise alone. Reaching into the otherwhere, she pulled out the broadsword Roux had helped her assemble back when she'd first met her mentor. The sword of Joan of Arc.

Roux and his young protégé, Garin, had been responsible for Joan of Arc's safety five hundred years ago. The saint's death by flame and the destruction of her sword had been defining events in both Roux's and Garin's lives. As in, they didn't seem to have an end date anymore, and for the past five hundred years, Roux had scoured the earth for the sword's pieces.

And then Annja's touch had forged the blade anew.

Now it was Annja's. Three feet of double-edged steel, naked and plain, with a broad hilt and a leather-wrapped pommel, it was a warrior's blade.

With the sword in her hands, Annja immediately felt more confident. Since acquiring the sword, her life had become action-packed, a constant struggle to right wrongs and punish the wicked.

She sprinted back toward the approaching Russians, staying to the shadows of the crypts and taller tombstones. Bullets chased her, gouging holes in the ground, tearing the bark off trees and shattering stonework.

Ducking to the side of a mausoleum, Annja took the sword in both hands and waited. The weapon, as always, felt light as she readied herself.

Two men ran toward her position. The others were in pursuit of the fleeing ghosts. Evidently the Russians didn't want to leave any potential witnesses to whatever it was they were doing.

The Russians came around the corner of the mausoleum in a two-man staggered group so that each of them had a clear field of fire. Annja dropped into a half crouch and launched herself at the first one. A stream of bullets ripped through the air only inches above her head.

She planted her shoulder into the man's midsection and felt the almost bone-breaking impact of flesh and blood striking body armor. With her headlong drive, she managed to lift the bigger man from his feet and propel him backward for a couple yards like an offensive tackle. Then her legs became tangled in his and they went down in a heap.

The other man jockeyed for position, trying to get his weapon lined up on Annja without accidentally shooting his partner. Annja did a forward roll toward the second man eight feet away to avoid the withering bursts of fire from his weapon, then came up in a crouch. Using both hands, she swung the sword and cut through the assault rifle between his hands. The weapon dropped in pieces from the man's hands as he stared down in silent surprise.

Continuing up into a standing position, Annja shifted onto her left foot, then kicked the man's head with her right. The Russian's head snapped back and he was unconscious before he hit the ground.

When Annja had both feet on the ground, she was facing the first Russian. He tried to get up, but his balance hadn't returned to him, and he was an easy target as she swung her leg and caught him full in the face with a snapkick. Blood running from his broken nose, the man flopped back but immediately tried to get up again. Annja swung her sword, catching him in the temple with the flat of the blade and stretching him out unconscious.

Letting go of the sword so it could return to the otherwhere, Annja picked up one of the fallen assault rifles, quickly recognizing it as an AK-47. She checked the magazine, discovered it was half-depleted and changed it out with a fresh one from the man's chest ammo rack. She dropped two more magazines into her pants pockets, then sprinted in pursuit of the screaming ghosts, the Goths and the remaining Russians.

SECONDS LATER, ANNJA caught up with the first of the Russians. She pulled up short, lifted the AK-47 and sprayed bullets at his legs. As a general rule, something to separate her from the people she often found herself fighting, she tried not to kill unless she had to.

The 7.62 mm rounds caught the Russian below the knees and cut his legs out from under him. He squalled in pain and fell headlong into a four-foot marble obelisk, taking it down with him.

Annja vaulted over him. Ahead of her the two other Russians stopped and swung around, bringing their weapons to bear in blistering bursts.

Annja ducked to one side and took shelter behind the thick trunk of an elm tree. Bullets embedded in the trunk and ripped splinters from the bark. The two men called out to each other, but Annja didn't understand them. Her Russian was limited but she was sure they weren't discussing their surrender.

She feinted to her left, rolling out just far enough to be exposed for a second, then rolled right and sprinted toward a mausoleum fifteen feet away that would place her out of the field of fire and out of sight. Bullets pursued her across the cemetery grounds.

Instead of staying put behind the small stone building, Annja retreated twenty yards and threw herself behind a double headstone. She hated using the grave marker for cover, because it was someone's stone, and because it looked old. She'd seen a lot of headstones in Boston cemeteries that British soldiers had used for target practice during the American Revolution. She mourned the loss of such history.

The Russians came around the mausoleum from opposite sides and nearly shot each other. They cursed— something Annja understood clearly enough—and started searching for her. One of them pointed toward the mausoleum's roof.

Breathing out, Annja aimed at the one on the left and took up trigger slack. The AK-47 went off with a loud retort and the man she'd aimed at went down as his knee buckled beneath him. The other Russian scrambled for cover behind a rosebush. Annja chased him with three shots just to keep him busy, then rolled away from her position, knowing the man had marked her from the muzzle flashes.

A hail of bullets smacked into the headstone where she'd sheltered and tore divots from the graves. Rising to one knee, Annja took aim low and fired. He screamed and the rosebush shivered.

She had the Russians' attention now. Her guides and the ghosts were surely back to the road and the ghosts' vehicles by now. She just had to stay alive long enough to get lost in the shadows. She shifted and studied the area. At the same time the rifle jumped in her hands and two more shots struck the tree beside her.

Rolling away to a new position, Annja rose to a crouch and sped through the headstones. She pointed the AK-47 toward muzzle flashes off to her left, but when she squeezed the trigger, nothing happened.

Hunkering down behind a statue of a robed saint, Annja dropped the magazine and tried to work the bolt but it wouldn't move. Without enough light to see by, she examined the rifle with her fingertips and discovered the action had been severely dented.

She should have checked the downed Russian for a pistol, as well. No time for regrets. Annja dropped the ruined assault rifle and scanned the night for the shooter. She didn't know if one of the men she'd left alive behind her had regained consciousness or if the man back on the boat had joined the sweep.

Reaching into the otherwhere, she pulled the sword to

her and got into a crouch. Heart beating like a snare drum, she stayed in the shadows as she circled around the mausoleum and headed for the cemetery's front gates. She had the keys to the rental car in her pocket. All she needed was a big enough lead to reach the vehicle. If everyone else had made it out, she would be gone in seconds.

Ten feet short of the wrought-iron double gates, Annja caught movement in her peripheral vision and went to ground, sprawling no higher than the freshly mown grass. Then rising to hands and knees, she scrambled for the nearest tree as bullets slammed into the ground and brush around her. She held on to the sword as she edged into a standing position with her back to the tree trunk.

Cautiously, the Russian gunman crept forward, calling out to his friends.

Knowing that her chances of escape were diminishing by the second, Annja found a baseball-size chunk of tombstone lying on the ground in front of her. She shifted her sword to her left hand and fisted the rock.

Taking a deep breath, Annja used the sword to shake the bushes next to the tree on her left. As soon as the man opened fire, she whirled to her left and threw the chunk of stone. Sister Mary Abigail at the New Orleans orphanage where Annja had been raised had been a big fan of softball, and a perfectionist pitching coach.

The rock caught the Russian in the chest instead of the face as Annja had intended, but it was enough to cause him to stagger back.

Before the man could recover, Annja sprinted across the distance. He shifted the AK-47. Annja dodged to her left and swung the sword, slicing through the rifle just ahead of the man's hand. Holding her ground, she stopped her forward momentum, whipped her sword back in front of her in a fluid motion, then spun and slammed the hilt into the back of the man's head.

His eyes rolled up, and he dropped.

Before she could take another step, Annja heard the helicopter rotors overhead. In the next instant, a spotlight picked her out of the darkness and illuminated her in bright light. A P.A. system blared out orders.

"Cape Cod Coast Guard! Stop right there!"

Annja did as she was told. The coast guard was used to dealing with smugglers, and they weren't gentle with them. She squinted and looked up at the helicopter as it lost altitude and hovered over her. Official markings gleamed on its sides.

Man, Doug is really going to hear about this.

The man's voice over the P.A. system got louder and more agitated. "Drop the sword!"

Seriously? Full-on assault rifles have been chewing up the real estate, and you're worried about a sword?

Annja held her arms out and let the sword drop, hoping they wouldn't see what happened next. It vanished back into the otherwhere before it hit the ground.

So did Annja's hopes for a hot bath anytime soon.

3

Standing in the long early-morning shadows that fell over Piazza della Signoria, Garin Braden was a man lost in time. Florence always had that effect on him. Pedestrians, bicycles and scooters hustled across the stone plaza as people made their way to work, but he was caught in the memory of the city as it had been five hundred years ago.

He had first seen the plaza in 1498 while still traveling with Roux. At the time, they'd already spent more than sixty years looking for remnants of Joan of Arc's shattered sword. Whatever magic made the sword—and its resurrection—possible had bound Roux and him to their lives, freezing them at the ages they had been at Joan's death. Well, at least it had done that for him. He still wasn't sure how old Roux was. The man had seemed ancient when Garin had first been apprenticed to him.

Even now, almost six centuries later, Garin still remembered the day Girolama Savonarola, a Dominican monk who accused Pope Alexander VI of being corrupt, had been burned at the stake in this place. That event had reminded Garin of how Joan had died at the stake and had sickened him. Later, during World War II, Garin had been in the city when freedom fighters battling the German regime and Mussolini were shot down in the plaza.

A lot of blood had been spilled on these stones. Garin

had taken lives here himself over the centuries. As long as the plaza existed, people would die here. It was too easy to make a point in this place.

He was convinced that was why the man who had engineered the meeting with him had chosen the area.

In his dove-gray Italian suit, Garin looked like a businessman collecting his thoughts or someone having an early-morning tryst with a mistress. His height and breadth set him apart, though. He stood six feet four inches tall before the boots added another couple inches, and his shoulders were wide enough that most men gave him a generous berth. His black hair hung straight and a carefully manicured goatee covered his powerful chin. Wraparound dark blue sunglasses hid his black eyes. He'd been told they were "magnetic."

He checked his Rolex. It was 8:03 a.m. If he hadn't been certain the man meeting him had what he said he had, Garin might have left and ordered the man killed as an example to future clients of how he did business.

The earwig in Garin's left ear crackled. "Sir."

Garin lifted his Styrofoam coffee cup to cover his response. "Yes?"

"I have identified the man meeting with you." The security leader's name was Emil Klotz, a very good man to have providing backup in a dicey situation.

"Good. So have I." Garin's eyes watched the crowded food carts off to his left. "He's at ten o'clock from my position."

"Yes, sir." If the man on the other side of the commlink was surprised, he didn't show it. Some of Garin's Dragon-Tech security people had worked with him for years, part of an international mercenary force that rivaled Blackwater. The good ones survived.

"I count three bodyguards who were already in position when I arrived."

"Yes, sir. The team confirms it."

"There will be others."

"We're looking, sir."

Garin sipped his espresso and discovered that it had grown tepid. That didn't bother him. Despite his current wealth, he hadn't always had money. When he'd first ridden with Roux, chasing after items the old man had claimed were made with Power—with a capital *P*—they had made do most of the time with what the land had provided, sharing their bedrolls with vermin. Hundreds of years had passed since, but he never felt far from those survivalist beginnings.

His satphone rang and the viewscreen showed Unavailable. Few people had his number. He picked up the device and watched the plaza, feeling the old familiar adrenaline in his veins. He was never more alive than when he stood on the edge of death.

"Yes?"

"You are at the plaza. I see you." The male voice spoke German with an Eastern European accent, and the husky tone advertised that he was a smoker. Eyuboglu was a Turkish name in origin, but the world was so transient these days that hardly meant anything. The accent meant more. He was a purveyor of ancient artifacts and by all accounts a dangerous man.

Garin resisted the impulse to look around. "If you can see me, why aren't you here? I thought this was to be an amicable exchange."

"We are searching for him." Klotz sounded unhurried and unperturbed, a professional consumed by his job.

The tall buildings ringing the plaza offered a thousand vantage points for a sniper. Garin knew that, and he knew that despite his longevity, he was still a man of flesh and blood. Yes, he had survived crippling wounds and come back whole. But Joan's sword was once more in the hands of a Champion and Garin wasn't yet sure what impact that had on his future.

"You are prepared to transfer the money we agreed on?" Garin heard a hint of anticipation in Eyuboglu's voice.

"You already have half of it." Garin baited the man who had been relegated to the role of go-between. "I've already been far too trusting in the matter."

Eyuboglu chuckled. "I've been told by others that you were a very difficult man to deal with."

"I am." Garin made his voice cold and hard. "I never forget a man who betrays my trust. Although I don't have to remember for long because those men don't live much longer."

"I've heard that, too. That's why I've sent an associate. He will be there shortly." Eyuboglu paused a moment. "You and I both know that this artifact you're buying isn't what you're really after."

Garin said nothing. He had expected further extortion. If he had been in Eyuboglu's position, he would have done the same thing. In fact, after he had his hands on the piece—and the knowledge of where it had been found—he himself intended to use it for leverage. It was the price of doing business.

"You want to know where I got it, and if there is any more of it."

Garin smiled. He hoped Eyuboglu could truly see him right now. "You and I both know that if you had any more pieces of this artifact to sell, you would trot them out and put a price on them. Don't act cavalier. I've paid a price to see this thing today. Keep me waiting and I'll simply take it."

"That would not be as easy as you think."

"Why?" Garin sipped his coffee. "Because you have the case your errand boy is carrying rigged with explosives? Because you've got guards in the plaza to protect your interests? Please. Do you think you're the only clever mind who has taken to the field this morning?"

Eyuboglu was silent.

Garin smiled again and dropped his empty coffee cup in a nearby waste receptacle. "Drop the charade and let's see if what you have is real. Because if it's fake, you're a dead man." He broke the connection. "Emil?"

Klotz responded immediately. "We have him, sir. Triangulated his cell phone signal to the fourth floor of the Palazzo delle Assicurazioni Generali. I've got a team en route."

Garin's eyes went to the blocky gray building. "Don't be overeager, and I want him whole when we take him. I can't question a dead man."

"Understood, sir."

Eyuboglu had thought the artifact was bait to get Garin to pay, but the payment Garin had made had been bait in a trap of his own. Even if he never recovered the money he'd spent to get Eyuboglu here, the price would be worth it if he could discover the hiding place of this particular artifact.

THE GO-BETWEEN WAS a nervous little man in his late forties who looked more like a clerk than a clandestine agent. He was scarcely five and a half feet tall, rotund with ferret features and thick glasses. His comb-over lifted and dropped in the wind like a flagman waving semaphore. His cheap suit didn't fit him well. He stood in front of a flower kiosk where an attractive woman with blond hair made change for a young man who'd purchased a bouquet of spring flowers.

The man looked up at Garin's approach, then pulled the briefcase protectively to his chest. "Mr. Braden?"

"I am."

"I was told to give you this."

Garin reached for the briefcase and immediately felt the solid heft of it. He turned to the flower kiosk and smiled at the young woman. "May I borrow your booth for a moment?"

She returned his smile and ran her gaze over him. "Of course. Perhaps after you conclude your business I could interest you in some flowers for your wife?"

Garin grinned as he laid the briefcase on the counter surface. "I'm not married."

"Really?" An arched brow lifted in speculation. "And you are not from here. I know this by your accent."

"No, I'm not."

"Perhaps this evening you would like to see more of our beautiful city. A private tour?" Her hazel eyes held a lot of promise.

"That does sound inviting."

She looked away, playing coy now. "Of course, if you find your schedule too filled with business, this might not work for you."

"Give me a moment to conclude this and we'll discuss the matter."

"I will be right here."

Impatiently, Garin waved at the briefcase's lock. The go-between fumbled through the combination and the lock clicked. The man stepped back.

Flipping the briefcase open, Garin surveyed the contents excitedly.

The piece was a mechanical butterfly made of a green-tinged metal. Twice as large as Garin's hand, the device lay nestled in cut foam. The body was as long as Garin's index finger and was filled with small gears that no longer quite meshed. That was disappointing. Eyuboglu had mentioned that the device was in good shape, but he had failed to mention that it no longer worked.

Gently, Garin prodded the thing with a fingertip. It was solid enough. He leaned forward and examined the stamped words he could make out. He thought they were Greek, which fit with what he knew of the original designer, but he wasn't sure.

The flower seller peered into the briefcase. "You're a collector of broken toys?"

"Something like that." With his forefinger, he shifted the foam and explored the bottom of the briefcase. The gray-green claylike substance that threaded across the space like a thick worm was plastic explosive. He let the foam drop back into place.

His satphone rang and he answered it.

"Is everything satisfactory?" Eyuboglu sounded anxious. Money meant a lot to him.

"Yes, everything looks fine." Garin closed the briefcase. He'd already memorized the combination.

Klotz whispered into Garin's ear. "We're moving in, sir. Don't worry about the remote control signal to the briefcase. We've already blocked that."

Unless there is a backup trigger. Garin reached under his jacket and fisted the Glock .45ACP he had holstered at the back of his waist. "You didn't mention that it wasn't working."

Eyuboglu chuckled. "After more than two thousand years, I would think that would be understood."

"I'm disappointed."

"Don't think of trying to take off without paying me

the other half. I have a sniper ready to put a bullet through your heart."

Turning, Garin faced the Palazzo delle Assicurazioni Generali. "Very nice. I hadn't expected that of you."

"Sir." Klotz's words came rushed. "We don't have the sniper."

"Understood, Klotz. See to your objective."

Eyuboglu didn't bother hanging up before issuing his order. "Shoot him! *Shoot him!*"

Lunging toward the flower kiosk, thinking of the beautiful young woman working there, Garin pulled the pistol and shot the little man between the eyes at point-blank range. The man looked shocked as his legs went boneless beneath him and he dropped to the flagstones. A small remote control dropped from his left hand.

A bullet cut through the space where Garin had been standing. Briefcase in one hand, the pistol in the other, he vaulted the counter space and wrapped an arm around the woman to drag her to the ground. He fell on top of her and the proximity was surprisingly pleasant. Her subtle perfume tickled his nose and made him think of that very private tour that was probably off the table at this point, though she was handling this turn of events surprisingly well.

He looked into her eyes. "Sorry."

She nodded.

Screaming had erupted in the plaza. The rifle shot echoed and rolled between the buildings. Then more bullets tore through the kiosk, ripping petals from flowers and turning them into bright confetti that floated down over Garin.

"Emil? The sniper?"

"A moment more, sir. We're fixing his position."

"At your leisure."

"Hardly the time for sarcasm, sir."

Garin grinned. "One thing I've learned, if you can't have fun when someone's trying to kill you, you're not enjoying life."

The woman held on to him. More bullets crashed through the kiosk as he listened to the screaming and the blast of scooter engines.

"Mr. Braden." Klotz sounded out of breath but calm. "Eyuboglu is ours—alive—and the sniper is dead."

"Excellent." Garin rose up with his pistol extended just as another gunman closed on the kiosk. "Emil, I am not amused," he said as he calmly shot the man twice in the face, just in case he was wearing body armor.

"Sorry about that one, sir."

Looking over the top of the kiosk, Garin scouted for other guards Eyuboglu might have had on the scene.

None of them appeared to remain.

At that moment, the woman thrust a small pistol into Garin's crotch. He looked down at her and shook his head. "Ah, and I had really started to like you."

"You'll like me more when I don't pull this trigger." The woman eased him off her but her weapon never lost contact with him. "Put your gun down, Mr. Braden."

Garin laid his pistol aside. "You know my name."

"I do." She picked up his pistol and tucked it into a large shopping bag.

"I do hope someone told you that I'm not a man to cross."

"Fortunately, after today you'll never see me again."

"I wouldn't bet on that."

"Give me the briefcase." She held out her free hand.

"Tell me who you're working for."

"That's not going to happen. Professional courtesy."

"I understand and respect that."

"Good. Give me the briefcase and be glad that I wasn't asked to kill you."

"Because you were told I would already be dead? That Eyuboglu would betray me?"

"Give me the briefcase now or I'll pull this trigger," she said more forcefully. "I'm on a timetable."

Garin handed the case over. "Since I like you, I'll tell you that there's plastic explosive in the briefcase. And it's rigged to prevent a break-in."

"Not my problem." She took the briefcase and put it in her shopping bag, as well. Then she grabbed the straps and headed out of the kiosk as police sirens began to scream a few blocks away.

Garin remained on his back in case she had more people watching her back. "Emil?"

"Yes?"

"Evidently we're going to be flushing out the other buyer today, as well."

"Never a dull moment with you."

Garin chuckled. "And I thought you said this wasn't a time for sarcasm."

"You have to keep a sense of humor in this job, sir."

4

"I know about the Abenaki people." Captain Hiram King of the Cape Cod Coast Guard was in his early sixties and still manned a desk job. "When I was a kid, I used to look for arrowheads and tomahawks in the forest. Found a few of them, too."

He was a thin, compact man with a long face, lantern jaw and big ears. Although his face was weathered from sun and wind, and wrinkled from the passage of years, Annja could still see in him the boy that he had been.

He sat behind his desk in a crisply starched uniform. "I'm not trying to tell you your business, Ms. Creed, but a story about the Abenakis would probably be a lot more interesting than that witch's ghost."

Annja was still eating her half of the cheese sandwich King had shared with her from his lunch. She'd been starving and wasn't looking forward to eating out of the vending machines while the coast guard sorted out the Russians. "I know. That's what I'd tried to sell my producer on when he gave me this story. I was hoping to do some research on the Abenaki while I was here."

"Those people have a tragic history, if you ask me." King pulled a grape from the bunch in the plastic container between them and popped it in his mouth. "They were an Algonquin-speaking tribe, but separate from the Algonquins."

"They spoke Eastern Algonquin."

King nodded. "I learned a little when I was a kid. My mother, she was part Abenaki and her grandmother tried to make her hang on to the culture." He shook his head. "Didn't take, though, which was too bad. But my grandmother, she guarded her heritage fiercely. Used to tell me stories about Azeban."

"The raccoon trickster."

"Ah, Azeban isn't always a raccoon, though."

"Right. Sometimes he's a wolverine, but he's always a trickster, always doing something to get food or to get others to do something for him. He was the one Abenaki parents told their kids about the most when they wanted to get a point across."

King seemed quite pleased with her. "You do know your stuff."

"Thank you."

"My grandmother told me dozens of those old stories. Sometimes she told them to me after I got into trouble, but more often than not I think it was to keep me interested in the Abenaki."

"Evidently it worked." Annja nodded at the collection of arrowheads and two tomahawk stones in a display case behind the coast guard captain's desk.

King unscrewed his thermos and freshened Annja's cup of tea as well as his own. He'd warned her away from the office coffee. Studying her with his faded blue eyes, he said, "You shot a few folks out there in the cemetery."

"They shot first, and I didn't kill any of them. I think they were going to kill all of us."

King tapped the typed statement lying on his desk. "I

see that. I don't see a problem getting you out of this, but there are reports to file."

"Of course."

Puzzled, King folded his hands together. "Want to tell me where you learned to shoot like that, Ms. Creed? That's not something they mention on that television show."

"My first dig I was working on Hadrian's Wall. The Roman fortification that bisected England for a time?"

"I read a little history now and then."

"Well, some of the security people were ex–Special Air Service guys. They thought I might be interested in learning to shoot. I was a quick study."

"When did you learn to use a sword?"

That question gave Annja pause, but she hurried her answer to cover. "College. I took up fencing."

"Any particular reason?"

"It was more interesting than bowling."

King pulled at one of his big ears. "Those Russians aren't saying much, but a few of them mentioned you had a sword in that cemetery."

Annja bit into the cheese sandwich.

"The pilot and officer aboard the helicopter on the scene also stated that they thought they saw you with a sword. Had demanded that you drop it. Do you have anything to say to that?"

"No."

King's eyes narrowed. "Did you have a sword, Ms. Creed?"

"Your people have surely been all over the cemetery by now. Did they find a sword?"

King sat silent for a moment. "No. No, they did not."

"So why is there still a problem?"

Opening the file in front of him, King pulled out some color printouts and spread them across his desk for Annja to see. The images were of an AK-47 that appeared to have been sliced in two. "I can't account for the damage to this weapon."

Annja glanced at the pictures, then at the coast guard captain. "You like everything nice and tidy."

"I do."

"One of the things my study of archaeology and history has shown me is that we never get the whole story. Sometimes we don't even get very much of it. The rest? We have to make informed guesses, but we can't ever prove what really happened."

"You're saying that's what this is?"

"I'm saying that I don't have any answers for you."

After a long silence, King finally gathered the images and returned them to the file. "Interesting meeting you, Ms. Creed."

"IT'S TOO EARLY in the morning for this, Annja."

"Really?" Holding on to her satphone as she sat out in the large bullpen where the coast guard teams worked, Annja couldn't restrain her irritation. She was tired, still hungry, mud-caked and needed a bath. "It's only early for those of us who have been to bed. I haven't been to bed, Doug."

Doug Morrell groaned and sounded as though he was beating his head against something. He'd done that before during conversations with her. He was in his early twenties, had gotten the job at *Chasing History's Monsters* straight out of college because his father knew people and was more interested in pop culture than history.

"I want to go to bed," she persisted. "No, strike that. I want a shower."

"What did you do?"

"Seriously? You're going to blame this on me?"

"You're in jail. They don't put people in jail for not doing anything."

"I didn't—" Annja curbed her anger. "I didn't do anything. Except maybe interrupt a Russian smuggling operation. And I didn't even do that. The Goth twins did that when ghosts jumped out at us in the graveyard."

"Ghosts?" That sparked Doug's interest immediately. "There's more than one witch's ghost?" She could hear his grin over the phone connection. "That is wicked cool. See? I told you you'd be the one to find the witch's ghost. Did you get video?"

"No video."

"Annja!" The whine was piercing. "I've told you—I need *video.*"

"I know you need video. You're always telling me you need video. Trust me, one thing I'm going to remember is that you need video. In order to have video, you have to have a witch's *ghost.* There was no ghost."

"You said there were ghosts."

"College frat boys in sheets."

"What were they doing there?"

"They came out to scare the Goth twins."

"When you say Goth twins—"

"I mean Colleen and Victor."

"I didn't know they were twins."

Annja gripped the phone more tightly. "Colleen has had past lives. In one of them she was a witch. Maybe you could do something with that."

"She's not a ghost. I promised sponsors we'd have a witch's ghost." Doug sounded disappointed. "Annja, we have to have something."

"We don't. Except me in jail, Doug, when I should be sacked out in my hotel room, and if I don't get there pretty quick, I'm not going to be happy."

"You don't sound happy now."

"I can be a lot less happy."

"Well, I'm not very happy, either. I mean, guess who's going to have to go explain to production that we don't have the witch's ghost story?"

"You only get the story if there's actually a witch's ghost."

"Why do they have you in jail? They don't arrest people for stopping Russian smuggling rings."

"I'm not exactly under arrest."

"Then why are you calling me?"

"Because the coast guard hasn't let me go."

"Then you're under arrest."

"No. They're holding me for questioning."

"It's a no-brainer. I don't know why you bothered me with this. Answer their questions."

"I have answered their questions." Annja took a deep breath. "Get me a lawyer. Somebody to come down here and break me out of this place. Captain King gave me his good-old-boy 'let's talk about the Abenaki' schtick, and here I sit." Annja gazed across the room to where Colleen and Victor sat among hungover frat boys still in muddy sheets. They all looked miserable, but Annja wasn't very sympathetic. "The Russians were arrested, and I bet they've already had breakfast, *and* a shower."

"Don't they provide a lawyer for you if you can't afford one?"

"Doug, you've never been arrested, have you?"

For a moment, Doug was quiet. "No."

"Have you ever been to a police station?"

"No."

"I don't want them to assign me an attorney. That would take forever. I don't want to try my luck with the yellow pages or jailhouse graffiti written on the wall. I want you to contact the corporate lawyers, and get someone here. Now."

Annja punched off the satphone and leaned back against the wall. Sleeping in the chair wasn't a problem. She'd learned to sleep anywhere. But she wanted out of the coast guard office and as far away from this ghost quest as she could get.

She wanted something interesting to do, some real archaeological work. No matter how mundane. There were artifacts waiting for her back at her Brooklyn loft, waiting for her research and certificate of authenticity. Then there was that chapter in the book she was in the middle of. But more than that, she was ready to go out on a dig again. Go hunting again.

If only something would break...

5

Eyuboglu looked like death walking, a famine poster victim stretched over thin bones. His head was shorn smooth. He was in his late forties, a tall man with thick-lensed glasses and a thin-lipped mouth reminiscent of a moray eel's.

Emil Klotz propelled his prisoner ahead of him, aiming him at the dark blue Ferrari FF where Garin sat impatiently behind the steering wheel. Klotz was distinctly different from Eyuboglu, average-size enough to blend into a crowd, but well-built. Also, for those who had an eye for such things, he moved like a warrior, with understated power. His short cropped brown hair and easygoing expression took years off his actual age.

Over the centuries, Garin had worked with several such men, all professional and devoted to their craft because it gave them salable skills as well as identity and structure. Without war and struggle, these types would be lost.

Klotz opened the passenger door and shoved his prisoner into the backseat, then crawled in after him. Eyuboglu's hands were bound behind him and Klotz kept a pistol in his fist.

"Hello, Emil." Garin shoved the transmission into gear and let out the clutch, throwing the sports car into the flow of traffic. Garin narrowly missed locking bumpers as he shot across lanes to get the inside track long enough to pass a delivery van. Horns blared in his wake.

"Why am I not dead?" Eyuboglu sat uncomfortably in the backseat and banged against the side of the car as Garin took the next right.

"Because I don't wish you to be dead." Garin tugged on the leather driving gloves he was wearing. The invention of the combustion engine was one of his favorite things. "You don't have to be alive if you don't want to be. Emil will gladly amend that situation for you."

Eyuboglu cursed. He didn't look at the other man in the seat with him. "What do you want?"

"Where did you find the clockwork butterfly?"

Leaning back in the seat, Eyuboglu sat silent.

Garin pulled the Ferrari onto the sidewalk for a moment and narrowly missed a small group of diners on the patio of a café. They got up from their chairs and hurried inside. "If you don't tell me where you got the butterfly, I'm going to have my associate shoot you and dump your body out of the car."

"You're going to kill me, anyway."

Stepping on the brake, Garin downshifted and reduced speed, briefly dropping into a sideways skid. They stopped inches from colliding with a bus in the intersection. As soon as the bus cleared the space, he floored the accelerator and the tires barked as they grabbed traction.

"Actually, I have no intention of killing you." Garin calmly shifted gears. "You found the device and I applaud you for that. Over the years, you've been quite good at finding things. That's valuable to me. You don't come across people with such an ability every day. You tried to gouge me on the price—"

"That device is priceless."

"Nevertheless, you put a price on it."

"You only paid me half."

"True, but if I had paid full you would still have gone back on me to try to get more. I want to cut out the middleman."

"Then what use am I to you?"

Garin looked into the rearview mirror and shook his head. "That remains to be seen. There are still a great many things I would like to see found. I don't even know what some of them are. You have worth."

Eyuboglu cursed again.

"You're becoming repetitive." Garin glanced at the iPad strapped in the passenger seat. During his inspection of the briefcase, he had dropped a small tracking device under the foam. His car was a blue dot on the online street map. The vehicle he was pursuing was a green dot.

The distance between them had diminished, and he was now convinced he knew where his quarry was headed, but that destination didn't make sense. The Arno River ran through the heart of Florence, but at this time of year only the occasional small tourist boat navigated the river.

"There's a salvager in Genoa. He found the piece."

"Where?" Garin powered down, slipped the clutch and threw the Ferrari into another sideways skid that left them pointed toward a street that allowed him to cut over and shave off one more block in his pursuit.

"Off the coast of Rome. On a deep dive."

"How did he find it?"

"I don't know. He was reticent with the information. He's not a very trusting sort."

Not giving in to the impulse to ask if Eyuboglu had given the man cause not to trust him, Garin glanced once more at the tracking screen. He'd pulled to within a hundred yards of the target vehicle. Impatient, pressing his luck, he laid on his horn and cut through the morning traffic.

"What is the man's name?"

Eyuboglu remained defiantly silent.

Garin glanced at Klotz. "Emil, please."

Quick as a striking snake, Klotz rapped his pistol butt against Eyuboglu's nose, breaking it. Eyuboglu yelped in pain and surprise as blood gushed over his mouth and chin.

"The name. At this point, we don't have a lot of time." On the tracking screen, the blue dot slid in behind the green dot. Looking ahead, Garin spotted a sleek silver Alfa Romeo 159 cutting through the traffic. The woman from the flower shop sat in the front passenger seat.

Two men in the backseat turned to look back when Garin suddenly rammed the other car's back bumper. The Alfa Romeo twisted, crashing broadside into a parked maintenance truck with a screech of metal, and showering debris from the side and part of the rear bumper, but it kept moving. So did Garin.

"The *name*."

"Sebastiano Troiai." Eyuboglu slumped back and braced himself against the back of Garin's seat.

The name meant nothing to Garin. He tapped his earwig. "Amalia?"

"I heard. I'm researching him now." Amalia Hirschvogel worked as a DragonTech researcher. Today she was managing the recovery of the clockwork.

The two men in the Alfa unlimbered pistols and pointed them at the Ferrari.

Jerking the wheel to the left, Garin narrowly missed a taxi in the oncoming lane. The surprised driver didn't veer until the last minute and ended up clipping the Ferrari in the side.

Garin sped up, intending to cross lanes again ahead

of the Alfa, but the driver cut to the right down a narrow alley. Garin had a brief impression of the vehicle plowing through garbage bins, then he was looking for the next right turn. Downshifting again, he cut the wheels hard and smacked a cart selling gelato, sending colorful iced treats sluicing forward along the sidewalk. But he made the turn.

At the end of the alley, he had to hit the brakes again to avoid an older couple, then swung by them and roared out onto Via Por Santa Maria only a couple blocks from Ponte Vecchio. The vehicle and pedestrian traffic in the narrow street made escape and pursuit almost impossible.

Fifty yards from the river, the Alfa driver pulled to the side and the doors flew open. The two men in the back got out and opened fire with machine pistols. The bullets chopped into the Ferrari and burst through the windshield.

Garin threw the car into a skid and pulled the pistol from between the seats. Sitting up, he lifted the pistol and took aim at the nearest of the gunmen as the Ferrari slid toward the parked car. He squeezed the trigger three times, shattering the glass on the passenger's side, and put all the rounds into the man's hands and chest. The machine pistol dropped and so did pieces of the man's hands.

The Ferrari slammed into the Alfa's rear and came to a sudden stop. Powder from the deployed air bags blended with the smell of gunpowder. The seat belt tightened across Garin's chest with bruising force. Trying to recover his breath, he shoved the pistol into the air bag and pulled the trigger. The air bag deflated and the spent bullet ended up somewhere in the engine compartment.

The door was jammed, but Garin cleared it by throwing his shoulder against it. Metal screeched as he shoved the door open farther, then he was outside, taking cover behind the wrecked Ferrari, scouting for the other man.

"Emil?"

"I'm fine."

The back door opened with another screech. Eyuboglu toppled out onto the street, his lower face a mask of blood. He remained prone, cursing loudly. Klotz stepped over the man with his pistol in his fist.

"There's another one."

"You got him with the car." Klotz rose with the pistol in both hands and peered over the rear of the Ferrari.

Rising, as well, Garin saw the second man pinned between the two cars. Blood ran down his chin and dripped onto his chest as he panted for breath. The machine pistol dropped from his nerveless fingers. The impact had come close to cutting the man in half and he wouldn't survive his injuries, so Garin put a bullet through his brain.

Thirty yards away, the driver and the woman from the flower shop sprinted for the river. Pedestrians got out of the way as the driver brandished his pistol.

Garin took up the chase and Klotz matched him stride for stride. They gained on the fleeing pair immediately, but there was no clear shot to put either of them down.

At the bridge, the driver turned suddenly and brought up his weapon. Pedestrians who had already been backing away from the pair dove for cover. Garin didn't know whether he or Klotz hit the pavement first. They both came up firing and their bullets struck the driver in the chest, turning his white shirt bloody.

The driver fell in a loose sprawl. Behind him, the woman ran along the bridge. The briefcase only slowed her slightly.

Garin ran after her, leaping over the pedestrians that cowered on the street. "Amalia."

"Yes."

"I left an iPad in the rental car."

"Wiping it and crashing the drive now."

As he approached the bridge, Garin lengthened his stride. He wasn't worried about the police picking up his trail. He knew how to disappear, and there were no finger-prints or DNA left to track him. Eyuboglu didn't know his real name even if this Melina did, and the bank account wouldn't track back to Garin even if the police were able to get past the Swiss bankers.

All he had to do was disappear, and after hundreds of years of practice, he was good at that.

He'd do that immediately after he had the device.

Ahead of them, the woman evidently realized she'd never make it across the bridge because she halted half-way out. Then she glanced into the sky.

That's when he saw it. A small, four-passenger Cessna airplane with pontoons rapidly descended toward the Arno River. The river wasn't deep enough at this time of year for a powerboat to get far, but it was plenty deep enough to provide a landing strip for an amphibious aircraft.

The plane plunged down with full flaps and dropped like a swan toward the river as the woman threw herself over the bridge. The jump wasn't far and she hit the water feetfirst cleanly.

Without hesitation, Garin threw himself over, as well, followed instantly by Klotz. They struck the river only a short distance behind the woman. Garin held his breath as he sank and scanned for her, then his feet lightly touched the shallow river bottom and he pushed himself up. He swam with strong strokes, gaining ground rapidly.

The Cessna landed and came to a relative halt in the river as the pilot used the propeller thrust against the slow current. A man shoved his head and shoulders through the open door and fired an assault rifle. The bullets ripped through the water, missing Garin by inches.

"Emil, take the gunner."

Klotz pulled up, treaded water and lifted his pistol. The sharp cracks echoed across the river and the gunman toppled into the water.

Garin clasped the woman's ankle and yanked her under. The Cessna could hold a pilot and three passengers, so the possibility of another gunner remained, and the pilot would probably also be armed.

It made him wonder who was behind this effort to secure the device away from him. Not many would have known of its history.

The woman clearly thought he intended to drown her and fought like a tiger. Instead, Garin eased his grip on her and flicked through the briefcase lock's combination to retrieve the mechanical butterfly. Keeping himself turned away from the still-struggling woman, he closed the briefcase and abruptly turned and let her land a kick to his face, falling away as if she had stunned him.

She grabbed the briefcase and swam toward the plane with renewed vigor as Garin surfaced beside Klotz. He put a hand on the man's shoulder. "Let her go, Emil."

Klotz lowered his pistol.

Garin began to swim away from the plane. Another gunman was indeed aboard and a line of bullets stitched the river.

Together, Garin and Klotz dove beneath the surface. When they came back up ten yards away, the woman had already boarded the plane and the aircraft was taxiing back toward the Ponte Vecchio. Nearly a thousand feet of river lay between the old bridge and the Ponte alle Grazie, the next bridge to the southeast. A good pilot could get a four-seater airborne in that time.

The Cessna's pilot was good. The aircraft was climbing steadily into the sky after narrowly missing the Ponte alle Grazie when Garin took out the detonator they had recovered from Eyuboglu's man. He armed the detonator, then pressed the button.

Instantly, the Cessna turned into a roiling ball of orange and black flame as debris rained down over the Arno River and the surrounding city.

Still clutching his prize, Garin swam to the other side of the river. He had to get out of the city, then he'd find out what he and his mysterious competitor had fought so hard to acquire.

6

"Well, go ahead. Do something."

Sitting on the floor with her back to the wall, her arms crossed, Annja studied the large black woman lying on one of the few benches in the general lockup who'd just spoken to her. What had she gotten herself into?

As pleasant as Captain Hiram King had been to talk to, he hadn't been understanding of Annja's situation. He wanted the sword found. He wanted more answers. And maybe he was a little suspicious of how Annja had turned up in the cemetery in time to intercept the Russians.

Closing in on three hundred pounds, the woman with her in lockup looked like a Sumo wrestler squeezed into a bright, lime-green spandex outfit. She might have been a jogger, but her garish makeup suggested otherwise. One of her front teeth was missing. Another was capped with gold.

"You gonna say something?" A threatening tone underscored the woman's question.

Another half dozen scantily clad women of different races filled the remaining benches. Colleen was curled up in the corner of the cell, hugging her knees.

Uneasy at being singled out, Annja looked at the woman. "Are you talking to me?"

The large woman knitted her brow, which caused her multihued eye shadow to bunch up in pools of neon color.

"'Are you talking to me?'" she minced. "Don't go all De-Niro on me. I'll pull your hair out. Oh, yeah, I'll get real all over you."

Annja paused, thinking it was still a long time till morning if Doug didn't get a lawyer out of bed to spring her. "What is it you want me to do?" She couldn't want her space on the cold tile floor.

"Little Miss Thang over there said you were a television star." The woman's accent wasn't quite Bostonian, but she'd been in the region long enough to flatten out her *R*s.

"Do I look like a television star?"

"No, you don't."

Annja leaned her head back against the wall and hoped that the big woman had made her point.

"So you tellin' me Little Miss Thang was lyin' to me?"

In the corner, Colleen glanced up. She caught Annja's gaze and shook her head, pleading with her wide-eyed.

"Cause if she's lyin' to me, I'm gonna pull that black straw right outta her head."

Annja couldn't help wondering if the woman had some kind of hair fetish. "No. She's not lying. I'm on a television show."

"What are you? Like one of them girls that shows prizes on *The Price Is Right?*" The large woman glanced at the others and smiled. "Over here we got a brand-new car!" She mimed pointing to a showcase with a theatrical flourish.

On cue, the other women all smiled and nodded. "That's right, JuJu Bee. You tell her."

Annja didn't see why she needed to be told anything, or what—exactly—was being told. All in all, her stay in jail was becoming decidedly uncomfortable.

"Is that it, then? You some kinda game show hostess?" Juju Bee demanded.

"No."

"Weather girl, then?"

"No."

Juju Bee huffed. "I'm gettin' bored. You don't wanna see Juju Bee when she's bored."

"Archaeology."

For a long moment, Juju Bee thought about that, obviously stumped. She even checked with her peanut gallery, but nobody had any answers for her. Reluctantly, she looked back at Annja.

"It's a history show. I dig up stuff." Her professors would groan in collective unhappiness at her calling *Chasing History's Monsters* a history program.

Colleen chose that moment to speak up. "She looks for ghosts."

Juju Bee shifted her attention to the small Goth girl. "Who pulled your string, Bony?"

Colleen looked away.

"Ghosts, huh?" Juju Bee spoke to Colleen, who didn't know it because she was busy staring at her feet. "I'm talking to you now."

"Oh." Colleen smoothed the hair from her face with a shaking hand. "Okay. Yeah, she came up to see Horrible Hannah."

Juju Bee frowned in derision. "That old story? No truth in that. Story to scare kids." She looked back at Annja. "Take more'n some old ghost story to scare me. I've had a .45 shoved up into my face, an' I pounded the guy who done it." Juju Bee curled one massive fist and shook it. "That's power right there. That's what that is. *Power.*"

The other women nodded.

"What they lock you up for?" she asked Annja.

Colleen spoke up excitedly. "She got in a fight with Russian gangsters."

Juju Bee treated Annja to a glare that was equal parts doubt and disdain. "That right?"

Tired of the woman, Annja just smiled. "They locked me up because I didn't answer questions the way they wanted me to."

The peanut gallery drew back in shock.

"That right?" Juju Bee sat up on the bench, which creaked under her weight. "You tired of answerin' my questions?"

"If you had interesting questions, answering them might help while away the time, since you're not going to be quiet and let anyone sleep. But you don't have anything interesting to say."

Juju Bee got up ponderously and flexed her big hands. Stepping forward, she closed on Annja.

Annja rolled to the side and got to her feet. Even though she'd known Juju Bee was tall, she was surprised to learn that the woman was a full head taller than she was. Annja backed away, staying just out of reach.

"Don't make me chase you." Juju Bee kept advancing.

Not about to get hammered by an Amazon in neon-green spandex, she took another step back and felt the bars behind her. Immediately, Juju Bee swung a big fist at her head. Annja chop-blocked the woman's wrist and knocked her hand aside. Juju Bee's fist thudded against the bars. The woman yelped and drew back her bloody knuckles. She sucked on them, and Annja hoped that the woman would think again before continuing her attack.

"Just gonna make me beat you harder." Juju Bee set herself and swung again.

In these conditions it would play out in her opponent's favor if the fight was allowed to continue, so Annja ducked the blow—again with the right hand—and slipped behind

Juju Bee. She caught the woman's left arm, swept it behind her and levered it up between her shoulder blades.

Juju Bee yelled in pain and attempted to spin around, but Annja maintained her hold on the arm with her left hand, then placed her right behind the woman's head. Annja pulled up the trapped arm and shoved Juju Bee's head face-first into the bars.

Juju Bee's head slamming into the bars rang like a bell. The woman quivered like a mass of Jell-O, and the lime green looked suddenly more fitting on her. Somehow she found the strength to turn around.

Annja set herself again, surprised that the woman was still erect. Then she saw the glazed lack of comprehension in her dark eyes.

Weakly, Juju Bee collapsed in a huge, loose pool in the middle of the cell. A moment later, she spat out her gold tooth and passed out.

The other women gazed at her in disbelief.

Cautiously, in case one of the others felt like championing her fallen friend, Annja put her hands down and walked over to the empty bench. She sat down, discovering that it really wasn't any more comfortable than the floor. Yet there was a hint of satisfaction in claiming the bench.

"You knocked her out!" Colleen scrambled up from the floor and joined Annja on the bench like they were comrades-in-arms. "That was incredible."

"Thanks." Annja didn't know what else to say.

"She's really lucky, though." Colleen squeezed her hands into small, bony fists. "I was about to flip over into One-Eyed Myra. I could feel her there, just in the back of my mind."

Even though she felt positive she was going to regret it, Annja couldn't resist. "One-Eyed Myra?"

"A pirate. I sailed with Blackbeard before I got my own ship and crew."

"Oh." Annja leaned back against the wall.

The door at the end of the room opened and a young sheriff's deputy entered, followed by an older, graying man in a suit. The deputy looked at Annja. "Your attorney is here."

Sighing in relief, Annja got off the newly won bench and walked to the cell door as it clanged open.

The deputy looked down at the unconscious woman on the floor. "What happened to her?"

One of Juju Bee's friends spoke up quickly. "It was that TV woman. She done it."

The deputy stared at Annja.

Annja crossed her arms. "Really? This is going to be an issue?"

The deputy grinned. "No. It isn't."

He started to shut the door when Colleen cried out, "You're not going to leave me here, are you?" Colleen sat perched on the edge of the bench. "You can't just leave me."

Annja turned to the lawyer.

He held out his hand. "Thomas Costin. Your producer, Doug Morrell, called me." The lawyer looked as if he'd be more at home in a courtroom than a holding tank.

"Did Doug mention the guides I had with me tonight?"

"No."

"Will it be a problem getting them out, as well?" Turning, Annja saw Colleen standing at the bars of the door, gripping them tightly, her expression desperate. She looked like one of those big-eyed kids in Japanese animation.

Costin cleared his throat. "The charges against them aren't any more serious than they are against you?"

"Not to my knowledge."

Costin looked at the deputy and lifted an eyebrow. "Well, then."

The deputy shrugged and opened the door again. Colleen was through in a flash and wrapped around Annja. Although she was nearly bowled over by the younger woman's glee, Annja was observant enough to notice that Colleen held Juju Bee's gold tooth in one fist.

Must be One-Eyed Myra's piratical influence.

7

Gently, Garin placed his prize on the desk in the extravagant hotel suite. Immersion in the river hadn't hurt the
clockwork butterfly, but it hadn't washed away any of the
layers of blue-green encrustation, either. Wearing clean
pants and a turtleneck, still refreshed from the shower he'd
just had, he took a seat to study the object. A new Glock
pistol rode at the small of his back.

He ran his fingers over the encrustation, feeling the
jagged edges of it in some places. Evidently someone had
tried to clean it.

What are you? Garin turned the butterfly over. *Better
still,* what *were you and where did you come from?*

In the beginning, the butterfly had probably been a
work of art. Given the architecture of the thing—the small
wingspan to compensate for the weight of its composit
metal—it had probably never flown.

Probably. The possibility of the butterfly in flight was
intriguing. The object had obviously been underwater for
quite some time. It was possible the bits and pieces of the
original design had been thin and delicate, lighter than he
could imagine.

In the beginning, it might have flown. He liked to believe that.

Sighing in irritation, Garin shifted his attention to the

computer bag beside the desk. A DragonTech security team had brought it here. He opened it and reached inside.

Pulling out his iPad, Garin brought the device online and Skyped to an encrypted connection. A moment later, Amalia Hirschvogel appeared on the screen.

"Good afternoon, boss." She smiled, distracted. Round-faced and wearing black-framed glasses, she was a vibrant young woman who was one of the smartest people Garin knew when it came to computers. She was also an aficionado of pop culture, as evidenced by the Deadpool T-shirt she wore. A blue and white streak stood out starkly against her dark brown hair. "Still safe, I see."

"Yes."

"I heard about the airplane blowing up over Florence. Caused quite the stir. I suppose you had a hand in that."

"I did."

Her image went away for a moment, replaced by a You-Tube video of the Cessna exploding against the bright blue sky.

"That video has gone viral, by the way."

Garin grimaced. He didn't like calling attention to operations he wanted kept off the books. "In retrospect, perhaps I should have let those people get away."

The airplane footage disappeared and Amalia's visage returned. She grinned. "Not like you to let somebody get away after they try to kill you."

"No, it isn't. Is there any way to make the video footage *less* viral."

"Sure. Working on it now." The quick syncopation of her striking the keyboard keys echoed in the background. "I've got a team covering the video with viruses everywhere they find it. I've caused YouTube to shut down twice." She grinned again. "People hate it when you do that, and YouTube hates it even more, so it probably won't

be long till they dump it from their site. You've also purchased the original video, by the way. Under another name,
of course."

"Why did I do that?" Amalia's excitement was infec-
tious and Garin found himself smiling, as well. Or maybe
that was just because he had secured the butterfly.

"You did that because you've also issued a cease and
desist order to YouTube in order to maintain your rights
concerning that property. Now that you own it."

Fascinating how quickly the young woman worked, and
how many different strategies she could come up with in
such a short time.

"I also notified CNN and other news networks that they
couldn't air it, either. There were three other tourists with
cameras out at the time. They got footage, as well, not as
good as the first, but you now own those, too, because they
were good enough."

"Always wise to have a monopoly."

"I thought you'd like that. Other people got shots of
debris falling after the explosion, but that's not nearly as
interesting as watching a plane turn into a fireball in mid-
air. Those videos will drop out of sight quickly enough on
their own because they don't have the pizzazz they need to
remain viable. So you'll be protected there. It's just hard
to go unnoticed in the digital world."

"I've noticed." Sometimes, Garin missed the old days.
Not as often as his former mentor, though. Roux was forever griping about new technology. Clandestine arrangements were at greater risk these days. Being able to meet
a man in an alley behind a bar and fill his guts with a
length of steel had often been a solution for Garin back in
the day. It had allowed him to be more personally hands-
on in business transactions.

Garin, however, wouldn't give up today's technology for

anything. Not when it had created digital dollars and bank accounts that could be accessed by computer…and a variety of ways and means to hide or ferret out fortunes. A man just had to be more patient, more careful, in his dealings.

"What have you found out about Sebastiano Troiai?"

"The background the woman gave you checks out. Troiai is a salvager based in Athens. Does a lot of work around the islands."

That news further excited Garin. Everything about the butterfly find was falling into place.

On the iPad's screen, Amalia disappeared and a website for Troiai Salvage popped up. Initially, the site showed up in Greek, then changed over to German.

Garin read through the information quickly, knowing Amalia would have a summary ready for him, as well. Sebastiano Troiai was featured in several of the photographs on the site.

He seemed to be in his late twenties or early thirties: athletic, trim, with a headful of dark ringlets. A five-o'clock shadow covered his lower face. He had tribal tattoos on his biceps and wore gold chains the site claimed he had found on salvage jobs. Judging by his seeming ease in front of the camera, dressed in swim trunks and standing in profile with his arms crossed in front of a sailboat, Troiai had a narcissistic streak.

"Troiai is a fourth-generation salvager." Amalia reappeared on the iPad screen. "He also offers day trips and fishing cruises to help fund the marine expeditions. Evidently the salvage business isn't terribly solvent, based on the peek I took at his financials. He's a risk-taker, in the water and out of it. He was fifteen years old when he and his father got trapped in a sunken cargo ship. His father died. But that didn't keep him from getting back in the water with his grandfather. When his grandfather passed away, Sebastiano inherited the salvage business. Over the years old ship's logs indicate that he's managed to put together a group of investors on occasion. They've missed more times than they've hit, but he's made enough money to stay afloat. Pardon the pun."

Garin's respect for the man rose. "Is there any mention of the clockwork butterfly on his site?"

The website returned to the iPad screen and Amalia quickly flicked through the pages. "Just one. It was brought up in a collection of odds and ends that Troiai scraped up from the ocean floor."

Touching the screen, Garin manipulated the image, expanding it. A blue-green lump, the butterfly—and he only knew that's what it was because it was listed as a model of some sort, presumably decorative—lay amid shards of pottery and three intact amphora. The containers weren't as encrusted as the butterfly, suggesting that perhaps they had come from a later time period.

"Want me to get rid of the image?" The screen went back to Amalia.

"I don't think it will matter," Garin replied thoughtfully. "You can hardly tell what it is. Is Eyuboglu's name mentioned in Troiai's files?"

"I've got a copy of a sales receipt here."

Almost instantly, the sales receipt showed up on the screen. It listed the "model" and four other items, including one of the sealed amphoras. Amphoras were always a mystery and a gamble, depending on how much a buyer was willing to pay for one. Usually they only contained seed, dry foods, oil or spice. But occasionally they had been used as hiding places for coins and jewelry. Eyuboglu had probably had buyers for the other things, but he'd realized that the butterfly would be ideal bait for an assassination attempt on Garin.

"Can you get rid of the receipt?"

An instant later, the receipt vanished, melting away to reveal Amalia's self-satisfied expression. "Done."

"Thank you."

"I'm here to serve." She pushed her glasses up her nose. The statement held just a hint of sexual entendre. Garin knew the young woman was infatuated with him. Even with her exceptional cyber skills she couldn't dig up the truth about him. Part of her attraction to him, he knew, was the mystery he presented.

"I'd also like to find out who convinced Eyuboglu that setting me up was a good idea." It would probably turn out to be someone he'd bested in business, or love. People with money tended to have long attention spans.

"Already working on that. I've got someone digging through Mr. Eyuboglu's recent business dealings. We'll find out who it was."

Garin nodded. "In the meantime, do you have anything on the third party to our transaction?"

"I identified the flower woman." Amalia tapped at some keys.

An image of the beautiful woman who had been in the flower kiosk took shape on the screen.

"Her name was Claudia Golino."

"Italian?" Garin had thought so, based on the accent.

"She was." The image shifted, running through a series of scenes featuring the woman in different roles, including one with her firing a pistol into the face of another woman. "For a time, she was a contractor for the CIA and MI6."

"Pedigreed." Garin was impressed. The woman had not been cheap, and she'd be missed by the contractor who'd set her on Garin's trail. *Not my trail. On the trail of the butterfly automaton.* That was an important distinction to keep in mind.

"Very pedigreed. Golino specialized in reacquisitions of things that had gone missing. Government documents. People, et cetera."

"Do we know who she was working for?"

"Not yet."

"But we know people in the CIA and MI6."

"We do."

"Let me know when you find out."

"The very instant."

Garin broke the connection. He pulled the iPad closer. All of his files were heavily encrypted and password protected. Within a few minutes, though, he'd opened up what he was looking for.

The folder contained several drawings of clockworks copied from ancient texts and scrolls. Putting that collection together had been a very expensive enterprise, and it had taken him over a hundred years of meticulous research. Despite the arrival of the digital age, that task had not gotten any easier.

During his time with Roux, the old man had constantly been on the lookout for artifacts. Since even before Joan had lost her sword. Those forays into the lost parts of the world had been filled with danger and excitement, and Garin had learned a great many things. In addition to martial prowess and battlefield expertise, Garin had also become educated about several aspects of history. He knew he would never know everything Roux knew, but Garin had learned more than the old man had counted on.

In Constantinople, more than thirty years before the fall to the Ottoman Empire in 1453 and the city's subsequent renaming to Istanbul, Roux had come across an automaton that had fascinated him and put a fear in the old man that Garin had never before seen. At that point, they hadn't yet lost Joan to the English. That fear lay ahead of them.

The automaton had been a silkworm. When it was wound, the clockwork had "spun" a wire strand, then folded in on itself and reopened as a silk moth. Still little more than a boy at that time, Garin had been enraptured by the mechanical creature. It had been impossibly small and delicate, and so cunningly made he hadn't been able to fathom it.

Once he had found out about the clockwork from gossip, Roux had killed four men and one woman to get it. Garin hadn't thought anything of the bloodshed. He and the old man had killed their way through several parts of Europe and into Russia. Roux had always seemed to be following an agenda, but Garin had never been privy to it.

Back in the rented rooms they'd taken, Roux had examined the clockwork, made notes about it in one of the thick journals he had always carried.

That clockwork, and other items like it, had been some of Roux's deepest mysteries.

And now Garin felt certain he had his hands on one of them. He took out a new cell phone from the electronics bag and turned it on. While it downloaded his files, he went over to the room's wet bar and checked out the supply of beer. By the time he'd made his selection and poured it into a glass, the phone was ready to go. He brought up the number for Roux and punched the call through.

Of course, the old man didn't answer. Roux insisted that he was the master of his time, not some electronic handheld. The attitude made getting in touch with him an exercise in frustration.

Irritated, Garin tapped in a text, then took a picture of the butterfly and sent it along, as well. Then, knowing there was nothing else he could do at the moment, he settled in to wait.

Roux would see the message and the image. Then he would call back. Garin felt certain about that.

8

Idly stirring his glass of Scotch with his cigar, Roux sat at the card table, his mind clear. He loved games of chance, and he especially loved Texas Hold 'Em.

He had maneuvered himself into this game in the small room of the magnificent penthouse in one of Paris's largest hotels for two reasons. The game, as it was, created a welcome diversion and tested his skills on a level that didn't often get challenged. Primarily, though, he was there to deliver punishment. Making money off the arrangement was a secondary concern and merely counted, to Roux, as a means of keeping score. He was wealthy enough by any measure.

A frequent player in Texas Hold 'Em tournaments, Roux's face was known to diehard fans of the game. He had, however, avoided the attentions of ESPN. He loved playing cards, and he hated that he could never allow himself to become a champion. That would have put him too much in the limelight and he couldn't have that. It was getting increasingly harder to hide the fact that he'd lived hundreds of years.

Over the past few centuries, several legends and half-truths had sprung up about him, about the things he'd done on occasion. Some of those stories were outright lies, of course, yet the hint of magic clung to them, and rightly so.

In the dining room last evening, he'd worn a nice suit and had settled in for a dinner with a couple of charming young women. He'd gone to the hotel with a plan to get into this very game. The women had been there as his backup plan, in case things hadn't turned out as they had. Young women could sometimes be as exciting as wagering and watching the River shift as the cards were turned in Texas Hold 'Em.

Halfway into the meal, Faisal bint Saud, a cousin—he claimed—to the princes of the House of Saud, had approached Roux's table. He was an elegant man with impeccable manners and a memorable baritone he'd cultivated to suit his suave appearance. Tall and good-looking, dark complexioned with soft brown eyes and a meticulously trimmed beard at his jawline, Faisal had introduced himself.

"I have seen you play in Vegas. Twice. I was there as a player, as well." Faisal had ignored the attentions of the young women with Roux, even though he'd known they were watching him, of course, because he was a peacock. The man was well aware of himself and liked the impression he made on the opposite sex.

Roux had looked at the younger man and smiled benignly. His white beard made him look somewhat feeble, especially because he also had a thin physique and wore a suit that didn't fit. "I'm sorry, I don't remember you. Did we play each other? I try to remember other people I play cards with."

The reply was designed to offend Faisal as well as convince him that Roux wasn't exactly the sharpest tool in the shed.

Faisal's smile had been forced, but he'd made the best of it. "No, no, we never played each other. Though I have to say I was impressed by your skill at the tournaments."

"Thank you." Roux had gestured a little broadly, just enough to convince Faisal he'd perhaps been drinking too heavily that night. He'd known the hook had been set when a feral light gleamed in Faisal's eyes.

Now that it was the middle of the afternoon the next day, he no longer felt certain getting a seat in the game was a desired event. Playing for so many hours against the odds and against the machinations of his host was becoming tedious. Still, he sometimes enjoyed playing with his prey before springing his trap.

The other men at the table looked haggard and worn. Faisal and two of his cronies remained in the game, and they'd had to give one another a pot to keep them all in the game. Two other players had already left, cleaned out and disgruntled by the evening's outcome.

Faisal, his tie askew and his eyes hollowed from drinking and nearly sixteen straight hours of playing, looked at Roux. "The bet is to you."

Deliberately, Roux shuffled through the stacks of chips in front of him. He'd more than doubled his stake, and the men had intensified their efforts to separate him from what they considered to be their profits for the night.

Roux plucked chips from the stacks and pitched them into the pot in a spray of color, adding to the already considerable pile. "I'll raise five thousand dollars." He never even checked his cards.

Faisal remained motionless in his plush chair and inhaled slightly, nostrils pinching for a moment. That was one of the tells Roux had spotted during the game. The other men had them, too. They were, possibly, decent players, but together they made an excellent tag team of cheaters.

The three of them glanced at one another, then at the

dwindling chips in front of them. Roux was steadily taking their money and they hadn't yet found a way to stop him.

Roux yawned, all part of the game. Then he smiled easily. "Sorry, gentlemen. I guess I'm more fatigued than I thought." He took another sip of his Scotch, then lit the cigar and blew a plume of thick, blue smoke into the air.

Evidently Faisal and his cronies reached a decision. They tossed their chips into the pot, as well, figuring with three-to-one odds that one of them would come out ahead.

Roux turned his cards over, exposing the four tens he'd managed to put together counting the two in his hand.

Faisal looked decidedly unhappy and one of the other two men, the young one named Otto who spoke with a German accent yet sounded like he'd spent time in South Africa, cursed vehemently and threw his cards on the table.

Faisal leaned back and sipped his drink. "You've got an incredible streak of good fortune going."

Grinning magnanimously, Roux raked in the pot and began stacking chips. "It's just experience. I told you that." He shrugged. "Let me know when you've had enough."

"I would like to take a small break."

"Of course."

As one, Faisal and his partners got up from the table and wandered over to the wet bar in the corner of the room.

Roux hummed happily, but he was wondering how much further he could push his luck with the men. According to what he'd learned about them during the game, they weren't necessarily dangerous. They were just cheats, banding together to fleece less experienced players.

Roux took out his cell phone. He'd missed two calls. Both from a number he wasn't familiar with. There were very few people who called Roux on this number.

He also had a text. Curious, and knowing that paying

attention to his cell would gall the would-be malefactors, he pulled up the message.

I have found a clockwork.

Surprise and consternation tightened Roux's chest. Memory of the clockwork creations plagued him. They were some of the worst things that had been set loose in the world, and there were a great many things out there that shouldn't be.

And now Garin had one?

Roux prayed that it wasn't so. Noticing that there was an image attached to the text, he brought that up, as well, having to struggle to remember how to perform that particular task. Once he'd accomplished it, he stared at the misshapen thing. Despite the buildup of age covering it, he could tell what it was. It looked disturbingly familiar. He was certain he remembered the clockwork, but it had been years since he had referenced those images. A clockwork hadn't shown up in over two hundred years.

He tapped out a laborious text to his driver, letting her know he would need the car, then put his phone away and stood, drawing Faisal's attention immediately.

"Is something wrong?"

Roux picked up his jacket from the chair behind him. "I'm afraid I have to leave. An emergency has come up. I need to cash out."

That drew the other two men over, as well, and they clearly weren't happy about the prospect of Roux leaving. The South African man bowed. "You can't just leave."

"I don't have a choice."

"Correct." The man stepped closer to Roux, making the most of his size. He was half a head taller and at least fifty pounds heavier, all of the weight muscle. Blond and blue-eyed, he looked the epitome of an Aryan warrior. "You're going to stay here and finish the game."

"Otto, please." Faisal stood in front of the man. "Keep this civil. This was a friendly game. Nothing more."

"'Nothing more?'" Otto pushed Faisal back. "All night, despite everything the three of us have been able to do, this man has been winning. Can you explain that?"

All pretense at being a gentleman dropped away from Faisal. He shrugged and grimaced at Roux. "I'm afraid my friend has said too much and tipped our hand. Misfortune, it seems, lies in wait for you."

Roux didn't say anything. Truthfully, he was paying the three men scant attention. They had been a diversion, nothing more, even as targets for his sense of fair play. In light of Garin's potential discovery, they were even less interesting now. He held on to the walking stick he'd carried into the room. Like the ill-fitting suit and the two beautiful women who had accompanied him, the ornate stick was part of the disguise he'd chosen to wear. Last night and during the infrequent breaks from the game, he'd leaned on the stick as though he needed it to get around.

Faisal gazed at Roux. "I'm afraid we're not letting you leave here with the money."

Otto pulled a small Walther from behind his back and pointed it at Roux.

Seeing the pistol, Roux smiled. "Ah, the trademark weapon of James Bond. How exciting for you. I suppose that means that not only do you fancy yourself as something of a cardsharp, but you're an international spy, as well."

Otto narrowed his eyes in disbelief. "That's all you have to say, old man?"

"As a matter of fact, no, it isn't." Moving with deceptive speed, Roux swung the walking stick up suddenly, catching Otto between the legs with a sharp rap.

9

Letting rip a high-pitched, pain-filled yelp, Otto started to double over and struggled to bring the Walther to bear at the same time. Roux snatched the pistol from the man. Miraculously, the South African straightened and lunged forward, recovering much more quickly than Roux had surmised he would.

At first, Roux gave ground, stepping back as he pocketed the Walther. He didn't intend to use the pistol if he didn't have to. Corpses were so much harder to explain than a good thrashing. Twisting, Roux whipped the walking stick from his left side to his right at an angle. The stick slammed into Otto's face, breaking the man's nose and splattering blood, then slid on by, free for another blow. Dazed, the big man dropped to his knees.

Mercilessly, Roux drove the walking stick's heavy handle against his opponent's temple. Eyes rolling up into his head, Otto sprawled across the floor.

Cursing, the third man pulled out a Derringer. He thumbed the hammer back as Roux drew a previously hidden sword out of the walking stick's sheath. Naked steel flashed in front of the man's face and drove him backward fearfully.

With the next pass, Roux pierced the man's right shoulder, expertly slicing into the brachial nerve and causing his arm to go limp. The pistol fell from his numb hand. When the man turned to run, Roux stepped forward rapidly in a fencing move and hammered the base of his skull with the hilt. The man dropped.

Spinning with the grace of a ballet dancer, Roux slashed the blade across the front of Faisal's trousers, deliberately not cutting into flesh, but pointing out how easy it would have been.

"Drop the gun." Roux's voice now carried as much of an edge as the sword blade.

The pistol dropped onto the carpet, which muffled the impact.

Holding the man at bay with the bloody sword tip just inches from his chin, Roux addressed the silent dealer still seated at the table. "You. Gather up the money. You're coming with me."

The dealer, a nondescript man with quick hands and a cheap suit, stood and with trembling hands picked up the small suitcase that held everyone's money. "Look, I don't want any trouble. None of this was me."

"Then do as I tell you. Otherwise, I'll kill you along with your friends."

"They're not my friends."

Roux returned his attention to Faisel, who stood at stiff attention against the wall. "I know you. If you send hotel security after me, I'll be back, and when I'm finished, no one will ever find your body. Do we have an understanding?"

Wordlessly, Faisel nodded.

"Good." Roux grinned. "And remember this, playing cards isn't a gamble. Luck and some skill, yes. Sitting down at a table with opponents you don't know? That's the true risk you take. Find another city to play your shoddy game, or I'll be back."

Terrified, Faisel just stood there with his hands raised.

Roux followed the dealer, walking through the door and heading down the hallway to the elevators. He slipped the blade back into its walking stick sheath, then wiped the pistol he'd taken with a handkerchief and dropped it into a waste receptacle beside the elevator as the doors opened.

The dealer, much calmer now, led the way inside, then handed Roux the small suitcase. "Here you are, sir."

"Thank you, Devore. I trust you saw to your share of the proceeds?"

Patting his pocket, Devore nodded. "Yes, sir. And I must say, sir, it's been a pleasure working with you. I hardly ever had to mechanic the cards during the game. As I'd already known, you're an excellent player. You read those men magnificently."

As the elevator dropped toward the lobby, Roux waved away the compliment. "Thank you. I'm just glad we could come to terms regarding the matter."

"I don't like cheaters, sir," he said disdainfully. "After I hired on to deal for Faisel and found out how he conducted his 'business,' I immediately knew you wouldn't tolerate it. I've seen you deal with such matters before." He shook his head. "I was eager to see them get their comeuppance." He grinned. "And they certainly got that."

GARIN SAT IN the elegant bar of the hotel where he was staying and watched the casual afternoon crowd that filled the booths and tables. Most of the people here were doing business, talking about stock portfolios and options and impending mergers in a half dozen languages. None of the chatter was interesting to Garin. He caught himself checking his phone again and grew more irritated.

Once Roux saw the message and the image, Garin had been certain the old man would contact him. Since Roux had not responded, Garin was also certain that Roux *hadn't* seen the image or the text. Waiting was a singularly unappealing event, and it was something he still hadn't mastered even after hundreds of years.

During the past half hour or so, Garin had pondered calling Annja Creed and revealing his find to her. Then he realized she had no knowledge of the history of the clockwork and having to cover all of that information while waiting on Roux to call back would have been even more irritating.

So he'd decided a few drinks would take the edge off his anticipation. He'd drunk enough to more than take the edge off, though, and was working on maintaining a buzz that let time pass more easily.

He finished his latest drink, then held up his glass to the passing cocktail server. Young and pretty, if a little tired, the woman took the glass from his hand, mumbling something pleasant. She returned in short order with a fresh drink.

Out in the lobby, a beautiful redhead caught Garin's attention. She was dressed for business in a charcoal suit, but a pearl-gray turtleneck clung to her shapely curves. Her hair, so dark it looked as black as coals, fell across her shoulders. She gazed briefly around the lobby, her features strong and calculating, and she made Garin think of a lioness in its hunting ground. She spoke briefly even though no one was around, revealing that she wore an earbud.

She was immediately...*interesting*.

Taking a sip of his drink, Garin watched the woman walk to the front desk. But more than her looks drew him. She was dangerous. The promise of violence radiated from her and resonated within him like a tuning fork.

His cell vibrated on the table and the caller ID told him it was Amalia. He picked up the phone and growled into it.

"Hey, don't kill the messenger."

Garin took his Bluetooth earbud out of his pocket and linked it to the phone. He activated the FaceTime app and looked at Amalia. "If you're the messenger, then you have something."

"I think I located who Claudia Golino was working for, but I don't think you're going to be really happy about it."

"I'm not really in the mood for riddles, Amalia." Garin only let a smidgen of his irritation seep into his words.

Amalia's image went away and a photograph of a woman took shape on the phone. The same woman he just happened to have been studying in person when he took this call. "Her name is Melina Andrianou. She's a board member of an historical preservation society. Very hush-hush. They don't have a dedicated web presence, don't advertise—except to the superrich."

The name stirred a fleeting memory in Garin's mind, but he couldn't nail it down quickly enough before it was gone. With hundreds of years of experiences in his past, it was sometimes hard to remember everything. But there was something about the name.

More images of her shuffled across the phone's screen: indoors at extravagant parties, on the decks of yachts.

He watched as Melina Andrianou in real life talked briefly at the front desk. The clerk went away while she waited, gazing around the room, her eyes never settling on any one thing. Taking stock of her environment.

In his peripheral vision, Garin also noted that three men had filed into the hotel lobby shortly after the woman. Even though they made an effort not to move at the same speeds and they'd dressed differently, from street casual to business attire, Garin sensed that they were together. If he hadn't spent hundreds of years dealing with violence, seeing it take shape before the moment of action, he wouldn't have noticed the web they were weaving.

"I haven't been able to discover what Andrianou's business is, or why she would have been tied to Claudia Golino. However, I was able to establish the connection between them because they had been named in a civil suit three years ago in Amsterdam. The plaintiff maintained that Golino and Andrianou conspired to replace a piece in his collection with a fake. He caught Golino at it red-handed. Andrianou had introduced them."

"What was the piece?"

"According to the civil suit, it was believed to be a child's toy."

"A toy?"

"That's what it says here."

"Are there any pictures?"

"None."

Garin snarled and took another sip of his drink. He kept watching the woman out in the lobby. What was Melina Andrianou doing here? He wondered that, but he was certain he knew the answer. Just not how she'd been able to find him. Doing so meant she had considerable resources.

"I'm still digging into the court case because that appears to be our best leverage point. I'll let you know what I find out. I have to say that I'm quite pleased with what I've been able to dig up so far."

"Of course. As am I. Hold on just a moment." Garin lifted his phone, opened the camera app and captured images of two of the men he believed to be with Andrianou.

The third man had disappeared.

Garin texted the images of the men to Amalia. "See if you can dig up anything on these two men."

"Sure. Images are coming through now. Who are they?"

"If I knew, I wouldn't be asking you."

"Testy, testy, aren't we?"

"Ms. Andrianou is standing in my hotel lobby."

"You're kidding!"

Garin captured another image, this one of the woman in profile, and sent it along, as well. "Would I joke about something like that?"

"No, of course not. How did she get there?"

"I'd like you to find out. We left a trail somewhere."

"*I* didn't. All your financials are clear under the cover identity you're using at the hotel. The woman didn't track that."

"Perhaps I was not as circumspect in my arrival here as I'd hoped." Garin squashed his rising irritation. After all, he'd killed Claudia Golino and believed he'd blown up her cohorts, as well.

But if Andrianou were as practiced as she appeared to be, she might have had a second team waiting in the wings. Garin had done that before himself.

"See if you can find out anything about these men that connects to Andrianou and get back to me as soon as you can."

"I will."

Garin broke the connection and watched the lobby. Things were definitely taking an interesting turn. He'd left the clockwork piece in the safe in his suite. He hadn't been worried about losing the piece, but now it bothered him that he didn't have it to hand.

After all, the only thing that tied Andrianou to him was the clockwork butterfly. She hadn't happened along so soon after losing her employee by some happy coincidence.

Garin took another drink and considered his next move, wondering if he wanted the woman alive or dead.

10

When the elevator arrived at the lobby level, Roux bade Devore goodbye and walked away with the suitcase of money in his left hand. He took his cell phone out of his pocket and hit one of the speed dial numbers.

"Good afternoon, sir." The voice was female and had an Australian accent that Roux thought was positively delightful.

"Good afternoon, Honeysuckle. Bring the car around front, would you?"

"I'll be right there."

By the time Roux reached the hotel entrance and stood out in the cool Parisian spring breeze, Honeysuckle pulled the Rolls-Royce Silver Cloud to a smooth stop in front. One of the nearby valets hurried forward and opened the car door for Roux. Sliding inside, Roux handed the valet a hundred-franc note and sat back as the man closed the door.

Honeysuckle Torrey was in her mid-twenties, a stunning strawberry blonde whose hair barely brushed the liveried shoulders of the chauffeur's uniform she wore, along with cap and gloves. She was Australian by birth, a child of the world by luck and adventuress by choice.

Roux had crossed paths with her a few months ago in Taiwan while playing in a Texas Hold 'Em tournament.

She'd been working as a bodyguard for a man who had turned out to be contemptible in many ways. The man had also made the mistake of thinking he could kill Roux. Roux had disabused the man of that notion, and Honeysuckle had lent a hand. After viewing the young woman's quick thinking and prowess, as well as her calm in the face of danger, Roux had immediately offered her a job as his driver and sometime bodyguard.

"Everything went well?" Honeysuckle accelerated into traffic effortlessly.

"Yes, I was pleased." Roux set the suitcase aside. "Did you get some sleep as I suggested?"

"I did. The room was quite comfortable."

"Good. Once I'd settled in with those people, I knew it was going to take a while to set everything up."

Honeysuckle glanced into the rearview mirror, meeting Roux's gaze. "You're agitated."

Irritated that he'd been caught out, realizing that he'd been drumming his fingers on the door, Roux made a fist.

He wouldn't be able to keep this young woman in his employ for long. She was too restless and far too observant. Only Henshaw, Roux's majordomo at his manor house, knew much about his employer's personal life. Roux had worked hard to prevent more from getting close.

"Something unexpected has come up," he said.

Honeysuckle arched a perfect eyebrow. "Do you have a destination in mind? Let's start with that."

"Home. There are some things I must look at." Roux caught himself drumming his fingers again and cursed beneath his breath. He took out his cell phone and called Garin back.

"Well," his former apprentice said upon answering, "it took you longer to call back than I thought it would."

Garin's shortness was almost too much to take given

the circumstances. On some cold and lonely mornings, Roux often thought of the boy he had raised, and of the way that boy's father had come close to killing him before he apprenticed him to Roux. On those days, Roux missed the way it used to be between them.

The man Garin had grown into was difficult, but Roux knew he'd come by that honestly. Roux had raised him the only way he'd known how, and he tended to be a demanding man himself.

Although he'd reflected over their strained relationship for hundreds of years, this wasn't the time. "Is the clockwork piece real?"

"I don't know them as well as you do. Perhaps you would like to examine it. I certainly didn't have it made to get a rise out of you."

Roux clamped down on his automatic response and chose to be more amenable. "I would like to take a look. Where are you now?"

"Florence."

"I could meet you there."

"I don't think that's a good idea."

Garin's tone caught Roux's attention at once. "What's wrong?"

"Getting the clockwork wasn't an easy thing. The event made the news."

"How many times have I told you that you can't simply walk in and take something? You need subterfuge." Roux leaned back in his seat and massaged his temples. He wanted to sleep, and he wanted nothing to do with a clockwork creation.

He was afraid of them.

"I had everything neatly arranged. Just a quiet buy. Then a third party interrupted. In fact, she tried to kill me."

"She?"

"Yes. Quite a beautiful woman."

Roux felt like a vise had centered on his chest and was tightening. "Was she redheaded?"

"No."

Roux relaxed a little. "Good."

"Do you mean redheaded like Melina Andrianou?"

His fear came rushing back, clouded in gunsmoke and the stench of blood. Roux had to force himself to speak. "How do you know that name?"

"Apparently she's trying to find me."

"You mustn't let her."

"She's standing in the lobby of the hotel where I'm staying."

"Then you have to get out of there. *Now,* Garin. What that woman will do to you is worse than death."

Garin chuckled. "If I didn't know better, I'd say you were afraid of her," he said, clearly intrigued.

"I am. She will stop at nothing to get what she wants. Get out of there as quickly and quietly as you can. Whatever identity you're using, whatever you've got that's associated with that identity, lose it. You won't be able to call me at this number again. I'll get another one to you through the drop."

"You're serious about her, aren't you?"

"Yes. We need to figure out where we're going to meet to deal with the clockwork. Where was it found?"

There was silence.

"Garin?"

When Garin spoke again, he sounded quieter and more intense. "I'm going to have to call you back."

Then the phone clicked dead in Roux's ear.

Cursing, Roux emailed the images Garin had sent him to an address he could access without giving himself away.

Henshaw saw to such things. He didn't want this conversation to come back to haunt him.

If it wasn't already too late.

Roux took the cell phone apart, separated the battery and rolled down his window. He dumped it all out onto the street.

Honeysuckle caught his gaze in the rearview mirror. "Bad news?"

"Yes." Roux sat up and reached for his seat belt, pulling it on. "You'll want to be careful. I'm afraid things might get a little rough."

Honeysuckle nodded and sped up slightly, driving more aggressively through the traffic.

"May I borrow your cell phone?"

Honeysuckle handed the cell over the seat without hesitation. "Am I going to get it back, or is it going out the window, too?"

"I'll buy you another one, and I apologize for whatever inconvenience losing this one might cause you."

"No inconvenience. When I'm on the job, I never carry a personal phone."

For a moment, Roux gazed at the phone, only then remembering that Annja Creed's phone number had been programed into the other unit. He closed his eyes, summoned up the phone number out of centuries of memories and punched it in.

The phone rang three times, then went to voice mail. Cursing, Roux had to think even longer to remember his own house number. He punched it and was rewarded with an almost instantaneous answer.

"Hello. May I help you?" Henshaw's English accent rendered his French barely acceptable. He was ex-military and as majordomo he ran Roux's Paris home with precision.

"Henshaw, it's me."

"Ah, very good, sir." Henshaw didn't ask questions. Roux appreciated that about the man.

"I'm on my way home now, but I'm afraid I might be bringing some trouble with me."

"Understood, sir. I will, of course, take all the necessary precautions." That meant the house outside the city would quickly become a bunker. "Do you have an ETA?"

Roux looked at Honeysuckle. "How long?"

"With this traffic, forty, forty-five minutes."

"I heard, sir. Ample time to prepare."

"I need one thing further, Henshaw."

"Of course, sir."

"Contact Annja Creed. Tell her that Garin and I need her. Details will be forthcoming."

"Of course, sir."

"I have also uploaded a couple of images under the Basse identity. See that Annja gets those, as well."

"Shall I give her any information?"

"I have none at this point."

"Very good, sir."

"Thank you, Henshaw." Roux broke the connection, then he broke the phone and shoved it out the window. He gazed behind them, looking for tails, which meant the sanitation truck that came roaring out of the cross street at the next intersection caught him unprepared.

The impact sent a clangor of thunder through the Rolls-Royce. The heavy bulletproof glass fractured, filling the windows with spiderwebbing, but it didn't give way. Roux's head slammed into the window, then everything went hazy as the car turned turtle and ended up on its roof.

Dazed, his body not responding to his commands, Roux flailed for the walking stick as armed men wearing masks debarked from the sanitation truck.

11

"Keep your hands on the table or I will kill you."

Unhappy with himself at being caught so easily, Garin turned to face the man in the booth behind him. It was the third man on the search team, the one Garin had lost track of, and the man currently held a pistol pressed to the base of Garin's skull. The way he sat blocked the view of the gun from the server and the scattered patrons in the bar. Garin couldn't see the pistol, but he assumed it was of sufficient caliber to leave an unpleasant hole through his neck and an even more unpleasant mess in the hotel.

Garin kept his hands on the table. "As you wish, but are you sure Andrianou would want you to kill me?"

The man grinned at that. He was small and compact, very fit, but instantly forgettable. He had no visible tattoos, jewelry or scars.

"I was told you are a dangerous man. Therefore, whatever order I have been given will be superseded by my own desire to continue living." The man's eyes were a flat brown. "You, my job, my employer—nothing means more to me than that."

"I'm glad you brought up employment. Perhaps we could discuss career opportunities."

The man shook his head slightly. "Not for sale. If I was,

you wouldn't be interested in me any longer than it took to put a bullet through my head if I could be bought off."

Garin gave a small nod. "True."

"Get up slowly and I won't shoot you."

Garin did and the man stood with him. He roped his arm around Garin so that it looked like they were two friends. The man was tall enough that having his arm over Garin's shoulders wasn't too awkward.

"Now stay very still." With his free hand, the man searched Garin's clothing, making it look like he was adjusting his jacket, and removed the pistol from the holster at the small of his back. It disappeared into his jacket pocket. "Just the one weapon?"

"You trust me?"

"If I spot another weapon you're holding out on me, I'm going to shoot you where you're standing. I hate surprises."

Garin nodded. "So do I."

The man grinned.

Garin met the man's gaze. "Do I get to meet your boss?"

"She's looking forward to it, Mr. Braden."

The use of his name bothered Garin immensely. The false identities he used were deep and hard to break. The one he'd used to collect the clockwork had a longer lifespan than most, had even been something of a sacrifice to lose, but there was nothing substantial connected to it. Nothing that would tie that name to Garin Braden.

Melina Andrianou knew more than he'd expected anyone to. Roux's words reverberated through his skull. *What that woman will do to you is worse than death.* In all their long relationship, Garin had been given opportunities to meet several sadistic and cruel people. Roux generally didn't deal with the average selfless person in his hunt for Joan's shattered sword—or the other items he gathered.

The man gave Garin a small push toward the main

lobby. Garin went that way, but remained loose and ready, knowing that he was about to have a small window in which to reverse the situation.

Even though she was tired, the server was alert enough to keep an eye on her tables. "Hey!" Her voice rang out behind Garin. "What do you think you're doing? You can't just walk out of here without paying the bill!"

Garin made it a point to not have anything he did in a hotel amended to his bill. Doing so made it too easy to check his movements. He'd known the young server wouldn't let him walk away without paying.

His captor turned toward the server. As the man shifted, the pistol muzzle sliding along Garin's neck, Garin stepped back and spun to his right, keeping contact with the weapon, blocking the man from employing it, then tried to spin out of harm's way.

Still up against Garin's neck, the pistol barked. True to his word, the man had shown no compunction about shooting. The heated gas from the spent cartridge singed Garin's skin and the loud detonation deafened him. He kept turning, swinging around the man's hand like it was a pivot point, till he was facing his would-be captor. Garin swept his left hand up and jabbed the man in the right eye with his forefinger.

Squalling in pain, clapping his hand to his eye so that his forearm partially blocked his vision, blood leaking down his cheek, the man stumbled back and fought to bring his pistol to bear. Garin grabbed hold of his hand gripping the pistol and twisted violently as another round of bullets cored into the ceiling. He chopped the man in the throat, creating an instant choking spasm that took away his breath. The man's wrist shattered in Garin's grip and the pistol slid free.

Deftly, as he swept his gaze around the hotel and saw

guests and staff running for cover, Garin reached into the man's jacket pocket and recovered his pistol. Then he slammed his borrowed weapon into the man's forehead. The man fell.

Garin followed him down and took a moment to kneel and search him, turning up two more magazines for his captured weapon. He thrust those into his pockets and caught a flurry of movement at the bar's open doorway leading to the lobby. Another man peered over the sights of a pistol, firing even as Garin threw himself to the side over the guy he'd knocked out.

As he rolled, Garin thrust the pistol out and opened fire. Two of the bullets struck the woodwork beside the shooter's cheek, driving splinters into his flesh. The third and fourth bullets crunched through his face and snapped his head back as his body went slack.

Garin retreated behind the bar. A moment later, a hail of bullets shattered several of the bottles on the counter at the back. The large mirror went to pieces and came down in a deadly, glimmering rain.

The bartender pulled himself into a tight ball and gazed fearfully at Garin.

Garin swapped out magazines in the ensuing silence. "Don't worry. I'm not going to hurt you."

Nodding out of fear, not trust, the bartender eased away, putting more distance between him and Garin.

Leaving one of the pistols temporarily on the floor as he sat hunkered down, Garin tapped his phone and dialed Amalia.

"Hello." She sounded bright and alert. "I'm guessing you're the reason the hotel is blowing up the emergency services numbers?"

"Not directly. I need you to kill the camera feeds and eradicate the records over the past couple days." That should get rid of any video footage of him arriving at the hotel.

"Already in progress. I'm downloading the files to my computers, though. You can have them later if you need them."

Garin peered over the top of the bar but the redheaded woman was nowhere in sight. "Did you happen to notice which way Andrianou went?"

"Upstairs. She made a beeline when the action started."

Across the lobby, the doors on two elevator cages dinged open. Garin watched as hotel guests stumbled out in confusion. "Not by the elevator?"

"The elevators are now shutting down. Emergency procedures are in place. However you want to go up in the building, it's got to be the stairs. Andrianou took the stairs."

"My room is on the twelfth floor." Garin left the bar, holding pistols in both hands and moving into a comfortable jog.

"Yes, it is, so if you want your mysterious toy, you'd better hurry."

A few hotel guests streamed down the stairs, either curious about what was going on or too scared to stay in their rooms. Word about the shooting had spread quickly. Garin felt like he was moving upstream even though most got out of his way.

The panicked mob thinned out on the third floor.

Garin pushed himself, hearing his lungs heaving like a bellows, but his legs remained strong. His ears still rang. He made the fourth-floor landing, turned and charged up the next flight of steps.

"HE IS COMING your way."

Melina Andrianou raced up the stairs with a compact

.45 gripped in her fist. Her thighs and calves burned from the effort, but she never missed a step. She wasn't running full out because she needed her wind intact the rest of the way up. Her life depended on staying in shape.

"The surveillance cameras are still down?" She rounded the sixth-floor landing and heaved herself forward, throwing herself at the next flight of steps.

"Yes. We don't know what happened to them." The voice at the other end of her earbud sounded calm and unperturbed.

Her grandfather, Georgios, hardly ever lost his aplomb. He was as fierce and determined in his late seventies as he'd ever been when she was a girl. She pictured him standing in the nerve center of the family business, a button-down shirt with the sleeves rolled up to midforearm, and his white hair carefully brushed back, barely controlling the unruly curls that had once been black like her father's. Lean and spare and bronzed, he'd always reminded her of a pirate. For a time, he had been.

"This man Garin Braden has many resources, *kopela mou.*"

Her grandfather had always called her *my girl* in Greek, though they usually spoke English when she was in the field. The mercenaries they employed came from all over the world because they hired the best, and English was the only common tongue among them because they mainly worked with European and American employers.

Melina kept charging up the stairs. She would have been better prepared for what had taken place in the bar if she'd known their quarry better. All she knew is that these men she pursued were her grandfather's enemies, and they had killed her father.

At the next landing, a uniformed hotel security guard stepped through the door. When he saw Melina racing up the stairs toward him, he raised his hands and said in Italian, "No, miss. You must go the other way. It would be best if you return to your…"

She understood the language. She understood many languages. Like her physical prowess, her knowledge was also something she worked on.

Raising her pistol and firing by instinct, Melina put a bullet between the security man's eyes. He fell backward, trapping the door open with his body. The body count on this particular operation had already been running high. Dropping civilians was going to run it higher. Her grandfather would not be pleased. Plans went better when she operated in the shadows.

A small crowd gathered at the door, staring down at the dead guard, then at Melina as she crested the steps. She shot into them and a man fell, crying out in surprise and agony, blood suddenly staining his light green shirt. The rest of the hotel guests scattered like mice before an owl.

Her grandfather's computer teams had been working on hacking into the hotel. "Do we have the room number where Garin Braden is staying?" Melina reached the eighth floor, her wind still holding steady. She pushed herself harder, faster.

"Room 1236."

"Location?"

"Southwest corner."

Picturing the blueprints of the hotel in her mind, Melina oriented herself. When she reached the twelfth floor, she would need to turn left and follow the hallway to the end. "That is a suite."

"Yes."

"There will be a safe." She raced up to the tenth-floor landing, no longer having to dodge guests. She assumed people staying in the top floors weren't aware of the gun battle that had taken place below. For a brief instant, she wondered if Garin had killed Bolger. The man deserved it for letting the German get the upper hand. This should have gone easily.

"I have a demolitions team en route to you. They will reach the room ahead of you."

Of course they will. Her grandfather was always planning, always thinking things through five and six moves ahead. He had been a chess grandmaster at an early age. Some said Melina got her intelligence from her grandfather.

She had been a good student in university for a time. Her father had wanted her to stay out of the family business, though Melina had been fascinated by the stories and legends her grandfather had told her when she was a little girl. Her father had accused her grandfather of luring her into their business, and maybe that was true. After her father was killed six years ago, Melina had been grateful for the chance to take revenge on the man who had killed him. This man Garin Braden would put her one step closer.

She considered the way she had shot the hotel security man down. There had been no reticence, no hesitation. Just a single trigger squeeze and the man had been blown out like a candle flame. She hadn't cared if he had a wife and children. That didn't matter. He'd almost gotten in her way, would have caused her to break stride if he'd taken another step. That wasn't acceptable.

Her grandfather would have done the same thing. She had seen him do it. Her father, though, he would sometimes consider consequences before he took action, and some of those consequences bothered him. Iron will took a lot of focus. It wasn't possible to consider others. That was weakness.

Her grandfather didn't allow weakness, but hadn't been

able to weed it from her father. He'd been killed in front
of Melina by the old man everyone had discounted, a man
who had been—*should* have been—dead on his feet. She'd
taken that as an object lesson. She had no such weaknesses.

Driving herself up the final flight of steps, Melina
reached the twelfth floor and shoved through the doors
into the hallway with the pistol extended before her. Her
eyes were gunsights.

Three men stood at the door to room 1236. One of them
knelt in front of the door and was hooking up a digital
lockpick to the ecard reader. The other two held H&K
MP5 submachine guns they'd taken from duffel bags at
their feet.

They acknowledged her with nods.

Melina raised her hands behind her neck, opening her
lungs so she could bring her wind back under control
faster. The man kneeling by the door stood and the electronic lock flashed from red to green. He gripped the knob,
leveled his MP5 and entered the room.

Gun in both hands, Melina followed.

12

Annja's cell phone rang.

Holding her breath underwater in the deep bath in her hotel room, she barely heard the ringing. She'd planned on staying under until just short of drowning. After spending most of the night in lockup, she'd felt certain that a long soak in scented bathwater was what it would take for her to feel clean.

The phone rang again.

Reluctantly, Annja rose from the water, swept her hair back from her face with her hands and blinked her eyes clear. She hadn't bothered turning on the lights in the bathroom because she could see well enough in the ambient light that leaked in from the street outside. She was alone in the darkness with the lilac-steeped bathwater.

Her cell phone lay on a towel on the floor within reach of the bath. She snatched it as it rang again, then gazed at the too-bright light of the viewscreen.

The number was to Roux's manor house outside Paris. Her heart beat a little faster, her imagination already fully engaged. Roux didn't make a habit of calling her and it wasn't yet 5:00 a.m. in Boston. She picked up as she did the math, figuring that it was 11:00 a.m. in France.

"Hello?"

"Ms. Creed?" The man's voice was officious and very

British. He didn't sound stressed, but then Annja felt certain he never would. He was cool under fire and threat of imminent death. She'd seen him in both those instances.

"Henshaw."

"Yes. Do you have time to talk?"

Annja relaxed a little. If anything had been wrong with Roux, Henshaw wouldn't have asked the innocuous question. Or, on second thought, maybe he would have.

"Yes, I have time to talk." She thought she detected the sound of a racing engine, but she wasn't certain.

"Sorry to catch you at this ungodly hour." Henshaw paused. "I assume, that wherever you are, it is an ungodly hour."

"Boston."

"Then, yes, it is quite an ungodly hour."

Annja lay back in the water till the level rose nearly to her chin again. She loved the fragrance and warmth, but thought the water could stand a little more heat. She'd amend that when the call was ended. "I assume you called for a reason."

Henshaw cleared his throat. "I was instructed by himself to alert you to a matter he requires your assistance in resolving."

"Roux needs me?" That didn't often happen.

"So it would appear."

"Where is he?"

"In Paris."

"Why isn't he calling?"

"He's...otherwise engaged."

Annja frowned. Her relationship with Roux—and with Garin for that matter—was on a slippery slope. Nothing was simple with any of them. She still didn't know if that had more to do with the sword or with their own abrasive natures. "Henshaw, meaning no disrespect, but if *himself* needs me, then *himself* needs to call me. Tell *himself* I'll talk then."

"I'm afraid things are not quite that simple, Ms. Creed. Himself is currently under duress and I'm not quite certain how he's faring. I have lost contact with him."

"Hold on a sec." Annja pushed up from the water and stepped out of the bath, putting the cell on the counter. Taking one of thick, plush towels from the sink where she'd placed them, she quickly toweled off, then used another towel to wrap her hair. She pulled on a terry-cloth robe hanging on the bathroom door and picked up the phone as she walked into the bedroom.

She crossed to the window and pulled the drapes aside to peer out over the city. Cars threaded through the streets, headlights and brake lights gleaming. It was cold enough outside that her breath frosted on the glass.

"What kind of duress is Roux under?"

"Regretfully, I have no information for you concerning that. I wish that I did."

Annja knew that was true. Now she finally heard the strain in Henshaw's voice. Not for the first time, she wondered how Henshaw had become majordomo for Roux. There was a story there, and her curiosity wouldn't allow her to ignore it. On occasion, she picked at the history between the two men, but both of them ignored her questions.

"Is Roux in trouble?"

"He seemed rather vexed when he called and insisted I get in touch with you."

"On a scale of one to ten, how vexed?"

"Ms. Creed, I assure you, this is no whim on his part nor on mine. When he contacted me, he called me from his chauffeur's phone. I believe he disposed of his own."

That fired up Annja's synapses. She released the drapes and turned to the bed where her backpack lay. She'd checked the contents back at the jail and had been relieved to find everything there.

"Does Roux need me to come?"

"No. I forwarded you the images of an object he was most interested in your seeing."

Annja dug her Surface Pro tablet PC from her bag and powered it up. "An object, huh?" She took out the miniature satellite receiver she carried and powered it up, as well, connecting it to the PC through the USB port, quickly logging on to the internet.

"Yes."

"Have you seen it?"

"The images, yes."

Annja brought up her mail client and quickly flicked through the emails. Even discounting the obvious spam, there were a lot. She searched through the most recent.

"Butterfly?"

"That's the one."

"So this is a butterfly?" Annja almost felt disappointed. The subject line couldn't have been more pedestrian. Well, it could have. Foot, for instance, could have been more pedestrian. Her Latin pun cheered her somewhat. "Did he say where he got it?"

"I'm afraid not. There didn't appear to be time. We were…cut off rather unexpectedly."

"Don't you have a way of tracking the car?"

"I do. In fact, I'm doing that even as we speak."

"Okay."

"I should probably let you go. Traffic has gotten more severe and I think I'm nearing the trouble spot. There are several gendarmes on the scene and there appears to be some sort of running gun battle in play."

Annja caught her breath. She hated being so far away when Roux was in trouble. He and Garin had their own lives, and she accepted that. As a matter of fact, they'd each had several lives before they'd ever met her. She wasn't their keeper. Neither of them would have stood for it. She wouldn't have wanted them prying into her life, either.

But they were the closest thing she'd ever had to family since the orphanage. No one had ever truly understood her the way Roux and Garin did, though those individual relationships were much different and sometimes caused problems she didn't want in her life.

She double-tapped the image to magnify it. With the enhancement, she could see the small gears and wheels within what looked like a very ancient mechanical butterfly. The image instantly captivated her. She'd never seen anything quite like it.

"What is this?"

Henshaw's unflappable demeanor started to slip. "I really don't know, and I'm afraid I must end this call. The situation here is pressing."

"What am I supposed to do with it?"

"I was not told, Ms. Creed. As I said, my communication was rather truncated. I would assume that you should do what you do best—research and discover. Let himself know what you find out, provided that he survives whatever he now faces. If he does, I'm sure he will be in touch." The phone clicked dead in Annja's ear.

Anxious, wondering what was going on with Roux, Annja called the special number she had for Garin Braden. He had set it up so that no matter what phone he had on him, she was always patched through without interruption.

She paced back and forth, staring at the butterfly on the screen. Finally, just as she was convinced the connection was about to dump her into voice mail, Garin answered.

"Not a good time, Annja." Garin was so preoccupied that he spoke in German, a barbaric version Annja could barely translate. Gunshots punctuated his words. "However, I do want to talk to you the moment it becomes convenient."

Noticing the light shifting on the viewscreen, Annja looked at the phone, realizing that Garin had left his camera operational. She caught a glimpse of an empty hallway, then movement swept the perspective around a corner, briefly revealing a man with a submachine gun in front of what looked like a hotel room door. The man opened fire just as the perspective changed again. This time the phone connection switched off on the heels of a gunshot, like a bullet had ripped through the cell.

Annja hoped that it hadn't ripped through Garin somewhere along the way.

Her anxiety through the roof, she felt utterly impotent. She didn't even know where Garin was.... Taking a deep breath, she slowly turned her attention to the mechanical butterfly.

Several cultures had developed automatons, all seeking to duplicate the marvels of nature. The Renaissance inventors had been driven to create imitations of flesh-and-blood beings.

Pushing aside her worries, Annja brought up the alt.archaeology and alt.history sites she favored, then started a thread, introducing herself and framing the subject matter.

Looking for information about early automatons. Focus on mechanical insects.

Leaving the computer on, Annja got up and started to get dressed. She wasn't going to be sleeping anytime soon.

13

Roux cursed as he struggled to release himself from the seat belt. The locking mechanism remained jammed despite his best efforts. The masked men came closer with their weapons in their fists. He didn't know if they wanted him alive or dead, but they moved like professionals.

One of them knelt beside the door window that was now empty of glass. The mask over the man's face shifted and his eyes crinkled, giving Roux the distinct impression he was grinning beneath it.

"Hello, gramps," he mocked in English with an American accent. "Hang on a sec. We'll get you right out of there." He reached into the car with his free hand.

Roux finally managed to curl his fingers around his walking stick. He ripped the sheath free as the man fisted his shirt roughly. Roux twisted and drove the sword cane with both hands. The point pierced the man's unprotected throat, then—because of the angle he was at—slid down into his chest cavity and pierced his lungs, as well. Blood spurted from the man's mouth through the mask as Roux pulled the blade free again. Sputtering, the man dropped to his knees, blocking the man behind him from reaching the window. Desperately, the man held on to his gushing throat with his free hand and trained the pistol on Roux.

Constrained by the car, Roux barely managed to thrust

the sword against the man's forearm to knock the pistol aside. The detonation of the gunshot was deafening inside the vehicle, almost rendering Roux senseless.

Releasing his hold on the sword, Roux gripped the man's hand, broke his thumb and two of his fingers and freed the pistol from the man's grip. Roux fisted the weapon, then used his sharp blade to saw through the seat belt in one quick slice. He dropped heavily to what had been the top of the Rolls-Royce just as someone squatted down at the opposite window. Roux raised his pistol, as the other man pointed his.

Two quick gunshots erupted inside the car, but these didn't sound as loud because he was still partially deaf from the previous one. In the shattered window, the masked man suddenly sat back on his haunches. The ski mask served to hold together the fragments of the man's face and skull left by the passage of two bullets.

But Roux hadn't fired yet. He glanced over his shoulder.

Pistol gripped in her fist, Honeysuckle hung upside down from the driver's seat. A cut over her left eye dripped up her forehead toward her hairline.

Roux flicked the sword across her seat belt and the material parted instantly. On the other side of the spider-webbed windshield, three men walked toward the over-turned vehicle.

Honeysuckle put a hand on Roux's shoulder and shoved. "Get out!"

Although it didn't sound like it through the thick cotton in his ears, Honeysuckle's face was contorted like she was shouting as she threw herself along what had been the car's overhead and into the backseat. The cut over her eye had reversed direction, running into her eyebrow.

On his belly, Roux managed to slither through the window, knocking free more glass fragments that fell around him. Once out of the car, he pushed himself to his feet, already feeling the twinges and aches that would settle in after the horrific collision. He turned to check on Honeysuckle's progress only to receive a thrust to his chest that almost bowled him over.

She lifted her weapon and aimed at one of the men on the other side of the Rolls-Royce. A bullet cut a strand of hair from her head and the red lock drifted toward the ground, then caught in the blowback from the pistol she fired.

Her bullet caught one of the masked men in the chest and caused him to stumble and fall. The other two trailing after him dove for cover as she swept her weapon toward them.

Spinning, Honeysuckle stiff-armed Roux again. *"Move!"*

Roux ran, smiling in spite of the danger. Honeysuckle was quite the woman. He would be sad to see her move on, but he knew she would. She would tire of his secrets because he would not share with her who he was and what he did. Women, he'd found, were like that. They weren't content to settle for part of a man's life.

Even Annja got frustrated with him over his secrets. And those secrets were only part of what had set him and Garin apart.

Traffic had stalled in the intersection, blocked by the wrecked Rolls-Royce and the sanitation truck. The truck had continued to roll after striking the car, finally coming to a rest against a musical instrument shop just past the intersection where it had partly crushed through a display window and scattered guitars and horns across the sidewalk. Other drivers recovered from being stunned by the wreck and realized that it had turned into a gunfight. They tried to back away, running into other vehicles in the process, or simply abandoned their cars.

Reaching the secondhand clothing store on the other side of the intersection, Roux plunged inside. The circular racks just inside the store were heavy with winter wear, which he hoped would help block bullets.

He navigated through the narrow aisles toward the back door. He burst into the stockroom, where two young clerks, one male and one female, had hidden. They had cell phones in their hands and were texting as they stared at him with wide, frightened eyes.

Roux grabbed the back door, but it was locked. He whirled on the two clerks and asked in French, "Do you have the key?"

Blankly, they continued to stare at him. The female lifted her cell and took Roux's picture. He snatched it from her and threw it on the floor, then smashed it to pieces.

"Hey! You can't do that!" She gawked at the cell in disbelief.

"It's done. Do you have a key?"

"It's in the register."

Snarling an oath, Roux leveled his pistol at the lock. "Step back."

The two fled.

Roux fired, shattering the lock. Kicking the door open, he shot into an alley and headed left, away from the intersection.

Honeysuckle lagged behind him, covering their retreat. "Do you know who those people are?"

"Not for certain, no." Roux ran for the end of the alley. "But I've got a good idea why they're here. Garin stumbled across something that's going to make life difficult for us for a time, I'm afraid."

"Who's Garin?"

"I'll explain later." But he wouldn't. The number of

people who knew about him and Garin was small. "We need to find a phone."

"The police are already on their way."

He listened for the shrill sirens of the police vehicles. Heard them.

"We can find somewhere to hide until they arrive," she suggested.

"I'd rather not talk to the police. That's what I hire lawyers for. I've got more important things to do."

At the end of the alley, Roux stopped and scanned the street. A quick glance behind assured him their pursuers hadn't yet gotten through the secondhand clothing store, either. He shoved the pistol under his belt at the small of his back, straightened his disheveled clothing, then walked to the right down the sidewalk.

It was irritating that public phones were no longer readily available, but four doors down on the left, a small electronics boutique advertised Disposable Mobiles. He crossed the street and headed for the shop.

MELINA CLOSED AND locked the hotel door behind her, throwing the dead bolt and the security chain. She didn't expect either would keep out someone determined to get into the room, but it would slow them and at least alert her that they were about to have company.

The demolitions team sent by her grandfather ignored the outer room and went to the bedroom. According to the blueprints, the safe would be there.

Instead of following them, Melina walked through the outer room, trying to get some sense of the man who had so explosively destroyed her attempt to claim the clockwork butterfly. Although she had read through Garin Braden's records, what there were of them, she knew the true man was hidden from those files.

Everything the computer search had turned up on Garin Braden was false. A public face he wore, though she supposed some of it was based on truth. The man lived a reclusive life for the most part, but he had gotten into trouble on several continents. Those troubles had been covered up by lawyers. Investigators could never quite figure out exactly what the man had been doing.

Melina felt certain she knew, based on the knowledge her grandfather had of the man. She believed that the clockwork her grandfather searched so diligently for was only a small fraction of what lay out there for someone to find. If only they knew where to look.

During her twenty-eight years, she had seen many impossible, wondrous things, and she had known a lot of men. Most of them had been deadly and violent, men whose lives hung in the balance at any given moment, depending on how fast they could move or kill, and how quickly they could think. A few times, those men had nearly killed her.

Garin's suite was immaculate. Five newspapers lay neatly folded on the desk. Two were in English, one was in French, one was in Italian and one was in German. By the smudged fingerprints, she could tell the papers had been thumbed through.

She was impressed. It was one thing to be able to speak a language, and quite another to read it. She used her phone to capture images of the papers. She'd review them later and try to figure out what Garin Braden had been so interested in.

Moving quickly, aware that the man was even now closing in on them—because her grandfather had told her he'd killed the mercenaries she'd brought with her to retrieve him, proving that he was more dangerous than expected—Melina entered the bedroom.

The demolitions team had set up in front of the floor

safe. The vault was built into the floor. The men had removed flooring and were placing charges around the safe door.

Melina had to restrain herself from pointing out how delicate the clockwork might be. Her grandfather would have impressed that upon them already.

She stepped into the bathroom, still trying to puzzle out the man who stayed here. If someone was going to make a mess, it would be in the bathroom. Instead, the toiletries were carefully put away. The used towels had been left in the tub. There was no hair in the sink.

But are you neat? Or just careful not to leave any DNA behind? She wondered what his relationship to the old man was. They did not look like father and son.

"Ms. Andrianou."

Melina returned to the bedroom. The three demolitions men stood in the doorway to the outer room.

"The charges are set. We're ready."

Nodding, Melina stepped past them into the outer room.

Just then something slammed into the door from the hallway.

Melina tightened her grip on her pistol and slid to the wall to cover the entrance. In her peripheral vision she saw two of her grandfather's team draw their weapons and spread out around the room.

"Blow the safe." Melina never took her eyes from the door as the handle jerked and twisted. For the moment, the dead bolt held.

After a muffled explosion in the bedroom, smoke boiled from the room.

The attempted break-in at the door halted. Melina waited, not giving in to the temptation to go see what was happening out in the hallway.

Behind her, the man at the bedroom door went to check on the safe. Melina held her pistol steady.

Inside the bedroom, the man cursed, then a loud *boom!* swallowed his voice and deafened Melina as a concussive wave hammered her against the wall and knocked her forward. Her senses swam as she fought to keep from striking the floor face-first.

"Melina! *Melina!*" Her grandfather spoke in her ear, barely audible even right there inside her head. "What is going on?"

Struggling, Melina forced herself up, glancing at the bedroom in disbelief.

The wall separating the two rooms hung in tatters. Flames broke out in curling twists even as Melina stared in shock. The charges used to break the safe couldn't have done that much damage. Even as she was thinking that, the sprinkler system gushed to life, deluging the suite in artificial rain.

The man who had been inside the bedroom now lay scattered in bloody chunks around the suite. The large windows in the bedroom gaped open and wind sucked the smoke out, stoking the flames to life. Fractures lined one of the windows across from Melina. As she pushed herself to her feet, the fractures gave way, glinting in the sunlight briefly as the pieces fell. The outside air chilled her down to her bones.

She checked the room's door, but it remained intact.

"Melina."

"I'm all right."

"What about the clockwork?"

"I don't know. There was another explosive rigged to the safe." Melina strode toward the bedroom on shaky legs. Her ears rang so loudly she could scarcely hear herself think.

Only one of the men in what had been the outer room moved. The other was dead, impaled by a shard of wood.

"Two of the demolitions team are dead." Cautiously, Melina walked toward the hole in the floor where the safe had been. She couldn't believe Garin Braden would have destroyed the object he'd killed over only that morning.

"Is the clockwork still there?"

Melina peered at the floor. Instead of a burned, twisted mass of safe as she'd expected, a hole opened to the floor below. Debris lay scattered across the bed on that floor. Through the smoke she could just make out the cylindrical shape of the safe canted to one side, but otherwise undamaged.

"He rigged the safe—which your so-called demolitions experts didn't notice. When we attempted to open it, we set off a second explosion that took out the floor and dropped it down one level. Who is in that room?"

"We've lost access to the hotel records. It doesn't matter. Recover the clockwork."

Melina didn't point out that accomplishing that task was going to be difficult with two-thirds of the demolitions team dead. Her grandfather wanted results, not excuses. Judging from the circumference of the hole left in the floor, she thought she could get through.

She stepped forward, threw her arms over her head and dropped.

14

Outside room 1136, Emil Klotz stood on guard. A wheeled luggage carrier sat beside him. A bright red fire extinguisher sat in the middle of the carrier alongside a canvas bag.

Garin crossed the hallway and joined the man.

Klotz produced the room card, slotting it quickly. "This is turning out to be an interesting day."

"I prefer them to boring days, Emil, but this is getting to be too much of a good thing."

"Do you know who the woman is?"

"Not entirely. Amalia is working on it."

Klotz handed Garin the fire extinguisher. "You'll probably need this. And the safe will be hot." He passed over a pair of asbestos gloves, as well.

Garin took the extinguisher and gloves, then pushed the door open and went inside. The suite was set up exactly as the room above it. He'd taken both rooms as a precaution. It was always better to have a planned withdrawal route.

Pulling the luggage carrier after him, Klotz followed.

Smoke streamed from the bedroom. Garin holstered his pistol and pulled the fire extinguisher's pin, readying the device. He hoped he could still open the safe because that would make leaving with the clockwork much easier, but he doubted it would be so simple. Melina Andrianou had complicated his life a lot in a short time. That made her even more interesting.

Small flames darted and twisted across the bed, growing larger as Garin watched. Through a gaping hole in the ceiling water streamed in from the sprinkler system above. He peered at the hole, but nothing seemed to be moving up there.

Aiming the fire extinguisher at the bed, Garin depressed the trigger and smothered most of the flames—as far as he could tell through the resulting thick smoke. Just as he was about to put the extinguisher aside, a lithe figure dropped through the hole and landed on the bed in a crouch.

Melina Andrianou lifted a pistol and aimed point-blank from six feet away.

Garin quickly raised the fire extinguisher and covered the woman's face, temporarily blinding her. She fired, anyway. Four shots dug into the wall behind where Garin had been standing. She was starting to adjust, fighting the uncertain footing of the bed, when Klotz opened fire from the doorway.

Crumpling under the bullets, the woman rolled off the bed and onto the floor.

Garin started to go after her, but an arm appeared through the hole in the ceiling and a man started blasting away. Ducking to one side, Garin pressed himself up against the wall. Klotz traded shots with the man for a moment, but there wasn't much of a target and their opponent was firing an MP5 submachine gun. Garin threw the fire extinguisher aside and pulled on the asbestos gloves.

When the weapon cycled dry, Garin darted forward, grabbed the floor safe in both hands and manhandled it to the luggage carrier Klotz had brought with him. The floor safe thudded onto the carrier just as the MP5 wielder thrust his weapon back into the room and opened fire again.

Cursing, Garin shoved the luggage carrier ahead of him and raced for the door. Klotz had wedged it open so it was a straight run to the hallway.

Outside the room, Garin kept pushing the carrier ahead of him. The safe teetered precariously, but the remaining corners of the mortise work prevented it from rolling off the carrier. He reached the elevator and stopped.

"You did a good job on the safe, Emil." Garin waited while Klotz shoved a knife into the slot between the elevator doors and created a gap he could dig his fingers into.

"Didn't kill enough of them, though, did it? That woman lived through it."

"I'm betting there were others who didn't."

Klotz shoved the elevator door open and held it.

Picking up the safe, Garin leaned over and peered down the elevator shaft. "Do you think you killed her?"

"I don't know. That fire extinguisher fogged up the room a lot. Couldn't tell for sure what I was hitting."

"She went down quick enough."

"Let's hope." Klotz shook his head. "She's not someone I'd like to see again anytime soon."

Garin grinned. "Nor would I." The elevator cage sat at the bottom of the shaft. "This is going to make a big impact."

"The safe will survive the fall. What about your butterfly?"

"I packed it in nice and tight. That thing isn't as fragile as it looks. Evidently it survived centuries on the ocean floor." Garin heaved the safe into the elevator shaft and watched it tumble slowly through the air as it plummeted, skidding now and again against the cables and creating a shower of sparks in its wake.

When the safe smashed through the top of the elevator cage it sounded like a cannon going off. A cloud of dust swelled up into the elevator shaft.

"That's going to draw attention." Klotz took a pair of carabineer's cable descenders from the canvas bag. The units had been engineered for mountaineers traversing difficult emergency descents from mountains after a route had been established. Klotz clamped them to the elevator cage support cables with practiced efficiency.

"Amalia?" Garin took hold of one of the descenders and tentatively stepped into the shaft.

"I'm here." She sounded tense.

"Do you still have eyes outside the hotel?"

"For the moment. Local law enforcement is a minute and twenty seconds away."

Slipping the brake on the descender, Garin dropped into the darkness. The cable sang through the device and Garin felt the growing heat caused by the friction. Short seconds later, he reached the elevator cage.

Abandoning the descender, Garin drew his pistol once more and reached for the emergency access panel at the top of the smashed elevator cage. Crumpled folds from the safe's impact area stretched out across the door, causing it to stick. With a final growl of effort, Garin ripped the panel open and climbed inside. As broad as he was, he barely passed through.

The safe lay on the broken surface of the elevator cage floor. One of the elevator doors leaned outward, bent from a secondary impact with the safe.

Klotz dropped down just as Garin heaved the safe over one shoulder, precariously balancing the weight. Taking the lead, Klotz shoved through the buckled door—startling an employee who had clearly been studying the damage—

and walked out into the lobby, which was nearly deserted.
A young manager stood behind the guest check-in counter
on the phone, his eyes on them, and two uniformed valets
had come in through the revolving front door, probably
to find out what the noise inside the elevator had been.

"Amalia, you have a car at the back of the building?"
With the safe over his shoulder, Garin loped down the
hallway toward the rear of the hotel.

"Yes. In position now."

Garin ran as fast as he could, staying behind Klotz,
passing a few curious guests. The stink of an indoor pool
filled Garin's nose, then he was past it and the fogged glass
door that led to the area.

Klotz held open the back door, revealing the black SUV
idling in the narrow alley. Garin caught the driver's eye
and pointed to the rear of the vehicle. The hatch opened
and he thrust the safe into the cargo area. He took the seat
behind the driver and buckled in as Klotz sat up front.

The driver put his foot on the accelerator and roared
out of the alley.

Turning in his seat, Garin watched the hotel recede behind them. Nobody. He turned back around as the driver
merged with the traffic out on the street.

"Amalia."

"Yes?"

"Get Annja Creed for me." Even if Melina Andrianou
was dead, whoever sent her wouldn't give up so easily.
Garin wanted to get out in front of whatever storm was
descending on him. To do that, he was going to need help.

"MELINA? CAN YOU hear me?"

Face numb from the cold, her eyes felt as if they were
full of glass shards. Melina Andrianou made herself

breathe. She regretted the effort instantly as pain racked her body. Still, she filled her lungs with oxygen again and again. Running a hand over her abdomen, she felt the two hot bullets that had lodged into the low-profile bulletproof armor she wore from chest to midthigh.

Trying to remain quiet, she felt for her pistol and found it on the floor next to her. She closed her hand around it and listened, hearing nothing. The smoking ruin of the bed filled her nostrils and she had to fight not to sneeze. She wiped her free hand over her eyes, clearing more of the stinging chemical. Squelching the fear that the fire extinguisher might have done permanent damage to her sight, she sat up, following her pistol, ready to shoot anyone in the room.

No one was there.

Making herself breathe, Melina took stock of her situation. Garin had sprayed her with the fire extinguisher, but there had been another man behind him.

"Melina?" She could hear her grandfather's concern and annoyance.

"I'm here."

"And the clockwork?"

The bed was empty. Bright embers were woven into the sheets, glowing orange defiantly. Fire extinguisher foam stood out in spots.

"Gone."

"What happened?"

"I was shot." Melina forced herself up and out of the bedroom. A wedge held the door to the hallway open.

"Are you injured?"

"Only bruised." Tears ran down Melina's face from the trace of chemicals still in her eyes. "Do you know where Garin Braden has gone?"

"Unfortunately, no. However we have had some success tracking down Eyuboglu."

"The man who sold the clockwork butterfly to Garin Braden."

"Yes. If we don't know where the clockwork is, maybe we can get closer to it by figuring out where it came from. In the meantime, you need to clear out of the hotel before the police arrive. A car will be waiting in the street."

Melina remembered the bodies in the room upstairs. "We're leaving dead behind."

"None of those men can lead back to us."

"Garin Braden knew who I was. You heard him talking to Erskine in the bar."

"He tracked you through the Golino woman."

She heard the reproach in her grandfather's voice. He had warned her to take no chances with Garin Braden, had told her the man was dangerous, but she had chosen to go with Golino. Claudia had been the best woman for the job. Melina would miss her. They had done some good work together.

"The police don't have the resources of Garin Braden and the old man."

"Have you found the old one?"

"We did." Her grandfather was silent for a moment. "In Paris."

Melina's stomach tightened as she went quickly down the stairs. She remembered him as he'd been in that dark dungeon: alone, beaten and half-starved, naked and wild-haired. Yet his gaze had been electric. He'd been afraid. Anyone would have under those conditions.

The old man had also been cunning. Despite all the torture she'd doled out, he hadn't broken. His secrets had remained his, and Melina still didn't know what it was he was hiding.

The next memory hurt. Her father's blood all over her.
    She would face the old man again, and this time she
would kill him. She didn't care if he gave up his secrets
or not.

15

The ringing phone startled Annja out of her studies. Jerked back into awareness of the silent hotel room around her, she broke her gaze from the tablet PC and checked the viewscreen. She didn't recognize the number. "Hello."

"Annja?"

Relief flooded Annja as she recognized Roux's voice. He sounded like himself, short-tempered and in a hurry. "What's going on?"

"Nothing you should concern yourself over."

"I heard there were people trying to kill you."

"They didn't succeed. Otherwise, you'd be hearing from me through a crystal or scrying bowl, wouldn't you?"

Evidently his snarkiness is still intact, too. Traffic noise filtered in over the connection and Annja knew he was walking along a street. She ignored his sarcasm. "Where are you?"

"Paris."

"I know you're in Paris. I talked to Henshaw earlier. He was on his way to you."

"Well, that's a waste of time."

"He thought he was being helpful."

"I'm perfectly capable of finding my way back home."

"He was worried about you. You might try being a little more grateful when gets there."

"Henshaw should have stayed at the house. With all of this nonsense going on, it needs to be watched. I don't know what's safe and what's not."

Annja was curious about that, but she had other matters she wanted to know about first. "Have you heard from Garin?"

Suspicion darkened Roux's tone. "Why? Has he been in touch with you?"

"Actually, I called him."

"Why would you do that?"

"I wanted to know more about the images you sent me. I figured he might know."

Roux snorted disdainfully. "And what did he have to say?"

"Not much. He was in the middle of a gun battle."

"He never could take advice when it was given to him. I told him to get out of there."

"There *where?*"

"Florence."

"What was he doing in Florence?" Annja wanted to scream. She would have thought she'd be used to Roux's petulance and half answers by now, but she wasn't.

"It has to do with the image I sent you."

Annja touched the tablet PC and brought up the image again. "The butterfly?"

"Yes, the butterfly. Have you found out anything about it?"

"I haven't exactly had it very long." Annja's phone buzzed and the viewscreen showed Garin's face. She had taken a picture of him and stored it in her phone, but it had mysteriously been erased and replaced by a different one. She'd assumed Garin hadn't cared for her picture, and she wasn't surprised that he had someone who could hack her phone. She also wasn't surprised that he'd be egotistical enough to improve his picture. "Hold on a minute. Garin's calling."

"What does he want?"

"I don't *know.* I haven't answered the call yet." Annja put Roux on hold because she knew he was safe, then answered Garin's call, listening carefully for the sharp crack of gunfire or bombs going off. With Roux and Garin, anything was possible.

"Good morning, Annja." His voice sounded pleasant and relaxed, as though he hadn't been dodging bullets only a few minutes ago.

"What are you doing in Florence that has people shooting at you?"

Garin paused. "How did you know I was in Florence?" He sounded slightly paranoid, which was unusual for him.

"Roux told me."

"You've talked to Roux?" His paranoia fled as anger took over.

"He's on the other line."

"Why did you call him?"

"I didn't. He called me. *Both* of you called me. I've been sitting here worr—wondering if you were alive or dead."

"Oh ye of little faith. I'm not that easy to kill. You should know that by now."

"I also know that when it happens, the two of you are going to be more surprised than anyone."

"'The two of you?'"

"You and your ego. Together, you've got to be the biggest target I've ever seen. I don't know how anyone shooting at you misses."

"Well, someone's not in a good mood."

"No. I'm not. I've been locked up in jail most of the night, and I've been getting mysterious phone calls from you and Roux."

"You called me."

"You're calling now."

"What were you in jail for?"

"It's a long story. Let's get back to why you and Roux called."

"What has Roux told you?"

"He sent me an image of some kind of…mechanical butterfly."

"Clockwork. A clockwork butterfly."

Annja sighed as she sat cross-legged on the bed. "Fine. A *clockwork* butterfly. An automaton. Call it whatever you like. What's that all about?"

"I don't know. You'll have to ask Roux."

"He has the butterfly?"

"I have the butterfly."

"Then why is Roux sending me pictures of the butterfly?"

"Because I sent the pictures to him and he probably wants your help figuring out exactly what it is."

"I want to know what is going on," she said in exasperation. Neither Roux nor Garin trusted the other very much, but she'd seen both of them in situations where they'd risked their lives for each other. "Otherwise, I'm going to hang up, turn off the phone and get some sleep that I really, really need."

"As I said, you'll have to ask Roux about the significance of the clockwork. Maybe he'll tell you, because he certainly won't tell me."

"Why are people trying to kill the both of you?"

"Someone tried to kill Roux?" Garin sounded surprised.

"Yes."

"When?"

"Just now."

"Interesting." Garin paused. "Obviously the woman isn't operating alone."

"*What* woman?" Annja knew for a fact there was a very thin line between exasperation and insanity. She had a toe over that line now and momentum was an irresistible force.

"She may be dead right now, so it won't matter."

"She may be dead?"

"One of my associates shot her, but the moment was very hectic."

Memories of the general lockup haunted Annja. This smacked of something that would land her in custody—somewhere—if she wasn't careful. She wasn't ready to go back to jail. "Look, whatever the two of you are doing, maybe you should just keep it to yourselves." Even as she said it, she knew she couldn't walk away. Garin knew it, too.

"Can't do that, I'm afraid. If Roux sent those pictures to you for some kind of consultation, then he's flummoxed, too. He needs help. I need help. You're going to have to choose one of us."

"No, I don't. If you've got something, and he knows something, you're going to have to work together."

"We can't. Not on this. That old goat is insufferable when it comes to these clockwork things."

The other line buzzed. Annja told Garin to hold on, then added his call to Roux's. "Okay, now we're all talking together."

"You've got Garin on here, as well?" Roux sounded put out.

"I'm here against my will." Garin didn't sound happy about the three-way call, either.

"Annja," Roux said in a calm, about-to-explode tone, "if I'd wanted to talk to Garin, I would have called him. I called *you*."

"*Why* did you call her?" Garin demanded. "You're willing to talk to *her* about the clockwork, but you're not willing to talk to *me?*"

"This isn't about you."

"Of course it's about me. I've got the clockwork and you want to talk to Annja about it."

Annja flopped back on the bed. "Guys. Maybe we could all talk this through. Like *adults?*"

Roux ignored her. "This isn't any of your business, Garin. Hang up."

"Not my business?" Garin roared into the phone. "I *found* this clockwork. It's *mine!* You wouldn't even have known of its existence if I hadn't contacted you!"

"I knew of its existence."

"Then why didn't you get it?"

"I didn't know where it was. By the way, where did you find it? I know it wasn't in Florence."

"How do you know that?"

"Tell me where you found it."

"No."

Roux took a deep breath and let it out. "Garin, this is no time to act like a child."

The effort Garin made to talk calmly strained his voice. "This is no time to act like an old fool. Melina Andrianou is a dangerous woman."

"You don't know the half of it."

"Then tell me what I'm missing."

Roux was silent.

Annja took that opportunity to wade into the discussion. "Me. I'm still here."

"Annja, I wanted you to look into the clockwork butterfly," Roux said.

"I am."

"But you haven't learned anything."

"Not yet. It's been—" she looked at the time/date stamp on the tablet PC "—all of eighteen minutes. Many of them spent listening to the two of you. These things take time. If there were easy answers, you'd probably already know them."

"He'll never tell you what he knows about the clockwork," Garin said. "This is one of his big secrets."

Roux sighed. "Obviously it isn't secret enough."

"Because *I* know about them?"

"Wait," Annja interrupted again. "*Them?* There's more than one of these butterflies?"

"There's more than one clockwork device," Garin said. "I've seen two others. I didn't, however, get to see them for long. Roux is quick about making them disappear. That woman very nearly killed me—*twice*—to get this one. I want to know how she knew they were so important."

"Her family probably found out about the clockwork from someone you told," Roux accused him. "Subtlety isn't your style, and you were never any good at discretion."

"I can be the soul of discretion," Garin argued.

"Then how did Melina Andrianou get on to you so quickly?"

"How should I know? Until today, I'd never heard of her."

Roux harrumphed. "You don't know her, but you know her family. You just don't recall."

"When did I meet her family?"

"A hundred years ago, give or take, on a salvage ship in the Aegean Sea."

16

"A *hundred* years?" Garin was nearly shouting. Annja took the phone from her ear, put it on speaker and laid it on the bed. "Do you truly expect me to remember someone I met in passing a hundred years ago?"

"It wasn't in passing," Roux argued. "We had business with the Andrianous. Or, I suppose I should say, *I* had business with that wretched family. Thieves and murderers were what they were. And they still are."

Annja took in a breath and let it out. "*Who* is Melina Andrianou and *what* is her interest in the clockwork?"

"She's a stone-cold killer," Garin answered. "Apparently Roux knows all about her."

"Not all about her." Roux sounded distracted. "She is one of the most vicious, cruel women I have ever met. It would have been better if you killed her."

"If she isn't dead, it's not from lack of my trying."

"If I had been there, she would have been dead. I would have made certain of it before I left."

"You weren't there, though, were you? It was me, and I was up against her without benefit of your knowledge."

Roux ignored that. "Do you still have the clockwork?"

"Yes."

"Good. Because I'll need it."

"No."

"'*No*'?" Roux's growl tore through the phone line.

"No. The clockwork is mine. I have it. I'm not about to give it to you."

"You don't know what to do with it."

"Then tell me."

Roux cursed. "That clockwork isn't for you."

"Then who is it for?"

Annja wanted to know the answer to that, as well. Although she was having a little trouble tracking the conversation because it kept shifting from English to French to German and back again. She didn't think Roux and Garin even noticed the shifts.

After a tense moment, Roux said, "That is one of the things I hope to find out. With Annja's help."

"But I've got the clockwork," Garin said.

"Garin, surely you can see this is beyond you. Listen to me regarding this. It's very dangerous."

"*I've* got the clockwork."

Roux cursed again.

"Not only that," Garin said, "Melina Andrianou knows me by name. I was staying at the hotel under an alias. I dealt with the man who found the clockwork under a different alias. Yet she was able to find *me*. And she found you, as well."

"She found me because you called me. All it took was for someone to hack phone records to get to me. That was no big feat. You unleashed her hounds on me."

"For someone to hack me—" Garin cursed "—is bigger than you realize."

Sitting on her bed in the hotel room, Annja knew she was relatively safe. But her gaze kept straying to the clock butterfly on the tablet PC screen. "Guys, hold on. Stop the bickering."

The other two quieted.

"Evidently this clockwork butterfly means something to both of you, and now you've got me interested. You've also got this Melina Andrianou on the hook, and she's trying to kill you both. Maybe we should pool our resources and—"

"Nonsense," Roux huffed.

"I'm not working with him," Garin replied. "No matter what, he's not going to tell you the truth. He'll look you squarely in the eye and lie about these clockwork devices. In almost six hundred years, he's never told me why artifacts like this strike such fear in his heart. We're better off trying to figure this out ourselves. Now that I finally have one of them."

"I'm willing to help," she continued, "but trying to help only one of you is going to mean letting go of some piece of this puzzle. And with someone on your tail, you're running out of time." She smiled. "*Clockwork. Running out of time.* See what I did there?"

Obviously Roux wasn't impressed with her wordplay. "What you're suggesting isn't going to work."

"We're not interested in working together on this. I have the clockwork." Indignation laced Garin's words.

"Remember there's a third party," Annja reminded them. "Garin, does Melina Andrianou know who you got the clockwork from?"

Garin hesitated. "Possibly. She used the buy as an opportunity to try to kill me this morning."

"Obviously she didn't manage to do that."

"It was a valiant effort."

Roux harrumphed again. "You don't know what a true effort is until you've sat in one of their dungeons. Then you would know."

Annja hurried on before Garin could one-up Roux. "Why would she try to kill you?"

"I don't know," Garin said. "To get the clockwork, I suppose."

"She might have been able to get that without killing you. She made an effort to kill you."

"*Two* efforts."

"Which begs the question—what made this so personal for a woman you say you've never met?"

"Because," Roux said, "Melina Andrianou knew who he was."

"What do you mean?"

Roux sighed. "The Andrianou family's involvement with the clockworks goes back a hundred years. The head of the family lived in the Aegean Sea at the turn of the twentieth century. Even back then, the Andrianous were salvagers, though they didn't mind the occasional act of piracy. They would attack boats out in the islands, kill everyone aboard, then claim the boat as salvage."

"Not exactly your average family."

"Certainly not. They were a bloodthirsty lot back then, and obviously subsequent generations haven't improved with age."

"And yet you worked with them."

"I didn't know about their history of violence till later. I barely escaped with my life then, and six years ago Melina Andrianou nearly killed me. If it weren't for Garin, I would have probably died. If, indeed, that is possible." Roux's voice dropped. "I owe her a great deal of anguish. Of course, she feels the same way about me."

"Why?"

"I killed her father six years ago."

"You…ah, I see. And she was there?"

"She was. She had tortured me for days. When I finally had the chance to escape, I took it. Her father got in the way. I tried to kill her, too, but she was quick."

"Let's go back to a hundred years ago. How did you come to know the Andrianou family?"

"I hired them to work for me."

"To rob and kill someone?" Garin asked.

"For a salvage operation. I found a sunken ship I wanted searched. They provided the means. I didn't know about their penchant for piracy back then."

"Wait." Garin finally sounded calm. "The shipwreck in the Aegean. I remember that. I was there."

"For part of the salvage," Roux replied irritably, "yes, you were. But not for all of it. You departed rather suddenly."

"I remember there was a girl," Garin mused. "A very beautiful girl."

"You were along for the expedition for a few days. Then you met Iambe."

"Iambe." Softness infused the name when Garin said it. "I'd forgotten her name." He chuckled. "She was a fine, fine young woman. Really good in the—"

"Stop," Annja interrupted him. "We get it. You met a girl."

"Yes, he did," Roux said in accusation. "At the time he couldn't get enough of her. He disappeared shortly after meeting her."

I'll bet that happens a lot. Annja chose to keep her observation to herself.

"I never saw you again till after the Andrianou family nearly killed me."

"She was a beautiful girl," Garin replied.

"She was," Roux agreed. "Yet you should have been with me."

"I didn't know you found a clockwork."

"I did."

"What was it?"

"A snail. A wonderfully intricate African snail. It was over a foot long, life-size. Truly one of the most elegant creations I have ever seen."

The idea of foot-long snails didn't sit well with Annja. Especially since having come across them in the sub-Sahara in Africa.

"What happened to the snail?" Garin asked.

"They tried to steal it from me, doubtless thinking that it would be worth a fabulous sum. To the right people, it would have been, but they didn't know those people. During the scuffle for the snail, it…*imploded*…I guess would be the best description."

Annja looked at the image of the butterfly again. She didn't see anything in it that looked in any way like an explosive.

"Almost capsized the salvage vessel in the process," he continued. "Killed a few of the crewmen, as well as two members of the Andrianou family. That was when they swore eternal enmity toward me. And Garin."

"Why me?" Garin protested. "I wasn't there."

"The Andrianou family thought we were related. Father and son."

"Father and *grandson*."

Roux sniffed. "Whatever. That's really not important. What is important is that the Andrianous intend to see you and me dead. Me and my family. If we had not left Greece immediately, you would have seen that." He paused. "And perhaps now they'll want to kill Annja, as well."

That surprised her. "Me? I wasn't even born when you guys met the Andrianous. And by their reckoning, you should be dead…or at least in a nursing home. Both of you, by the way."

"It won't matter. If the Andrianous can find Garin under his Braden identity, we have to assume they will eventually *pinpoint you,* as well. *They're really* very lethal, Annja. You will be in danger till we resolve this."

"Terrific." Annja took a deep breath and let it out, thinking furiously. "It doesn't make sense that Melina Andrianou would pursue a clockwork butterfly so hard if all it's going to do is implode."

"Self-destruction wasn't something the device had been constructed to do," Roux said. "That was surprising. Of course, there may have been other factors in play that I didn't know about."

"What factors?"

"How would I know?" Roux snapped.

"Then what had the snail been designed to do?"

"I'm not certain, but the clockwork snail had...*qualities*...about it that affected several people aboard the salvage ship."

"What qualities?"

"Each of the affected crew had a dream that revealed something of their future to them. At least, each was under the impression it did. They were alarmed to discover they had all dreamed portentiously the night after our discovery of the clockwork." Roux sighed. "Unfortunately, not all of those revelations were happy or peaceful things. Two people foresaw their own deaths. One of them saw his death in the implosion of the device during the scuffle over it."

"If he saw that, then why didn't he leave the salvage vessel?"

"He saw it," Roux explained, "but that doesn't mean we understood how it was going to happen. Or when. But seeming manifestation of power like that hooked the Andrianou family. Captain Andrianou had a dream about me, and that dream revealed certain things I had hoped would remain in my past."

"Like what?"

"Other clockworks I have found over the years."

"How many?"

"That's not relevant."

"See?" Garin complained. "I told you. Stonewalls you every time. Never gives you a straight answer when he can lie."

Annja forced herself to be calm in spite of having to put up with Roux and Garin at their worst. *Second worst,* she amended. *At least they're not trying to kill each other at the moment.* "What about you, Roux?"

"What about me?"

"Did the clockwork snail reveal anything to you in a dream?"

"He's not going to tell you," Garin snarled.

"I did dream," Roux replied in a beatific tone. "I dreamed Garin was a seething, enflamed hemorrhoid that had no cure."

"All right," Annja said quickly, "that's enough. You're both so wound up over each other that you're forgetting you have bigger problems. Melina Andrianou and her family. While you're sitting there talking, she could be closing in on the man who sold the clockwork butterfly."

That stopped them.

Then Roux said, "Garin?"

"It's possible. She paid him off to allow her a chance to kill me."

"Do you know where this man is?"

Garin hesitated before answering, "No." He sounded contrite.

Roux cursed. "Do you know where this man got that clockwork?"

"Yes."

"I'll need to get a few things from my house, then I'll

join you. Are you going to see to Annja's travel needs? Or shall I?"

"I've already got a jet standing by at Logan International Airport. All she has to do is get there."

"Fine," Annja said. "Where am I going?"

Garin reluctantly gave up the destination. "Genoa."

Annja smiled. "The beach. I'll need clothes. I'd only packed winterwear."

"It will be taken care of. When will you reach the airport?"

Annja rolled from the bed and stood. "I'm packing now." She opened the drawers and scooped the few things she'd brought into the carryall. "I'll be out the door in five minutes." Sleep was forgotten. "I'm going to need better pictures of the clockwork butterfly so I can work on the flight over."

"I'll get them to you."

"I'm on my way." Annja broke the connection, grabbed underwear, khaki cargo pants and a pullover sweater out of her bag, then zipped it closed and got dressed. She put on her coat, shoved the tablet PC in her backpack, which she then slung over her shoulder, grabbed her carry-on and headed for the door.

17

"I know what you're thinking, Bahadir Eyuboglu."

Seated in an uncomfortable chair with his hands tied behind him, Eyuboglu was actually thinking many things. He was thinking that he wished he'd never met up with the man who had bought the strange mechanical butterfly. That making the deal to kill that man was perhaps the worst thing he could have done. That he should have left Florence and returned to Turkey, and that the men there who had sworn to kill him could not possibly be as frightening as the woman standing in front of him.

And he was thinking he was going to die here in this decrepit basement with the water-stained stone walls that felt like a tomb.

"Do you want me to tell you what you're thinking right now?" The woman stared down at him without expression.

"I will do whatever you want."

"I know, but you see…that's part of the problem. You're very afraid."

"I am." Eyuboglu nodded. Sweat trickled down his face and into his eyes. That made him blink, and he was afraid to do that because he knew there was every possibility that he would die in that instant.

"You'll lie to me."

"No. Never. I swear." Eyuboglu could smell his fear, a

sour, pungent scent that made him want to throw up. But he was afraid to do that, too, because the woman might take offense.

"You will. You won't be able to stop yourself. In most people, lying is a necessary survival skill. With you, it's a vocation."

Eyuboglu shook his head as tears and sweat ran freely now. The plastic ties around his wrists bit into his flesh. The ones around his ankles that bound his legs to the chair had caused his feet to go numb. "I swear." His voice was a hoarse croak.

The single light that hung overhead felt hot and played tricks with his vision. When the woman leaned in just right, he could see her face. Then she would withdraw into the curtain of shadows just beyond the light.

"Where did you get the mechanical butterfly?"

Eyuboglu didn't hesitate even though the big man he'd sold it to had promised he would kill him if he told. He had believed the man, but he wasn't here in this small basement at the moment. That was a thing to be afraid of later, after he convinced this woman to release him. Eyuboglu intended to leave Florence and never come back. He would live a very small life in Istanbul. So small no one would ever find him again.

"From a marine salvager in Genoa. His name is Sebastiano Troiai. Check. I am telling you the truth." Eyuboglu prayed silently, listening to the woman talk to someone else in a language he thought sounded Greek.

She returned her attention to him. "How are you connected to him?"

"We do business together. He finds artifacts under the ocean. I know people who like to collect such artifacts. For a price, I put Troiai's findings into the hands of others."

"For two prices, you mean. You collect at both ends."

That wasn't something Eyuboglu would admit to under normal circumstances, but these were not normal circumstances. "Yes. Yes." He shrugged. "Neither party had to know. Neither truly cared."

"Where did Troiai find the clockwork artifact?"

In that instant, Eyuboglu knew he was in trouble. If he told the woman the truth, that he didn't know, she might not believe him. She would torture him until she was sure of his answer.

However, if he lied, she would believe him till she knew differently. By that time, though, he hoped to be long gone. "Off the coast. Two point three miles. Troiai found the shipwreck after a storm. He says storms sometimes do that to the seafloor, make it turn over so hidden things are revealed. He was there recovering a pleasure craft that had sunk during the storm."

"What was the name of the ship?"

Eyuboglu thought quickly, remembering that maybe Troiai had told him the name of a ship. He wished he knew if the woman was aware of what ship the mechanical butterfly had gone down on. Even if Troiai had told him the origin of the shipwreck, even if he could remember, the woman might think it came from somewhere else.

There was no correct answer.

He shook his head, his lower jaw trembling in fear. "I don't know. I swear to you, I don't know."

"That's all right. I believe you."

"Thank you. Thank you." Eyuboglu was so relieved that he was almost weeping. Then he saw the gleam of the long knife in the woman's hands.

"I believe you, but I have to make certain. We can't afford any mistakes."

Eyuboglu fought his restraints and screamed. Neither did any good. He did not get free, and his screams went no farther than the basement walls. His blood slid down his body, across the floor and oozed finally through the drain in the center of the room.

"YOU ENJOY THAT far too much for your own good."

Peeling the surgical gloves from her hands, Melina Andrianou looked at her grandfather. He stood there calmly, in dress pants and a button-down shirt with the sleeves rolled to midforearm. Some would mistake him for a university professor, and he could have been. He was smarter than all of Melina's professors had been when she'd attended.

The strong scent of the Turkish coffee he sipped permeated the room.

She threw the bloodstained gloves into a bright orange hazardous waste receptacle against the wall beside the door that led to the basement she'd just come through. She peeled off the bloody gown and tossed it in, too. They would be taken to the incinerator as soon as she left.

She was tired. The few hours of sleep she'd managed on the short flight from Florence to Athens by chartered plane hadn't been enough. Only the thought of torturing Eyuboglu had buoyed her spirits. But now reality had set in. Garin had vanished, and it was already the gray hours of the following day.

"It's work. It was necessary. There's no reason not to enjoy it." Melina crossed to the sink mounted on the wall on one side of the small room. On the other side was a computer workstation.

"Did you get the truth from that man?"

"Yes. In the end he didn't know as much as he claimed he did." She washed her hands in the sink.

"I didn't think he would. A man like him, he only cares about profit margin." Georgios Andrianou pointed at another cup on the small cupboard beside the sink. "I brought you coffee. I knew you were nearly finished when he no longer had the strength to scream."

Melina picked up the coffee cup and sipped. The strong aroma washed some of the blood scent from her nostrils. She hadn't minded the blood, though. Her father had taught her everything she knew about torture.

The whir of the bone saws coming from the basement provided background to their conversation.

Her grandfather gazed at her in quiet contemplation. "Your grandmother always insisted that something was wrong with our blood after my grandfather died in that salvage expedition in 1902. She believed the mechanical snail had infected all of those aboard the vessel with a sickness."

Melina shook her head. She'd heard the story before. "Do you believe my father was some sociopath, Grandfather? Or that I have a diseased mind?"

He smiled, the first true smile she'd seen on his face in weeks. "No, but your grandmother, may she rest in peace, would. She was a superstitious one, your grandmother. She said that the Andrianou family had become cursed that night when the mechanical device was lost, that the old gods had found disfavor in us."

Melina knew her grandfather had his own superstitions no matter what he said. Enchanted by the stories of his grandfather's death, the finding of the mechanical device and the fierce old man who had snatched his life from the jaws of death, Georgios Andrianou had chased the legends of the clockwork devices with an aggressive determination. He had built an empire solely to fund his search for them.

"What do you believe about my father and me?" Melina watched the old man's face, not sure if she would know a lie from him if she saw it. She would need her knives to know the truth for certain.

"I believe that I raised a strong son and helped raise a strong granddaughter. I am thankful for you."

"You would be more thankful if we knew the secret of the clockwork."

Her grandfather sipped his coffee. "That man Roux has not aged since 1902. He remains the same old man who hired Pavlos Andrianou."

That was true. She had seen the photographs taken aboard her great-great-grandfather's ship. Those images were in black and white, grainy, but Roux had been easily recognizable. "Garin Braden has not changed, either."

In the beginning, her grandfather had pursued the clockwork in an effort to solve the mystery of what happened to his grandfather, Pavlos. Six years ago, though, when they found Roux and discovered the man was—incredibly and inexplicably—still alive, the quest for clockwork artifacts had taken on an edge of frenzy. Her grandfather was an old man with few years left to him. Now he believed that the clockworks somehow had the power to stop time.

Melina didn't know what to believe, except that she wanted to kill the old man, Roux, and Garin Braden.

Her grandfather took a towelette from the sink and delicately dabbed at her face. Small traces of blood stained the towelette when he removed it. "You're going to Genoa next?"

"Yes. I have a team en route to watch Sebastiano Troiai. I will go there next."

"You do not know that Roux and Garin Braden will go there."

"I do not know any other place they will go. They will want to look into the origins of the butterfly, as well. Now only Troiai knows where he found it."

Her grandfather threw the towelette into the hazardous waste bin. "That's too bad."

"But I do have another clue."

He turned to her and folded his arms across his chest. "What?"

Melina dug a USB thumb drive out of her pocket. "Eyuboglu took several high-resolution photographs of the mechanical butterfly. There's an inscription on the device."

Her grandfather smiled again, something Melina had never seen twice in one day. "Magnificent."

She went to the computer on the other side of the room and moved the mouse, bringing it to life. Inserting the thumb drive into the USB port, she waited. A minute later, the search screen came on.

Eyuboglu's device held many pictures of diverse items he had for sale. Melina had to sort through a couple hundred before she found the images she was searching for. When she brought the photographs of the mechanical butterfly up on the monitor and increased the magnification, she was impressed with the quality. The details were all there.

Including the inscription under the butterfly's left wing.

Her grandfather bent closer to the monitor. "That is very small."

"Metalworkers were meticulous men, used to working on small surfaces. You've seen some of the metal scrolls we've recovered."

"Yes." Her grandfather's eyes narrowed and he peered more closely. "Can you make it out?"

"No. It looks like Greek, or some form of the language, anyway, but I can't read it. However, we have a friend who might be able to."

Straightening, her grandfather nodded. "Tell the cardinal I said hello. And let me know what he thinks immediately."

"Of course."

"I hope Roux and Garin go to Genoa. I hope we haven't lost them."

"We haven't. The hunt is only now starting. I'll find them. I'm sure of it." Excitement stirred within Melina. She didn't really care about the clockwork. She wanted another chance to kill the old man.

18

Hey, Annja, so it's robot bugs you want, huh? Ick! No, really, *ick!* Still, since you asked about automatons, I thought I'd throw this into the pot.

Have you heard about the *karakuri ningyo?* They were mechanized puppets created in Japan in the seventeenth century and used until the nineteenth century. They were pretty cool. They made the *zashiki karakuri* automatons to serve tea. They were small, powered by whalebone springs and carried cups of tea to guests.

Karakuri translates loosely to "mechanism" or "trick." *Ningyo* translates kinda into "person-shape." That included puppets and dolls. *Dashi karakuri* were used in religious events to act out myths and legends. *Butai karakuri* were used on the stage, mainly in Kabuki theater.

I don't know if there were any insects, but you might check there. After all, several Asian cultures believe crickets are good luck!

Still…ick!
Sailor Moon's Shadow

Annja sat cross-legged in the spacious seat of the private jet she'd boarded at Logan International Airport only minutes ago. The staff of three flight attendants had gotten her squared away quickly, then pestered her, trying to find things they could do for her. She'd finally chased them back to wherever it was they were flying, leaving the cabin just for her—*And here's the buzzer if you need anything, Ms. Creed. Please let us know.*

What she needed was peace and quiet. And answers. Lots of answers. She opened the journal she carried in her backpack and framed her questions on paper. Although the tablet PC could be used anywhere there was electricity, and for hours even when there wasn't, she wanted a blank space to think while she surfed the internet and trolled the alt.history and alt.archaeology sites.

Her mind had already fragmented the questions into different fields of research.

Where did the butterfly clockwork come from?
Who is/was the Andrianou family?
What are Roux and Garin most likely hiding?

She responded to the post on the alt.history site, typing quickly on the tablet PC's detachable keyboard.

Thanks for the reply, Shadow. Sorry, not in the market for Japanese bugs! I knew about the *karakuri ningyo.* Cool stuff.

Annja's computer dinged as she sipped a cup of chamomile tea the attendants had provided her. Opening her email, she found a new message from Garin's private researcher. The woman hadn't yet given her name, and the email address had obviously been set up to use and lose, but she was good at what she did.

Ms. Creed:
I've set up a Dropbox for all the news I could dredge up on the Andrianou family. Hope it helps.
Schrettinger

The woman had a sense of humor as well as a keen intellect. Martin Schrettinger had been a German librarian and a priest at the Benedictine monastery in Weissenohe, Bavaria. He was also considered the father of modern library science based on his work at organizing the great library at the church.

Annja surmised that whoever this "Schrettinger" was, she was a librarian by training. Probably more than that, though, since she worked with Garin. Annja knew her gender because Garin had referred to the contact as female.

Thanks, Marty!

That was just to let the woman know she'd identified the name.

Following the Dropbox link, Annja logged into the folder—"Schrettinger and the Archaeologist"—and opened up the files, copying them from that location into her own storage space on the cloud. The cloud location was new, as well, not one she was currently using on other projects. She wasn't going to give Garin—or his little librarian—a glimpse into her personal files.

Flicking through the various PDFs of newspaper stories, Annja discovered that Schrettinger had found articles relating to the tragic accident aboard the *Silver Cyclops,* the salvage ship owned by Pavlos Andrianou. The loss of the ship had been attributed to "a freak storm." There were a few black-and-white photographs of the family and of Pavlos. The man was stark and lean, hard-faced, but had an easygoing smile.

There were also police reports—copies of handwritten ledger entries—that mentioned the suspicion officials had about Pavlos's involvement in disappearing ships and boats in the areas. The original notes had been written in

Greek, which Annja could read a little of, but Schrettinger had provided English translations, as well. It was a lot of work and Annja was suitably impressed.

Another document showed the Andrianou family tree all the way down to Melina Andrianou. The family had remained small. There were a few assorted cousins, but none of them seemed to be involved with Georgios and Melina Andrianou.

Annja closed the family history and opened up the one on Melina Andrianou. The first photograph showed the woman walking in front of a bakery that specialized in wedding cakes. The picture was sharp enough to show her left profile as a darker image in the window glass. She wore business casual and was in midstride. She didn't have the humor of her great-great-grandfather. She was cold and distant.

The next picture showed the woman at some kind of social event. The little black dress she wore drew the attention of men and women around her and set her apart from the crowd. She was talking to a white-haired man that a digital note identified as Georgios Andrianou, her grandfather. In the picture, Melina was smiling and at ease.

She was a beautiful woman, as Garin had said, but Annja thought she could see hints of cruelty in the deadness of her eyes and the set of her mouth. Schrettinger had been good about building a personal history, as well, but there were a lot of missing areas. Melina had attended the University of Athens, but hadn't completed a degree. She'd studied history while she was there and had received excellent marks.

Schrettinger evidently had no problem hacking into university computer systems. Annja filed that information on Garin's liaison away.

Melina had also studied a number of martial arts, and was licensed to carry a weapon. Several weapons, as a matter of fact, and was listed as a security officer in the family business. Numerous documents showed she had a lack of respect for authority. She'd been arrested a dozen times, but the charges had been dismissed in each case, either pled out for a reduced fine or sentence served, or witnesses withdrew their testimonies.

Most of those brushes with the law were in regard to various artifacts, most particularly mechanical devices. Schrettinger had highlighted those sections on the reports. One of those reports revealed that Melina had been arrested at age twelve for breaking and entering and being in possession of burglar's tools. She'd been caught stealing a mechanical bull, which had later disappeared from the private museum she'd unsuccessfully targeted.

Okay, so you've been looking for the clockworks for some time, too.

Annja flipped through more pages and discovered the news report of Xydias Andrianou's death at the hands of unknown assailants. Xydias had been stabbed several times, and decapitated. That file included crime scene photographs of Xydias's body lying in an alley where it had been discovered by passersby. The dead man looked as if he'd been savagely mauled.

Roux had said Melina was there when he'd killed her father, but he hadn't mentioned that he'd removed Xydias Andrianou's head. That had to have left an impression on the woman six years ago. Annja would have thought it would leave an impression on Roux, too. That was pretty cold-blooded.

A chill drifted through Annja as she looked at the woman again. Melina Andrianou couldn't have weathered such an experience without emotional scars. *Roux and Garin are lucky to be alive.*

The computer dinged, and this time is was another post on the alt.history site.

Hi, Annja!
Big fan here! Love, love, love the show! Keep up the good work. BTW, have you heard of Tippoo's tiger? It was built for the Tippoo sultan, the ruler of an Indian kingdom called Mysore, which I always thought was a weird name. Anyway, Tippoo's tiger is really pretty cool, in a blood-thirsty mechanical way. That sultan had a real thing for watching Europeans get killed. I've attached a photo to this post so you can look at it. I know it's not the bug you were looking for, but maybe you'll find some in India? I'll keep looking.
Toymaker Tom

Opening the attachment, Annja studied the image. The orange-and-black mechanical tiger crouched on top of a mechanical man wearing a red shirt and a black hat. He was obviously *not* Indian. India hadn't been happy with England or any of the Western world at the time the toy had been made.

The man lying under the tiger was dwarfed by the big cat. The automaton contained an organ that created screams for the victim and growls for the tiger. As the organ was played, the victim lifted a hand in helpless terror at being eaten. The sultan had a macabre idea of what a good time was.

Tippoo's tiger had survived the British invasion in 1799 that had brought about the fall of Seringapatam during the Fourth Anglo-Mysore War. Annja had seen the actual mechanical "toy" at the Victoria and Albert Museum in London, where it had also survived World War II.

Hey, Tom, thanks for the help, but I believe the automatons I'm looking for were made in Greece. Or around Greece. I've studied the artifact, and there's an inscription on it that looks Greek.

Annja's phone vibrated and she took the call. "Annja Creed."

"Annja!" Thodoros Papassavas's voice was boisterous and jovial, deep and rich. It fit the man, a giant in personality and stature. "How are you doing, my dear?"

"I'm doing well, Thodoros." Annja leaned her head back against the comfortable seat. "How are you and Mina doing?"

"Fine, fine. Mina, of course, sends her love. She's busy these days with the children. They are constantly into things. She misses the days when she was in the field as an anthropologist, but the children are forever finding things in our backyard for her to 'authenticate.'"

Annja laughed. It was nice to talk about something that was normal, something that didn't have crime scene photographs and the threat of death attached to it.

Unfortunately, the small talk ended all too soon.

"I've looked at the image you sent me, but I'm afraid I can't help you with much more information than you already have."

Annja put her phone on speaker and opened the file she'd started on the inscription that had been on the butterfly. "I'll take what you can give me."

"The language is Greek, but it is a very ancient dialect. You've heard of Mycenaean Greek?"

"Yes." Annja paused a moment, assembling her thoughts. "The Mycenaean civilization flourished in the Late Bronze Age, around the second millennium BC. The language fragmented in the early Iron Age after the Mycenaean civilization collapsed. There were at least four distinct dialects. Primarily, though, the language we understand from that period comes from the Arcadocpriot dialect, as well as the Aeolic, Doric and Ionic, which were regional."

"You would shame my linguistics students, Annja."

"I brushed up on the language a little since I emailed you that image."

"Those dialects you mentioned fostered others. People speak differently regionally, based on experience and word choice. For instance, the Aeolic dialect was further divided into Boeotian and Thessalian. And the Lesbian dialect." Thodoros sighed. "My undergrads titter and giggle when I mention that particular dialect."

"Isle of Lesbos, right?"

"We know it well because of the writings left behind by the poet Sappho, whom Plato called the tenth muse, and who created new poetry by writing about her own thoughts instead of imagined adventures of the gods."

Annja's mind was already flying. "Lesbos was west of the Asia Minor coastline and north of Smyrna." She opened a map on her tablet PC and looked at the island in the Aegean Sea. "Separated from Turkey by the Mytilini Strait."

"Yes, it's the third largest island in Greece. Have you ever visited it?"

"No."

"If you get the chance, you should. Beautiful place. Mountains and olive groves as far as the eye can see. Unless you're looking out at the Aegean, then there's the ocean, of course. Wonderful people there, salt of the earth. All the rest and relaxation you could care for, and many historical sites to visit. You would love it."

"Do you think this language was from Lesbos?"

"I wouldn't know for sure, but I think it's a good possibility."

"Because of the dialects?"

"Exactly." Papassavas paused. "I also believe that the language is in a code."

"A code?"

"Yes, a simple one. Probably letter substitution. Much of Greek and Roman history was concurrent. And Julius Caesar invented the letter substitution code. Although the Jewish people would argue that because they had the Atbash cipher. You haven't said where you got this artifact."

"It turned up as part of marine salvage in Genoa."

"Fascinating. I'd heard they've had earthquakes again there. Those almost always make the sea give up something."

"They have a tendency to allow the sea to take things, too."

"True. Do you know what this was made for?"

"I have no idea. I haven't yet seen the actual piece."

"When you do, you'll have to let me know your impressions." Papassavas sighed. "Until then, I've got a desk covered in papers that I have to grade."

"I'll leave you to that, then."

"I'll be back in touch as soon as I have something for you."

"Thank you. I'll owe you one."

"When you get the chance, come see us, Annja. The children would be thrilled to see their favorite television star again."

"I will." Annja thanked him, then hung up and laid the phone aside. A quick glance at her watch told her she still had four more hours of flight. Eyes burning, she shut down the tablet PC and shoved it in her backpack. Then she put her seat back and closed her eyes.

In her dreams, clockwork ghosts rode witches' brooms and spoke in thick, Russian accents.

19

Melina parked her car as close as she could to the Archaeological Museum of Piraeus, then she walked to the new two-story building, which had been constructed in 1981. The museum had been a favorite of her father's. Xydias Andrianou had brought her there several times in his search for the mysterious clockwork maker. Before Roux had killed him.

She wondered if Cardinal Scuro had known this museum had been a favorite of her father's. It was possible, because the man knew a lot about a great many things. That was why she was here now.

It was only a five-minute walk down to the reception area for tourist ships in the port. Reaching her destination in front of the museum, yet not finding the man waiting for her, she took her phone from her jacket pocket and found Cardinal Scuro in her address book. When she pressed his name and the phone rang, the call was answered almost immediately.

"I see you." His voice was deep and melodic.

Even if it made her appear weak, Melina couldn't help glancing around as she put her phone away. Ten yards from her, Cardinal Scuro stepped from behind the corner of the museum and walked across the grass toward her.

His real name was Dino Corvo. Once upon a time, Cardinal Scuro had worked in the Vatican as a translator down in the private libraries. That was before he'd been discovered selling information from secret church documents. Although he no longer had access to those libraries, he still had translation skills and knowledge of arcane history no one could strip from him.

He was a young man, only a few years older than Melina, and wore his black hair in ringlets. A neatly shaved black beard covered his chin and helped him appear older than he was. Most people thought he was kind and gentle, a stolid man, a man who would listen to their problems without judgment. Melina had heard women speak of him that way. They only saw what they wanted to.

In Melina's opinion, it was Cardinal Scuro's eyes that gave him away. They were dark and flat, devoid of warmth. In some ways, his eyes reminded her of her own.

Dressed all in black with a calf-length duster to blunt the early chill coming in from the ocean, Scuro still looked like he belonged to the church. All that was missing was the clerical collar.

He handed her a takeout cup and kept one for himself. "Chocolate. I know you like it."

Melina accepted it and breathed in the heady scent of the chocolate. "Thank you. But I didn't come all this way for a hot chocolate." She sipped it, finding it just cool enough to drink without burning her tongue.

"No, you didn't." The breeze ruffled Scuro's duster.

Out in the harbor, boat klaxons rang. Fishing boats sailed on the horizon, in search of the catches they hoped to bring in to feed the tourists.

"I don't know why I'm here at all. We could have handled this over the phone."

"Because I asked you to meet me, and sometimes I like seeing you, Melina."

Meaning that there were other times he didn't like seeing her? Melina quashed the thought. She'd never been interested in Scuro. Men were a passing annoyance to her, something to do during downtime when she had it. At most, this man was a conundrum she hadn't quite solved.

"Did you find something on the clockwork butterfly?"

Scuro's lips flickered in a quick smile. "You're always so impatient."

She regarded him coldly. "I am more impatient concerning this piece. Someone else currently has it, and I want it back. More than that, I want to know where it came from."

"Who is the other person?"

There was no reason to withhold the information. If Cardinal Scuro wasn't able to suss that out, he wasn't worth asking. "Garin Braden."

Scuro frowned. "He's a very dangerous man."

"You know him?"

"We've had dealings."

"Face-to-face?"

He shook his head. "I've never dealt with Braden directly. Some of my acquaintances have…*encountered* Braden while acquiring items he also wanted. More than a few of them are no longer with us."

"Evidently they weren't equal to him."

"And you are?" Scuro's lips smiled again, but not his dark eyes. Amusement was just another of the masks that he wore. "I would hate to lose you, Melina. You provide interesting projects."

"I am more than his equal."

"Yet Braden has the butterfly that you are after."

Melina narrowed her eyes and took a moment to check her anger. "Tread carefully. My grandfather and I value your skills, but they are not irreplaceable."

"My apologies. I did not mean to offend."

Melina knew the man had intended to get a reaction from her.

"Walk with me."

She fell into step beside him as they crossed the grass.

"You've never said what it is that you want with the clockwork artifacts."

"They're a means to get to an old enemy."

"Someone other than Braden?"

"Yes."

"May I ask who?"

Melina hesitated only for a moment. Again, if Scuro didn't know the old man's name, especially when associated with Garin, then any information he had wasn't worth much. "A man named Roux."

"A French name."

"We believe so."

"'We'?"

"Roux has been an enemy to my family for a great many years." *He killed my father!* Melina put her hands in her jacket pockets so Scuro would not see how they'd knotted into fists.

"You don't have a surname for Roux?"

"No."

"Interesting."

Cars passed on the streets. Taxis took tourists toward the port. A few pedestrians used the sidewalks. Melina never knew if Cardinal Scuro was alone, or if he had someone watching over him. She had her own two men sitting in a car half a block away.

"Tell me about the butterfly," she said.

Scuro shook his head. "I don't know anything about the butterfly. I'd like to see it at some point. If you ever get your hands on it."

"By that time I might not need you."

He chuckled. "I doubt that's the case. There are things in the world that you have no clue about." He sipped his chocolate. "However, before you lose patience with me, I can tell you about the inscription."

Melina held her breath.

"The inscription was most likely not on the original butterfly."

"Why do you say that?"

"Because the inscription was put there by one of Julius Caesar's soldiers. A centurion named Gabinius."

After a brief search of her memory, Melina shook her head. "I have never heard of him."

"I would have been surprised if you had. Centurion Gabinius has no real historic distinction." Scuro looked at her with a mocking grin. "Except that he was sent on a secret mission by Caesar during the waning years of the dictator's rule."

"What mission?"

"Gabinius was sent to find a weapon. A fabled clockwork that would have tilted the odds against Caesar unless he stopped it and put them once more in his favor. Do you know much about Roman history?"

"Enough."

"About Caesar's last days?"

"He was preparing for war against the Parthian Empire."

"More than that, he was planning on laying waste to the Caucasus, Scythia, and take out Germania on the way through Eastern Europe. At the same time, relations with Egypt were rocky, though Caesar had taken Queen Cleopatra as a lover and might have fathered a child with her. His ambitions knew no bounds. That was why his detractors killed him." Scuro sipped his chocolate again. "During his travels, Caesar had seen many strange and wondrous things. At some point, he learned of Michalis the Toymaker. Have you heard of him?"

Melina reflected only for a moment. "No." But that didn't mean that the man wasn't mentioned somewhere in her father's journals.

"Not many people know about Michalis. Even I don't know what's truth and what's fabrication when it comes to this man. He is an enigma. According to *most* of the reports I've read, he lived some three hundred years before the birth of Christ."

Doing the math only took a moment. "That's well before Caesar's time."

"Two hundred and fifty years or so, yes."

"Michalis would have been dead." Even as she said that, Melina thought of Roux and Garin, how they both seemed to be over a hundred years old. How was that possible?

"Definitely."

But perhaps not. Not if one of those clockwork creations of his could stop a man from growing older. Melina knew her grandfather would be greatly interested. "Then how did Gabinius manage to find Michalis?"

He shook his head. "The centurion didn't find Michalis. He found the toymaker's workshop. That was what he had been tasked to find."

"How did Gabinius know where to look?"

"Lore. Fragments of tales. Whispers and rumors. The usual research when treasure hunters go looking for legendary things. Several centurions were sent in search of Michalis's wonders. Gabinius, perhaps, found where the toymaker worked."

"Where was that?"

Coming to a stop, Scuro turned and gestured to the sea. "Somewhere out there. From everything I have read about the man, it is believed that Michalis was Greek. It's rumored that he lived somewhere out in the Aegean Sea on a small, private island, and that his workshop was underground."

"How do you know this?"

"Because Gabinius reported this to Caesar. The church has two of his reports to Caesar in their files. And there are other memoirs that talk about Michalis's workshop. Only a few were ever allowed to visit him there. Usually the only visitors were models."

"Models?"

"Men, women and animals Michalis brought in so that he could sculpt them. He needed resources for his creations."

"His toys were supposed to help fight wars?"

"According to legend, yes. Some say he had an army of clockwork soldiers that would battle any who tried to come unannounced to his island."

"Do you believe that?"

Scuro stared out at the harbor. "As Hamlet says, 'There are more things in heaven and earth, Horatio, than are dreamt of in your philosophy.'"

"Michalis lived well before the Roman Catholic Church was established. Why would they be interested in a Greek toymaker?"

He dropped his voice. "Because the church found one of Michalis's clockworks at a village outside Rome that had been burned to the ground in 513 AE. Every man, woman and child had been killed."

"How?"

"No one knows. There were no survivors. All that was left was a clockwork goat."

"A goat?"

Scuro nodded. "The church investigator sent to look into the matter destroyed the goat and scattered the pieces.

Supposedly none of the clockwork remains intact." He paused. "Rumors began to circulate among the people and the church that Michalis was in league with Satan."

"Do you know where the location of the village is?" It might be worth sending a team there to investigate. After so many years, finding something was improbable, but with today's forensic tools it was worth trying.

"No. All record of the village's location was expunged even from the church's most secret records. After all, it's one thing to have people believe in Satan, but quite another to present evidence of it."

"Then the whole thing could be a lie. There's no village, no goat, no solid report."

"You're right, of course. But the story was tied to the file the church has on Michalis. There are rumors of some of his other creations killing, as well."

"Unsubstantiated?"

"They don't have any concrete data on anything recent. The last report was that village. The butterfly you *almost* had your hands on would be the first such discovery in over fifteen hundred years."

Melina frowned. "There was another clockwork."

Interest sparked in Scuro's dead eyes. "What was it?"

"A clockwork snail."

"Do you have it?"

"No."

"Did it exhibit any special abilities?"

Melina studied Scuro's face. Normally she wasn't able to discern much there, but this morning she could see his excitement. "You tell me."

"There is talk of one of Michalis's creations reaching the mainland. A snail that caused dreams of the future." Scuro looked deep into her eyes. "That was the snail you're referring to, wasn't it?"

"Tell me more about the snail." That clockwork had forever changed Melina's family. She wasn't going to give out information about it until necessary. "Who had it?"

"A fisherman caught it in his nets near Pylos, what was at one time called Navarino, where the Russians, British and French joined forces with Greece to destroy the Ottoman-Egyptian fleet during the Greek War of Independence. According to papers I have read, a ship's captain for Mehmet Ali of Egypt had the clockwork snail. Selim was supposed to have had an extraordinary run of good luck. *Almost as though he knew where his enemies were going to be on any given day.*"

"You think Selim was dreaming about those battles before they happened?"

He shrugged. "Not me, but the writer who recorded this story certainly did."

"If Selim could see the future, how did he lose the clockwork?"

"The story goes that as Selim was preparing to sail into battle against the combined European forces, he received word that his wife and son had died in childbirth. The snail never revealed that to him. Broken and humbled, no longer caring whether he lived or died, he reportedly threw the snail overboard, believing it was cursed."

"Maybe it was."

"Why do you say that?"

"Because my family found the snail in 1902. They took it aboard their salvage ship and began having terrible dreams. The next day, nearly everyone aboard lost their lives when the ship was destroyed. The survivors, and there were only a few, believed that the snail had somehow caused the destruction."

But Roux had been among the survivors, and it was he who had sent them looking for the clockwork. Georgios

Andrianou insisted that Roux had used the snail's power to destroy the ship.

"And this is why you're searching for the clockworks?"

"Yes." Melina pierced him with her gaze. "In all the years that my family has been searching for these clockworks, why have you never before mentioned Michalis?"

"Because I never had any reason to tie your search in with Michalis."

"It never occurred to you to mention the man?"

Scuro frowned, but he was careful not to show too much because he knew he was suddenly on dangerous ground. "Michalis is a very special case. The church has studied him and his works for years because of the goat incident. They believe Michalis made some deal with dark powers."

"That Michalis had made a deal with Satan? Christianity had not yet developed."

That made Scuro smile. "You don't just find the devil in the Christian Bible, Melina. The ancient Greeks believed in a supernatural personification of evil, as well. As long as there has been the belief in good, there has been a belief in evil."

Melina didn't care about that. She'd made her peace with gods and devils. All she wanted was a chance to get her revenge on Roux. "So you have no clue where I can find Michalis's island?"

"No. If I knew, the church would have already been there and picked it bare." Scuro paused. "Or destroyed it and sowed salt into the earth. Whichever they felt necessary."

That meant that the fisherman in Genoa was the only solid lead she had to Roux. She wasn't after Michalis's toys, anyway. She only wanted the old man.

Her grandfather, though, that was a different story.

"Keep me apprised of your research."

Scuro nodded. "Of course."

Melina left him standing there as she walked back to her car. She took out her phone and made arrangements to go to Genoa, hoping that Roux would soon be there.

20

"Ms. Creed."

Hearing the polite voice, Annja struggled up through layers of sleep to return to consciousness. Someone had draped a blanket over her at some point. When she opened her eyes, one of the flight attendants was gazing down at her.

"Yes?"

"We're about to begin final approach to Cristoforo Colombo Airport. You requested to be awakened prior to the landing."

"I did. Thank you." Annja stripped off the blanket and returned the seat to the upright position.

The attendant took the blanket. "Would you like a coffee? Or juice or tea? We have an assortment of beverages."

Of course you do. This is one of Garin's jets. "How soon will we be landing?"

"We'll begin final approach in ten minutes."

"Fine. Thanks."

The attendant started to leave.

"Wait."

"Yes?"

"You mentioned coffee?"

"I did. We have a selection of coffees, including lattes and espressos. Do you have a preference?"

"Black. Hot."

"Very well."

"The bathroom's still open?"

"Yes."

Annja assembled her gear in the seat beside her and got up. She took out her travel toothbrush and headed for the bathroom.

CRISTOFORO COLOMBO AIRPORT had been built on an artificial peninsula that stuck out from the mainland. The city crowded up into the hills surrounding the coastal area. When the time had come to put in a commercial air service, it had been easier to construct an airport in the sea than to plow through all the surrounding countryside looking for level ground.

Standing at the top of the gantry leading down to the tarmac, Annja paused to inhale the salt sea breeze. It was a lot warmer in Genoa than it had been in Boston, and a lot brighter. She adjusted her backpack and took a fresh grip on the carry-on she'd had to fight the flight attendants to keep.

The city looked cluttered, packed tightly together, and the verdant green hills rolled in all directions beyond it. On either side of the airport peninsula, sailboats and yachts occupied marina slips or cut across the blue-green water. There was no hint of danger. Of course, with Roux and Garin involved, there generally wasn't until it was suddenly life or death.

A dark sedan waited at the bottom of the gantry. Annja sipped coffee from the disposable cup she'd been given and headed down.

The sedan's back door opened and Roux got out.

Annja's heart sped up a little. Even though she'd known

from the phone call that he'd been all right, it was just so much better *seeing* him for herself.

He wore khaki pants, an obnoxious green bowling shirt and a creased fedora. "I take it your trip went well? I tried to reach you, but there was no answer. The attendants said you were sleeping." He seemed a little put out at that.

Annja ignored his attitude and gave him a beatific smile. "Good morning, Roux. And how are you today?"

He stared at her in puzzlement for a moment, then scowled. "I was nearly killed yesterday by some particularly nasty people. I was counting on you to help me find answers."

"No answers. Yet. But I have redefined the question. As to why you couldn't reach me on the phone, I had it turned off so I could sleep. If anything happened while I was in the air, it was pretty much out of my hands and I wanted to be fresh as I could be when I touched the ground here."

Roux only snorted and walked past her and into the waiting car. Annja walked to the back of the sedan where a female driver in chauffeur's livery stood military erect. "Good morning."

"Good morning, Ms. Creed." The woman spoke with an Australian accent. She opened the trunk. "I'll take your bags."

"Just the carry-on. The backpack stays with me."

"Very well." The woman took the carry-on from Annja and stowed it carefully. "Do you have anything else aboard the jet?"

"No. I travel light."

"Efficient. You don't usually find that in scholarly types."

Despite the boldness of the statement, Annja couldn't help liking the woman. "You're new. I was expecting to see Henshaw."

"My name is Torrey. Honeysuckle Torrey. I'm Mr.

Roux's driver. Mr. Henshaw is watching over the house."
Even in livery, the woman was beautiful. Her concealer
hadn't been able to hide the bruise along her left jaw,
though.

"You were with Roux yesterday?"

"I was." Honeysuckle smiled. "Quite exciting. For a
civilian matter."

"You're military."

"I was. Hope to be again. When a few small matters
get tidied up. I took this job as a bit of a lark, actually. Ran
into Mr. Roux and was intrigued with how he conducts
his business."

"Someone tried to kill him then, too, didn't they?"

Honeysuckle closed the trunk. "I'm afraid I don't discuss client's private matters."

Annja grinned. "I know Roux. I also know he goes
through young women when he has the chance."

Roux tapped impatiently on the window from inside the
car, then opened the door ajar. "Are the two of you quite
finished gossiping?"

"Not gossiping, Mr. Roux."

"You do realize that a sniper with a high-powered rifle
could end your employment." Roux cursed beneath his
breath and shut the door again.

"Well, the two of you must have an interesting relationship."

Honeysuckle nodded. "When I first heard him talk
about you, I wondered about your relationship. Especially
in light of the dalliances he sometimes keeps."

"No. I was not ever a dalliance. *Never* going to be a
dalliance."

"I didn't think that you would. He thinks of you more
like a daughter. You know, annoying but somehow en-
dearing?"

Annja didn't know how to take that, but it made her feel good to know that Roux had left that kind of impression.

Honeysuckle glanced at her watch. "We're supposed to be meeting Mr. Braden soon." She waved Annja to the other side of the car and opened the door.

INSIDE THE SEDAN, Annja took out her satphone and started checking the sites where she'd put out feelers about the clockworks. Roux sat on his side of the sedan and stared out at the harbor. His hands and the side of his neck were covered in scrapes, cuts and bruises.

"Are you all right?" Annja watched as the sites populated on her phone, then selected the first thread she'd created.

"I'm fine." Roux drummed his fingers on the armrest.

"You seem tense."

"I'm not tense. We're starting out late in the game on this."

"Garin still has the butterfly, right?"

"Yes."

"Then we've got more information than Melina Andrianou does."

Roux frowned. "She still managed to get pictures of the clockwork from the man who sold it to Garin. It's possible that she could have had the inscription translated by now." He looked at her. "I don't suppose your resources have come up with anything."

"They're still working on it." There'd been no email from Papassavas, and she figured he would call when he knew something, anyway.

"I'd expected to have something by now."

"Seriously?" Annja put her satphone back in her pocket. "I was asked to take a look into this less than twenty-four hours ago. You've had at least a hundred years."

"You're the specialist."

In all the time Annja had known Roux, from the time she'd found the last piece of Joan's sword in France, she'd known him to be crotchety and irascible, but she'd never heard him sound so demeaning.

"What's going on with you?"

"Nothing."

Annja didn't believe that for a moment. Intrigued, she watched him.

Roux scowled imperiously at her. "Don't stare. It's impolite."

"You haven't exactly been the paragon of 'politely correct' this morning. I'm beginning to think I would have rather had Garin pick me up."

"As would I. But he dictated the division of labor."

"Who made him king?"

"He has the clockwork. I didn't have a choice."

"Well, now I feel really wanted. I could have made my own way to you guys."

Roux sighed. "I apologize, Annja. I'm not in the best of moods this morning. Neither Garin nor I felt comfortable about leaving you to your own devices this morning. Events for both of us were extremely deadly yesterday, and as good as you are at extricating yourself from tenuous situations, we felt compelled to be with you in case something untoward happened."

It was more than that, though. Annja saw the quaver of fear in his blue eyes. That gave her pause. Roux had said the Andrianou family had captured him and tortured him only a few years ago.

"I'm having second thoughts about involving you in this," he said. "Seeing you here reminded me I have no right to risk you in this. It is, after all, a personal matter.

It might be better if we turned around and put you back on that jet before you get mixed up any deeper in this."

Tenderly, Annja reached out and took his hand. Despite his years, his fingers were supple and strong and warm. "I'm here. You can't get rid of me. This *is* a personal matter, and it's personal to me, as well."

"You don't know what lies ahead of you if this should go badly." Roux spoke in a soft voice. "That woman is evil incarnate. I've never met a darker mind. She is capable of anything."

"Yeah?" Annja squeezed Roux's hand and smiled. "Well, so I'm pretty capable, too. We'll get through this together. I'm not leaving you or Garin."

Wordlessly, Roux squeezed her hand back, but the fear in his eyes remained, although she knew he would never admit it.

21

Sebastiano Troiai worked out of a small but serviceable boathouse he shared with two other salvagers. Located in the Sampierdarena area, it was only a few minutes west of central Genoa. When it had first become a center of civilization, primarily fishermen, it had been named after the San Pietro d'Arena Church, Saint Peter of the Sands.

Garin had first seen the city when he'd been riding with Roux, before Joan had died at the stake and the sword had been shattered.

Sampierdarena had been beautiful, filled with wonders for a young boy verging on manhood. They had spent the summer there, enjoying the weather, the food and the sailors that had come far and wide to trade and make their fortunes. Roux had listened to the stories those ships' captains told over wine, and Garin had helped build ships, walked the decks imagining he was a pirate or a king's man chasing pirates, and he'd pursued young women his age. He'd never given his heart easily, but he had been more naive in those days.

These days, he was not. He parked his car in front of a small bar three blocks up from Troiai's salvage shop, reached over for the Glock .45 in the passenger seat and slipped it into a paddle holster at the small of his back as he got out of the car. He wore a pullover and a jacket over khakis and a pair of wraparound sunglasses.

Four teenagers too young to work the docks held skateboards and ate gelato while hunkered down in front of a small paint store next to the bar. They stared at the sports car with envy.

A boy in a faded soccer jersey looked defiantly at Garin, and Garin knew that look at once. Rebellious and cocky, the boy would risk a lot in front of his peers to prove that he was fearless.

"Sweet ride." He spoke in English, thinking Garin was a tourist perhaps, or just preferring the American slang.

"It is," Garin replied in Italian as he approached them.

They looked tense for a moment, on the brink of scattering and running.

"I want that ride to stay *sweet*." Garin used the English word. "In this neighborhood, maybe it needs someone to look after it."

The boy shrugged. "We're not in the car-sitting business."

"You look like an entrepreneur."

The boy ate some more gelato. "Entrepreneurs get paid well."

"They get paid well enough." Garin took four twenty-euro notes from his shirt pocket and handed them over to the boy. "If my car is in good shape when I return in a few minutes, I'll give you and your friends another twenty."

"Each."

"Yes."

The boy took the money and passed it out to his friends. "What if your car isn't in good shape?"

Garin took his phone from his pocket and took a picture of the four boys before they could move. He pocketed the phone and smiled at them. "Then I'll come looking for you. Entrepreneurs like you? Someone in this neighborhood will know you."

The boy paled a little, but he made a show out of shrugging. "Sure. Lucky for you we're in the car-sitting business today."

"It's that small-business ethic that's going to save the world." Garin left them sitting there and headed down toward the harbor.

Terns flew high in the sky and swooped down and around the masts of sailboats and the tall wheelhouses of cargo ships. Fishermen hawked the morning's catch at open bins filled with ice that was stained with blood. Music spilled out of the small shops, tunes from different cultures, but much of it American rock and roll. Several pedestrians were going about their business.

"You terrified those boys for no reason," Amalia protested over his earbud. "And you're keeping them from going to school."

"Nonsense. Those boys weren't going to school, anyway. They were hanging out and eating gelato. I just made their truancy more lucrative." Garin looked at one of the traffic cams in the intersection and winked, knowing Amalia had hacked into the system to watch over him.

"Hardly something a parenting magazine would appreciate."

"It's better than them keying my car while I'm gone."

"You don't even care about that car. When you leave Genoa, you're just going to dump it."

"I am, but while I'm driving it, I prefer that it looks good. Plus, those boys are locals. They'll know if someone who isn't a local comes prowling around the car." Garin crossed the street. "They're an extra layer of protection, and a filter to discriminate between the local thugs and Melina Andrianou's people."

"Do you expect them to be here?"

"Eyuboglu's people called one of my services last night and said Eyuboglu had been taken. That might have been because of some other business Eyuboglu had, but it's coming too closely on the heels of yesterday's confrontation. Since the Andrianous couldn't find me or Roux, they could have pursued Eyuboglu. And Eyuboglu knew about Troiai. Yes, I expect someone to be here. That's why I have Emil and his people around, as well."

"Knowing that, you're still going to walk into what could be a trap?"

"I'm depending on you to get me out of it. If you don't, I'll consider terminating you."

"Me? I thought you have Emil there."

"I do, but he's plan B. I'd much rather go with plan A and not get blindsided."

"What's the severance package like?" Despite the attempt at humor, Garin heard the tension in the woman's voice. She took her job very seriously.

"You don't want to find out. Where's my ship?" Garin had called in a salvage ship he owned under one of his subsidiaries. The vessel was crewed by men who were loyal to him, and who had stood by him during difficult and bloody situations before. They were his own private pirates.

"*Kestrel* is an hour and a half out as of this moment."

"Good. Now be quiet and let me work." Garin reached the corner and turned east to walk toward Troiai's place of business.

A HIGH FENCE surrounded the salvage yard proper. Razor wire topped the fence. On the other side of the barrier, several boats and yachts of different sizes sat up on blocks in various states of disrepair. A handful of men worked on some of the larger pleasurecraft, and the dull tang of diesel lay over the area, some of it from the immediate vicinity and some of it from the ships lying at anchor.

The salvage shop was housed in a large warehouse that fronted the water. Terns roosted along the peaked roof and added to the excrement already streaking the red tiles.

Garin waited at the large gate that opened onto the cross street. After a moment, he took out his phone and called the number he had for Sebastiano Troiai.

The man answered on the third ring. "Salvage."

"We have an appointment."

Troiai hesitated before clearing his throat. "Where are you?"

"Waiting at the gate. Evidently the men working on the salvage are too busy to see what I want." That actually relaxed Garin. If one of the men had addressed him immediately, the behavior would have been suspect.

"I'll get someone there."

By the time Garin put his phone away, Troiai had opened one of the multipaned windows on the building and shouted orders in an irritated tone.

One of the young men in a stained coverall stopped working on a diesel engine sitting on sawhorses and came to the gate. Without a word, the mechanic unlocked the gate and slid it aside.

Garin stepped through and headed for the building. He took in the salvage yard, looking for anything that didn't belong, any movement that appeared too sudden.

Amalia whispered into his ear. "I have you. You're clear here, but I'm going to lose you inside the building. They don't have any kind of CCTV."

"Understood. You'll still be with me audibly." Tension knotted Garin's stomach. Sometimes he still had nightmares about that night he'd gotten to Roux only minutes ahead of Melina Andrianou's hounds.

Roux had been in bad shape, more dead than alive. Garin had sat beside the old man, cleaned him, bandaged him and watched over Roux because he didn't trust anyone else to do the job half as well as he did. Less than two weeks before that, Garin had tried to kill Roux himself. That night, he'd wanted nothing more than to find the person who had hurt Roux, but the old man had never given him the name until yesterday when they'd been talking to Annja.

Garin's relationship with Roux was very complicated, partly because they had lived so long, and partly because they were so different, yet so much alike. That relationship balanced on the edge of a knife on good days.

Still, finding the sword, adding Annja Creed to their intimate circle, had tempered that relationship somewhat. The push-pull nature of their relationship was still there, but they hadn't tried to kill each other in a while. Things were getting better.

Except for instances when one of Roux's mysteries interfered. Those were enough to get either of them killed. Maybe both.

And Annja, too.

That wasn't a pleasant thought. He quite liked Annja, troublesome though she could be.

Sebastiano Troiai met Garin at a door labeled Office. He was a short, stout man with massive forearms and a complexion bronzed by the sun and the sea. Gray stained his unruly hair and the small mustache that curled up slightly at the corners of his mouth. He smelled of diesel and cheap cologne, and a wedding ring glinted as he cleaned his hands with a red rag.

"Welcome, welcome. Sorry about the gate. Those guys…" Troiai shook his head as he headed back into the building.

Garin nodded and followed him inside the small office where an older woman sat at a small desk and worked at an ancient computer. Trophies from salvage finds, some worthwhile and some evidently tangled remains of expensive yachts, hung on the otherwise plain walls.

"I would have been happy to meet you anywhere you wanted." Troiai kept on through another door into a large work bay that contained five powerboats and two yachts. Three of the boats and one of the yachts hung from chains attached to rigs on the high ceiling beams.

"This is fine."

"You said you wanted to talk to me about something I salvaged?"

"I do."

Sighing, Troiai stopped next to the hanging yacht, a sixty-two footer trimmed in teak and brass and looking like it was more someone's showpiece than a working vessel. "Look, I gotta ask, you know, if you're some kind of policeman."

Garin grinned. "Not even close."

Troiai pursed his lips. "The reason I had to ask, I know that you're supposed to claim all the artifacts you find and sell so the government can tax you on them, but I don't always do that."

"Government tends to cut deeply into the profit margin. I'm not a fan."

A relaxed smile split Troiai's face. "Excellent. Then what can I do for you?"

"A few days ago, you found this." Garin took out his phone and showed a picture of the clockwork butterfly to the man.

"Ah, the bug."

Garin put his phone away. "It's not a bug, it's a butterfly."

Troiai shrugged. "Okay, a butterfly. You bought that thing?"

"I did."

"How much did you give for it, if you don't mind me asking?"

"I do."

Troiai swore. "I knew I didn't charge Eyuboglu enough for it. I should have known because he kept talking the bug down. *Butterfly.* He talked the *butterfly* down. But he made sure he didn't leave without it that day. And for him to already have sold it to you, and for you to come here looking for it, that thing must be worth something, huh?"

"What else did you find when you found the butterfly?"

"Not so much. A few odds and ends I knew I could sell. Things that always go to somebody. I didn't get a real find on that salvage." Troiai looked slyly at Garin. "Except maybe I did, didn't I?"

"Can you tell me how you found this?"

"Out near a site I work every now and again after an earthquake. There are seven wrecks out there. All of them have paid off a little bit, but nothing significant."

"Seven wrecks?"

Troiai nodded. "A lot of ships have gone down out in the Mediterranean. Back in the day, Genoa was on one of the major trade routes. A lot of cultures sailed through these waters. Not all of them got where they were going."

"I'd like you to take me to that site."

Troiai looked around the warehouse. "I can't do that right now. I have a lot of work here to get out. A lot of people are depending on me. The only reason I was out there that day was because I had to pull up that boat." He pointed at one of the pleasurecrafts. "The owner's son went out there drunk, ended up running into a container ship while trying to impress the girls he was with. Boat went straight to the bottom. The owner called me, wanted me to get his boat back. I did. Now he's not sure he wants it in the shape it's in. He's thinking maybe he wants to trade up. The insurance company will pay me a finder's fee, but it won't do much more than cover the cost of the salvage, even if I get to sell off the parts." He shook his head. "I need to work. I have a family to feed."

"I'll pay you fifty thousand euros for playing guide for a week. Deposited into your bank. Or I can pay you cash."

That got Troiai's attention. "Cash?"

"That way you don't have to worry about the government taking a big bite of it. I'll give you half up front."

Once Troiai had it in his mind to do something, he moved quickly. "How soon do you want to leave?"

"Now."

"I'll have to get my ship set up to go out."

"We're taking my ship. It's already en route."

"Fifty thousand euros and we're using *your* ship?"

"Yes. I've got more equipment aboard than you probably do."

Troiai gnawed on a thumbnail. "What was that thing I found?"

"I don't know, but I want to find out. Are we leaving or not?"

"Sure, sure. Let me get the guys here squared away. Then I have to tell my wife I'll be gone for a week."

Garin nodded. "I'll wait for you outside." He walked back to the small office and Amalia called him over the earbud.

"Okay, you're in trouble. I just identified Melina Andrianou closing in on your position."

"Where?"

"Three intersections up in an SUV. She's going to be

on top of you any second, and she's got six, no...*ten* men with her."

Garin peered through the smoke-stained window at the street near the front gate. "Emil?"

"I heard. We are on our way. I have four men across the street who will engage her."

Garin turned back to the desk where Troiai was speaking to the secretary. He grabbed the shorter man by the shoulder to get his attention, then focused on the secretary. "You need to leave."

The woman gaped at him. "What?"

"Leave."

She looked at Troiai for support. He hesitated.

Garin pulled the Glock from the back of his belt and fired a round through the ancient computer monitor, scattering plastic and glass across the desk and floor.

The woman got to her feet and fled.

Troiai tried to leave, too, but Garin kept hold of him. "Is there a back way out of here?"

22

Melina tapped the brakes at the intersection to slow the SUV's headlong pace just enough to keep it from flipping over as she rounded the corner. The tires screeched as they fought to keep traction. Her colleague riding shotgun grabbed the seat belt and braced himself against the dashboard.

The other three armed men rode in the vehicle with her. None of them said anything.

Melina straightened the SUV, narrowly missing a delivery truck. She'd had no choice but to act quickly once Garin had been discovered on-site at the salvage yard because her quarry had a habit of disappearing. She'd hoped that Roux would also arrive.

The old man hadn't showed, though. Maybe he'd been more injured in yesterday's attempt on his life than she'd been led to believe. She hoped so because that would slow him down, but she also hoped he was still well enough to agonize over the torture she intended to inflict on him. The torture she'd put him through six years ago should have crippled him for life, yet he was able to kill trained soldiers yesterday and escape.

"There." The man in the passenger seat—she really should learn the name of her grandfather's employees, but she burned through them so fast, she didn't want to go to the bother—looked up from the GPS he held and pointed at the plain-looking warehouse behind the high security fence. He put the GPS away and readied his assault rifle.

Without a word, Melina steered for the fence. Metal screamed as the vehicle forced the fence back. Support posts pulled out of their concrete bases. Then the fence ripped just before she crashed into one of the boats and knocked it from the blocks.

Workers who had been aboard the boat tried to abandon ship, but they threw themselves overboard too late. The powerboat rebounded from the charging SUV and swung around, falling on top of two of them.

A large yacht blocked the way ahead. She stopped the SUV, killed the engine and grabbed the AK-47 between the seats. Snapping the safety off, she clambered out of the vehicle.

"Where is Garin?" she asked into the air.

"Still inside the building," one of her team stationed down by the piers responded through her earbud. "I do not have a shot at him."

Melina canted the rifle up, holding it in both hands as she closed on the building. She wore Kevlar from her neck to her knees under her pants and thigh-length jacket.

Sudden movement to her right brought her around. She saw a man duck behind a boat and fired a three-round burst that ripped into the vessel's gunwale. Seeing the man's legs beneath, Melina took aim again and squeezed the trigger. The rounds tore through the man's calves and knocked him to the ground.

He lay helpless and stretched out thirty feet away. His cell phone lay just out of his reach, but Melina could see enough of the screen to know that the police would be here soon.

Melina shot the man in the head, then blasted the phone

to pieces. The dead man's blood pumped out onto the ground for a few seconds before his heart got the message that he was gone.

Melina caught a glimpse of Garin Braden through the multipaned window at the front of the warehouse as he aimed a pistol in her direction. She dropped into a crouch immediately and yelled a warning to her team. "Down!"

The man standing next to her wasn't as lucky as the rest of them. Two rounds tattooed his Kevlar-covered chest and the third tore through his neck, ripping out his larynx and leaving him drowning in his own blood. One of the mercenaries behind the wounded man put his rifle to the back of the guy's head and pulled the trigger to put him out of his misery. They kept moving in a crouch as the man fell.

The man behind Melina then opened fire on the window, burning through a full magazine in a continuous, thundering roar. The bullets demolished the other panes that Garin's bullets hadn't already, and ripped away the latticework. Glass spun and shone as it spilled free and caught the light.

Emil's people across the street opened fire on Melina's team, but their field of fire was blocked by the SUV and the scattered marine vessels. As they started to pursue Melina, her second team of shooters in the other SUV engaged them. The driver put his vehicle sideways at the entrance to the salvage yard to help block shots as her second team got out and returned fire on Garin's men.

Melina picked up the pace to a jog as she closed on the front door. She waited beside the open entrance until one of the two men with her stepped into position on the other side. Then she swung around and advanced, following her assault rifle into the building, taking in the exploded computer monitor at a glance. Bullet holes decorated the wall opposite the window.

There was no sign of Garin Braden, but there was another door at the back of the office.

"Do you have Garin?" her grandfather asked through the earbud.

"Not yet. We have him cornered." Another team covered the rear of the building. "We'll have him soon enough." Melina kept advancing with short, tight steps. She peered through the doorway into the work area proper. Whether she took Garin Braden alive or dead didn't matter to her. Once she had him, Roux would come to her.

GARIN KNEW HE was in a desperate situation. He'd missed the woman when he'd shot through the office window. Thankfully one of her shock troops was down and not getting up again.

He kept hold of Troiai's arm as he guided the man through the building's maze of boats and yachts. He swept the surrounding area with his gaze, telling himself he was going to make it out of the ambush alive because that was all he could do.

"Garin," Amalia said into the earbud, "there are more men covering the back of the warehouse. They've killed Emil's observation team."

"I understand." Garin stopped in front of a row of metal shelves holding solvents and other chemicals. He scanned the Italian labels. Even if he hadn't been able to read the language, he could see the manufacturers' warning flames plainly enough.

When Garin took his hand from Troiai, the man started to run.

"If you go out there, they'll shoot you." Garin holstered his pistol and grabbed a couple of the alcohol-based solvents in five-liter plastic containers.

Troiai stopped and stood there nervously, poised to flee again. "Then what are we to do?"

"Get out of here." Garin opened the solvent and poured it over and around the chemicals. "Help me."

Grabbing the other solvent container, Troiai also began dousing the shelves. "What are you going to do?"

"You have insurance on this place?"

"Yes." Understanding dawned in the man's expression. "*Wait*. You can't set the building on fire."

"Sure I can." Garin produced a lighter, struck it, locked the button and tossed it onto the spilled solvent. The chemicals ignited with a soft surge and blue and yellow flames gently lapped at the shelves.

"My insurance isn't going to cover all of this!"

"Then be glad that I'm underwriting your insurance today." Garin grabbed him by the arm and pulled him behind the storage shelves.

"We're going to be trapped back here."

Already the flames were climbing the walls and spreading out across the floor in pursuit of the spilled pool of solvent running across the warehouse. Smoke clouded up instantly, acrid and thick.

"No, they're going to be trapped back there." Garin looked around the back of the warehouse and found the four acetylene tanks he'd seen chained to the wall earlier. Four oxygen tanks stood clearly marked beside them. "We're going to make our own door."

Garin opened the valves on the acetylene and oxygen tanks as quickly as he could.

"You're going to get us killed! That stuff is highly explosive!"

"That's what I'm counting on." Garin took the man by the arm and pulled him into motion.

A small bathroom occupied the rear corner of the warehouse. The room was constructed of cinder blocks, which left the walls structurally weaker than Garin would have hoped for, but the steel looked somewhat blast resistant.

He pushed Troiai inside and stood behind the door himself, then took aim with the pistol and started pulling the trigger.

MELINA STARED INTO the roiling cloud of smoke spreading from the back of the warehouse. A harsh chemical smell burned her nose and caused her eyes to tear. She peered into the room over the rifle sights, searching for Garin.

A string of small explosions rattled along metal shelving she could barely make out in the back of the room.

Cautiously, breathing shallowly, Melina stepped into the warehouse. All three bay doors were open to the harbor, all of them leading directly to the water. She called to her man watching the front of the salvage shop. "Have you seen Garin?"

"No. He has not come out. The building appears to be on fire."

"Watch for him in case he decides to use the smoke as cover." Melina continued moving forward, never crossing her feet so she didn't trip herself if she tried to shift quickly, and so that she presented a small profile in case Garin shot first.

Then four quick gunshots cracked in the confusion and the back of the warehouse exploded. Shrapnel ricocheted everywhere. A few chunks peppered Melina, thumping into her body armor and stinging her arms. The smoke whipped around in a frenzy and the concussive wave blew her off her feet.

Breath knocked from her lungs, Melina struggled to get back up. Next to her, one of the men with her lay quivering, howling in pain, except it came out in a gurgle because half his face and his lower jaw had been sheared away. Blood pooled around him.

On her feet, Melina went to put him out of his misery, but before she could he quivered a final time and lay still. She turned back to the rear of the warehouse, barely able to make out the hole in the building as two shadows disappeared through it.

Melina called the backup team, warning them that Garin had gotten free. She darted forward, hesitated only a moment at the wall of flame, then hurled herself through.

THE INSTANTANEOUS EXPLOSION of the gases igniting didn't give Garin any time to duck behind the steel door as he'd intended. The concussive force outraced the flames, though, blowing him back into the bathroom and slamming the door shut. Smoke instantly coiled in under the gap between the door and the floor. The chemical stink of it caused Garin's lungs to seize up and he fought to get his breath.

Growling curses in a pain-racked croak, he was afraid the fire had spread more than he'd anticipated and they were now in danger of being burned alive in the small room. Garin took a fresh grip on his pistol and braced his free hand against the wall to force himself to a standing position.

Troiai, wide-eyed with fear, appeared to be none the worse for wear. "We're not dead?" He ran his hands over his chest as if to prove that to himself.

"Not yet." Garin touched the doorknob cautiously. The metal was still cool to the touch. He swung the door open, then grabbed Troiai and pulled him out.

Smoke filled the immediate vicinity and Garin's lungs burned for oxygen and his eyes watered. He ran toward the corner where the acetylene and oxygen tanks had been.

Blunted sunlight streamed in through a hole five feet in diameter. He headed for it, letting the pistol lead the way.

Three cars had stopped in the middle of the small street as the drivers stared at the marine salvage yard. Several people in the nearby shops peered through windows.

Garin kept Troiai in motion, sprinting for the other side of the street. "Emil."

"Here."

"I'm on the street behind the warehouse."

"Affirmative. I'll be there in a moment."

As Garin ran through the stalled cars, bullets from an execution team hammered the vehicles, ricocheting from bodies and splintering glass.

"We're not waiting." Garin pushed Troiai ahead of him, firing his pistol dry and gaining the other side of the street as one of the Andrianou mercenaries behind him went down. "I'm going to try for my car. If you can, capture Melina Andrianou. If you can't do that, kill her." He dumped the empty magazine from his pistol and inserted another one as he ran.

23

Roux's phone rang at the same time Annja saw the pall of smoke hanging above the harbor. Her stomach tightened. She had the distinct feeling that the smoke was somehow connected to Garin.

Roux put the phone on speaker. "Hello."

"Mr. Roux, I work with Mr. Braden. I was instructed that if his meeting with Mr. Troiai went awry I was to contact you and advise you not to go there." The woman at the other end of the connection spoke matter-of-factly, professional in spite of the message.

"Schrettinger?" Annja asked.

The woman at the other end of the connection didn't miss a beat. "Ms. Creed, glad you made it. But to the point, Mr. Braden suggests that you make your way to the ship."

"What ship?" Roux asked irritably.

"*Kestrel*. One of Mr. Braden's salvage vessels. It's my understanding that you'll be joining the search of the area where the clockwork butterfly was found."

"I am."

"Then you'll need to know where to find *Kestrel*." She added the harbor listing where the ship would be found.

"Is Garin en route there?" Roux asked.

"Not at the moment."

Roux cursed and broke the connection. He looked at

Honeysuckle. "Maybe we could endeavor to get to the salvage yard more promptly."

The chauffeur laid on the horn and put her foot on the accelerator, surging through the sedate morning traffic. Faced with a reluctant taxi driver ahead of her, she pulled over to the left, dodged an oncoming car and rocketed through a small collection of empty chairs and tables in front of a café. Pulling back across both lanes of traffic, she easily zipped along the street, now suddenly clear of hesitant motorists.

The phone rang but Roux didn't answer. Hers rang a moment later, but she ignored it, as well, figuring it would be Schrettinger.

In the distance, she spotted the Lanterna, the main lighthouse for the port. It was one of the oldest lighthouses in the world, constructed on the San Benigno Hill. The hill no longer existed because it had been used for landfill. Only the scrap of a hill under the lighthouse remained.

Built of gray stone, the lighthouse looked like two long blocks from a child's play set, one stacked lengthways on top of the other. When the structure had been built, it had stood on a peninsula sticking out from the coast, but since the city had filled in the harbor, it now sat in the middle of the industrial area.

Roux reached into a worn satchel on the floorboard next to his feet. It looked like an old pet. He pulled out a wicked machine pistol that seemed like something from a science fiction movie and offered it to Annja. "Are you familiar with this?"

"It's an MP9. I've seen them before, but no, I'm not that familiar with them."

"You point. You pull the trigger. Whatever is in front of you is no longer a problem." Roux showed her how to work the action and the wire stock. "Garin prefers the MP5, but

I quite like these. About half the size of the German pistol, superior rate of fire, nightscope, magazine capacity of thirty rounds and fairly accurate out to one hundred yards. We're going to be in tight quarters today, so that shouldn't be a problem. I prefer the Austrian Steyr version to this Swiss model, but these were easier to get at the moment."

Annja took the pistol, surprised at how light it was. Roux handed her four extra magazines and she put them in her pockets. "Seriously? If we have to use this many bullets, we're in trouble."

Roux regarded her with his unflinching gaze. "This is the Andrianou family, Annja. They are very dangerous people, and they don't care how many people they have to kill to get what they want. We're already in trouble."

He reached into his satchel and took out another pistol that matched the one Annja held.

"They come in pairs like socks?"

Roux smiled grimly. "Hardly, but given who we're up against, I thought it best to be overequipped." He looked forward as Honeysuckle skidded around an intersection. "You can bet that Melina Andrianou did not come alone."

Annja checked over the weapon again, making certain she knew how to operate it. Then she slipped the safety off.

It's so much better to be unexpectedly fighting for your life than planning on doing that.

"There's the warehouse."

Roux's comment was unnecessary. The thick black smoke streaming from the building marked it instantly.

"Do we know where Garin is?"

"No."

"Maybe you shouldn't have hung up on Schrettinger so quickly."

"Is that truly the woman's name?"

"No. Is this car bulletproof?"

"Relatively. I learned my lesson yesterday."

"Good, because we just attracted someone's attention." Annja dodged back as a massive SUV pulled alongside them on the left.

"I see them," Honeysuckle called. "Hang on." She swerved, pulling over into the SUV. Gunmen at both the car's passenger windows opened fire. Bullets hammered their windows, fracturing the glass but not penetrating.

Metal shrilled as the car and the SUV fought for dominance. Finally, the SUV's greater weight pushed them to the side. Honeysuckle swore as she fought the wheel and plowed through market kiosks. The vendors had quickly run out of her way.

Rolling her window down slightly, Annja thrust the MP9's wicked snout through the narrow space and fired. The 9 mm bullets slammed into the SUV, but the driver remained locked onto the sedan.

"Brake!" Honeysuckle yelled, then applied the brakes forcefully. The antibrake locking system caused the car to jerk, but it quickly slowed and the SUV skid ahead of them.

Honeysuckle floored the accelerator again and pulled hard to the left, striking the SUV's right rear quarter panel with the front of the car and knocking the other vehicle sideways a little. She applied the brake and accelerator again, then nudged the attack vehicle again. With its higher center of gravity, the SUV's tires lost traction and the vehicle turned sideways, then flipped over onto its top. Honeysuckle braked and sped up again, catching the SUV across the front of the sedan and powering them both forward.

At the same time, a large van suddenly emerged from a side street.

As if expecting the tactic, Honeysuckle tapped the brake, pulled harder to the left and passed the SUV. The van clipped the sedan's bumper, sending a shiver through the length of the car, then continued on, coming to a miraculous stop just a few feet short of the end of a wharf surrounded by sailboats.

Honeysuckle brought the vehicle to a stop, set the transmission into reverse, then threw an arm over the seat and hit the accelerator again. She was smiling. "I saw that little trick yesterday. I was expecting it."

The sedan shot backward, then slammed into the van at the edge of the wharf. The tires spun for a moment as the sedan's motor and transmission strained, then the van toppled over into the harbor with a large splash.

"There." Honeysuckle smiled brightly. "Much better." She engaged the transmission again and roared forward. The salvage yard was just down the block.

Annja reloaded her weapon.

ON THE OTHER side of the flames, Melina got her bearings and headed through the hole in the wall, one of her team in tow.

Outside, Melina took a deep breath and scoured the neighborhood for Garin. Cars moved cautiously out in the street, then the drivers saw the rifle in her arms and decided to move more quickly. In the alley ahead of her, she spotted the backup team she'd ordered for the salvage yard. She launched herself in pursuit of them.

"Dettmer—" at least she'd remembered one of her grandfather's men's names "—where is Garin Braden?"

"He went into the alley."

"Do you have eyes on him?"

"Not yet. We're trying to catch him."

Her grandfather's voice carried over the earbud. "Melina."

"Yes?" The twisting alley had a sudden jog to the left.

Melina hit the wall with her palm, adding muscle to her course correction, and picked up her speed again.

"Roux has arrived at your location."

Excitement flared within Melina, immediately turning to bloodlust. She remembered leaving her father's head and body in the alleyway where it had been found. That had been one of the hardest things she had ever done. Part of her had died that night, but she had done as her grandfather had ordered.

And she had lived for the moment when she could take her revenge.

"Where is he?"

"Arriving at the salvage yard even as we speak."

"Dettmer, stay on Garin." Melina reversed her direction, waving to the man who followed her to do the same. "Where is Team Three? Have them close in on Roux and block his retreat."

"Team Three is at the bottom of the harbor. I already gave orders for them to bring Roux down. They failed."

"Roux is *mine!* You know that!" Melina redoubled her speed, the street now coming into sight in front of her.

"He is there."

"Send in the team from the ship."

"I have. They should be reaching you in a moment."

TROIAI COULDN'T HANDLE the pace Garin set, so he had to slow down to allow the man to keep up. They ran through the next alley, then reached the street where he had left the car.

Garin took out his key fob and punched the button. The car's lights flashed and the horn honked in response. The boys watching the car stood and looked around.

"Do you see the car?"

Out of breath, unable to reply, Troiai nodded.

"Get in." Garin shoved his gun into his jacket pocket and kept his hand around it. With his other hand, he fished euro notes from his pants pocket. He had more than four twenty-euro notes, but he didn't care.

When he reached the boys, he gave the money to the one he'd made the deal with.

The kid took the money and tried to look brave. "What's going on?"

"Better that you not ask. Better still that you're not here. There are some bad people coming."

Making a fist around the money, the boy nodded, then yelled at his companions. They put their skateboards on the sidewalk and shot in the other direction.

Garin slid in behind the steering wheel. Troiai shook so badly he couldn't lock in his seat belt.

"Do you know those people?" Troiai asked.

"They are with the competitors I told you about." Garin put the car in gear and peeled out down the street. "Aren't you glad you're doing business with me?"

"No. No, I'm not."

Garin laughed and the man looked at him as though he was crazy, which only made him laugh more. He shot past the group who had been following him, getting their attention too late for them to do anything to stop him.

He tapped the earbud. "Are Roux and Annja heading for *Kestrel?*"

"No. I told him the game plan and he hung up on me. I've tracked his car to the salvage yard."

Garin cursed as he took the next corner, watching closely for any other surprises Melina Andrianou might have whipped up. "Patch me through to Roux."

"He might not answer."

"Hack his phone. Put me on speaker." Garin's jubilation over his victory melted away as he thought about the bloody mess he had saved Roux from six years earlier. He didn't know how he truly felt about Roux after everything they'd been through, but one thing he knew for sure was that he wasn't ready for the old man to die. Not unless it was at his hands.

24

Roux's phone rang, then Garin's voice blasted from it. "Pick up the phone, Roux. Do it now!"

Fishing in his pocket, Roux brought the device out. "Where are you?"

"For the moment, I'm safe. I have the salvager and I have a ship. We're clear of the situation. You need to get out of there."

Feeling instant relief, Annja studied the confused mess ahead of them. A man lay dead in front of the marine salvage yard. A gaping hole glared out from the back of the warehouse, which she could see from the front because the windows had been blown out, too. A wrecked SUV sat idle next to an overturned sailboat, and a trail of carnage led up to that. Garin might be out of danger at the moment, but he'd certainly been in it.

"Where is Melina Andrianou?" Roux asked.

"I don't know, and I don't know how many people she has back there." Garin's voice was strained as he tried to speak calmly. "This isn't the place or time for a confrontation with her, Roux. The police are going to be all over that scene. Even if you kill her, you could get arrested."

"That's what we have attorneys for."

"If they charge you as a terrorist, you might never see the light of day again."

"They can't hold me."

"If they arrest you and put you in jail, you could be there long enough to die at the hands of someone else Adrianou's grandfather sends after you. They're not going to quit."

Sirens screamed, coming closer.

"More than that, Roux, whatever danger it is that these clockworks represent, that's going to remain out there till you find them. If you don't, someone else will. And if you're not around, no one's going to be left who understands the danger."

Annja sat quietly. It was strange listening to Garin counsel Roux, stranger still to hear him take the path of patience.

Roux sighed. "Perhaps you're right."

"I am. You know it. Get out of there. Meet me at *Kestrel*. Let's see what we can find. You've let that woman live for six years, Roux. A few more days isn't going to matter. She's not going to give up searching for you. So let her find us when we're ready, when we can control the situation—or when we don't have to worry about the police or collateral damage. Let it just be her and us."

"All right. I will see you at the ship." Roux hung up and looked at Honeysuckle. "Let's go."

Just at that moment, Annja saw a streamer of white smoke at a wharf nearly two hundred yards away. She knew from experience what the smoke represented.

"Go! Now!"

To her credit, Honeysuckle responded immediately, stomping the accelerator. The rocket screamed by only inches away to explode against the front of a Laundromat that was closed for reconstruction. Debris and flames spun into the air, and the thunderous explosion echoed between the buildings.

Annja watched through the back glass as a red-haired

woman with an assault rifle in her hands stumbled out of the alley across the street. Even though the woman looked like the pictures of Melina Andrianou Annja had seen in Schrettinger's folder, it was odd seeing her appear so... human. After everything the woman had done, and the fear she had instilled in Roux, Annja had expected the Andrianou woman to be ten feet tall and equipped with horns, fangs and a tail. Spitting fire wouldn't have been out of place, either.

"We have to lose the car," Honeysuckle said. "We're definitely going to attract attention if we don't."

"It has come to my attention," Roux said, "that you're extraordinarily unlucky with vehicles."

"Unlucky?" Honeysuckle looked at him in the rearview mirror and cocked an eyebrow. "You're still in one piece."

Roux shoved the MP9 into his satchel.

IN FRUSTRATION, MELINA watched the damaged sedan roll away. Roux and Annja Creed were visible from behind. She raised her assault rifle and took aim, then knew it would do no good because the glass was bulletproof. The fracture lines she'd seen in it gave that away.

She glanced back at the warehouse. Flames had claimed half the building, churning and twisting high above it. Garin had escaped, as well, and he had the salvage diver, Sebastian Troiai.

And she didn't know where to look for Roux.

She ran back into the building and went behind the secretary's desk. She hoped Troiai filed his reports with the woman. If not, he probably used the computer or the network to access his personal documents. She had people who could sort through that and find information about the dive that had turned up the clockwork butterfly.

Reaching into her pocket, she took out a USB equipped

with hacks to get into the computer. She slotted the device and called to her grandfather, "Tell the techs I have a machine I need them to gain access to."

Echoing over the harbor, police sirens screamed louder and louder.

"All right, it's come through. We have the computer," her grandfather said. "They will draw the information from it and destroy it. Now get out of there."

"I almost had him." The frustration that welled in Melina rendered her almost inarticulate.

"I know, *kopela mou,*" her grandfather said softly. "Perhaps it is better this way."

"How is it better?"

"It would be beneficial if we could take Roux and the secret of the clockworks at the same time. If we get him without the butterfly, he might prove as stubborn as last time and tell us nothing."

Melina said nothing. On Roux's fate, she and her grandfather did not agree.

"I repeat—get out of there."

Without a word, Melina left the warehouse, walking down toward the harbor where a boat was waiting for her.

KESTREL SAT AT anchor out in the harbor. Garin had a crew in a powerboat waiting to pick up Annja and Roux. Honeysuckle Torrey wasn't making the trip with them, and she clearly wasn't happy about that.

The woman, dressed now in casual street clothes they'd bought along the way, stood in front of Roux with her hands over her chest. "You're sure I can't come along?"

Roux smiled. "Not on this part of the trip."

"I have to tell you, I don't like leaving things unfinished."

"I understand. I sympathize. I'm not going to change my mind."

"Am I going to ever find out what this is about?"

"No."

Honeysuckle grimaced. "At least you're honest. Still doesn't make me happy." Her eyes flicked to Annja. "You know what this is about?"

"Not entirely."

"But you get to go because he says you can?"

"Yes."

Honeysuckle nodded. "Take care of him while you're out there."

"I will."

"Call Henshaw and he'll see to your needs," Roux said. "You can stay here or return to France. Whichever you prefer. Given the circumstances, though, I'd suggest a different venue. The people who are pursuing us may come looking for you."

"If any of them find me, there'll be fewer of them for you to worry about." She gave him a wink, then turned and walked away, turning heads as she went.

"That's a very strong woman." Roux took a deep breath and let it out as they headed for the waiting boat. "How many people have you told about that sword?"

"No one. People have seen it, but I never explain it."

"Why?"

"Because no one would believe it."

"Even if you pulled it out of thin air in front of them?"

"They'd probably think I'm *really* good at sleight of hand. But no one is going to believe this sword used to belong to Joan."

"Eventually, you'd lose whatever friend you trusted with that knowledge." He frowned. "You'd lose them even faster if you involved them in the things we do. I have learned that."

Annja passed her carry-on to one of the men aboard the boat, then followed Roux down the short ladder to the watercraft. She sat with Roux in the stern, but neither of them talked as the pilot took them out to sea. Annja watched the surrounding boats, looking for Melina Andrianou or anyone who might be working for her.

KESTREL WAS IMPRESSIVE. She was over a hundred and fifty feet long and had a swinging stern and A-frame for launch and recovery of submersibles. There was also a lifting jack and a weather station array.

"Welcome aboard." Dressed in white duck pants and a pullover, Garin looked at home on the ship. "I was beginning to think that witch had gotten you, after all."

The ship's crew dropped a rope ladder over the side while the powerboat skipper pulled his craft alongside.

Annja slung her backpack over her shoulder and climbed the ladder. At the top, Garin offered his hand and she took it. A moment later, she stood on the deck and felt the familiar sway of being on a big ship.

"You're looking good," he said.

Brushing loose hair back from her face, Annja frowned. She could smell the lingering scent of soap and shampoo coming from Garin and knew that he'd already showered. "For someone who's been shot at, slept overnight on a jet and hasn't had a shower in twenty-four hours? Maybe."

One of the crewmen clambered on board with Annja's carry-on. He looked at Annja with hard eyes that spoke of a military background. "I'll put this in your cabin, Ms. Creed."

"I've got a cabin?"

Garin smiled. "Of course you do. I'll show you. *Kestrel* is a deep-ocean research vessel. She carries fifteen crew under normal conditions, but since these *aren't* normal conditions, I've beefed the roster to twice that. She's capable of handling forty people easily."

"Does this cabin have a shower?"

"It does. Not only that, the cabin I've got you set up in has a whirlpool tub."

That sounded divine. "I don't suppose there's any reason I can't use it now?"

"None at all. Would you like company?"

Annja took in his guileless expression. "No."

"Too bad. I give a terrific backrub."

"I'll bet there are a lot of people who could give testimonials."

"As a matter of fact—"

Annja held up a hand. "I assume you have a ship's galley?"

"An excellent one."

"Good, because I haven't had breakfast, either. Or dinner last night for that matter."

FORTY MINUTES LATER, after a long soak with high-powered jets massaging her body and working out some of the stiffness from the long night in the Salem jail, Annja felt almost human. Except for the gnawing pit in her stomach that was threatening to consume her.

She opened her carry-on on the bed, which was surprisingly large yet still didn't overpower the room, when she noticed a note on the headboard.

There is clothing in the closet and underthings in the dresser.
G.

Wary of what she might find, though she knew from personal experience that Garin had excellent taste, Annja opened the doors to the built-in closet with trepidation.

Smiling, she chose a pair of charcoal pants that were just her size and a baby-blue turtleneck sweater. She took underwear from the built-in dresser as well as a camisole. The closet also held a selection of footwear, including soft calf-high boots.

Once she was dressed, she slung her backpack over one shoulder and left the cabin. Out in the passageway, she spotted one of the crewmen and asked directions to the galley.

25

Kestrel swayed more now that she was under way, and Annja could feel the engines vibrating through the deck. The ship was at cruising speed. Annja banked her fatigue for the moment as her excitement built.

A few minutes later she reached the galley and the wonderful smells coming from it made her stomach growl. She walked in and was surprised to see a large space outfitted with state-of-the-art kitchen equipment compactly placed on the wall and on the island near the stove and microwaves. Tables and benches were bolted to the floor, but were spread out to make seating comfortable. Four bar stools were mounted in front of the island.

A man seated at one of the tables looked up at her with frightened eyes. A nautical map of the Mediterranean Sea lay on the table in front of him.

Annja stuck out her hand. "We haven't met. I'm Annja Creed."

Hesitantly, the man shook hands. His palm was hard, callused. "Sebastiano Troiai."

Roux and Garin were cooking in the kitchen, working together without saying a word. They moved like parts of a machine even in the tight quarters, as if they'd been preparing meals together all their lives. Of course, over the past few hundred years, they'd perfected the routine. Rachel Ray, Paula Dean and Guy Fieri on the Food Network paled in comparison.

For a moment, Annja just watched them, trying again to imagine what being together for so long must be like for them. *You could really get to know somebody with that many years into a relationship. Of course, you could also build up a lot of intolerance.*

Garin looked up and caught her watching. He leaned back to reach around Roux to the glassware hanging from an overhead rack, took down a wineglass and lifted a bottle from beneath the counter. He filled the glass, then topped off his and Roux's.

Garin patted the island. "Join us."

Annja took one of the bar stools and dropped her backpack at her feet. She picked up the wine and sipped. "Nice."

Garin grinned. "Coming this close to death today, again, I thought maybe I'd open a bottle of the good stuff. Nothing like a near-death experience to sharpen the appreciation for the finer things in life. You're hungry?"

"Famished."

Roux took out a plate and put a folded omelet filled with red and green peppers, onions, cheese and sausage on it. "We thought since it was still early we'd have breakfast."

"Breakfast sounds awesome."

Garin took the plate, adding homemade hash browns and biscuits. He handed it to Annja, then slid over some cutlery.

"The buttermilk biscuits are heavy," Roux groused. "Garin rushed the dough instead of letting it breathe."

"I did not."

"You did."

Annja bit into one of the biscuits. "It tastes good to me."

"See?" Garin glared at Roux as he pointed the spatula at Annja.

"She's only being polite."

"No," Annja said. "Really. They're good."

Roux scowled. "To you, perhaps. You have an untrained palate and you're too hungry to care. You're responding with your stomach, not your taste buds." He returned his attention to the skillet and the next omelet.

Garin sipped his wine. "There's no pleasing him when it comes to biscuits or omelets. He usually insists on making both."

Roux pointed his spatula at the contents in the skillet. "I'm very pleased with how these omelets are turning out."

"Just make sure they're done in the center. I hate when you make them and they run in the middle." Garin winked at Annja.

"My omelets *never* run in the middle."

"Sometimes they do. You're not perfect."

"Give me an honest cooking fire and an iron skillet."

Annja ignored them as she took a bite. It was absolutely delightful. She pointed over her shoulder at Troiai. "What about our guest?"

"He's already had breakfast this morning." Garin took the omelet Roux handed to him and made a point of checking it with a fork to make certain it was done. "And he says he's too upset to eat."

Annja could understand that.

Roux sighed in obvious displeasure. When he had his omelet prepared, he allowed Garin to add the hash browns and biscuits. "Perhaps we could dine at one of the tables."

Backpack over her shoulder, plate in one hand and wineglass in the other, Annja followed Roux to the nearest table. Garin trailed after them. They didn't talk, concentrating instead on the meal.

A moment later, one of the crewmen entered the galley and addressed Garin.

"Yes?"

"Mr. Klotz says that Mr. Troiai's family is safe, and to let you know that some men came around to check on them. They also broke into Mr. Troiai's house and searched for the computer, but Mr. Klotz's team had already taken it."

"Good thing we got the family out of there when we did, then, isn't it?"

"Yes, sir," the man replied. Annja knew the question was asked for Troiai's benefit.

Troiai looked at Garin. "May I talk to my wife? She will be frightened."

"Yes, of course. This man will take you where you can call her."

"Thank you." Troiai got up from the table.

"A word of caution, Mr. Troiai."

Troiai waited.

"Your wife has been given the impression that you've received a good contract from a generous employer. One that paid off in a trip for her and your children."

Troiai appeared confused. "A trip?"

"Yes. I'm paying for it. An all-expenses-paid trip to Disney World in Florida. A surprise from you."

"Disney World?"

"It's the safest place I could think of that would keep them all occupied. Children can be exuberant, and hiding out in a safe house all day would be stressful for Mrs. Troiai. I also arranged for a nanny to help your wife with the children. Furthermore, that nanny is a trained bodyguard, one of the best in the business. She and a team of mine will watch over your family and keep them safe."

The man seemed torn between gratitude and distrust. "Thank you," he finally said.

Garin nodded. "Your wife will have questions about

the events at the salvage yard. I'd suggest saying that it happened after you left, that you don't know much about what occurred."

"I will. Thank you." Troiai followed the crewman out of the room.

Annja looked at Garin and raised an eyebrow. "Soft spot much?"

A scowl darkened his face.

"The kids will love it."

He shrugged.

She sipped her wine. "Do you have the location of Troiai's dive that led to the clockwork butterfly?"

"Yes. It will take us almost seven hours to get there."

Forking up another bite of the omelet, Annja swallowed it down with more wine. She studied Roux. "You never mentioned the name of the ship you were looking for when you found the snail back in 1902. Or how you knew that ship would have one of these clockworks."

Roux didn't say anything.

"I need to know if I'm going to help you find what you're looking for."

Garin also looked at Roux. "Yes, *we* need to know these things."

Sighing, Roux put his fork down and picked up his wineglass. "I found the snail the same way I found so many things back in those days—tracking down legends. In the instance of the snail, I'd heard stories from a merchant ship that had broken down in waters not far from Pylos."

"On the Bay of Navarino?"

"The city was once known as Navarino." Roux took a drink. "While the men were stuck there for two days, they dreamed things. One man dreamed of a wager he could make at a casino when he got back to shore. He made the wager and became rich. Another dreamed of a small fortune that had been hidden in ruins outside of Athens. He went there and found it. Another dreamed of his death after being shot by a jealous lover. He didn't leave her. He was shot shortly after his return to Pylos." He shrugged. "Stories like that, when you're looking for such patterns, get your attention."

"The Andrianou family lives in Athens. You could have hired a salvage crew in Pylos."

"I didn't want someone local. I wanted someone who would look at the waters with fresh eyes, as I did. Someone who—once the exploration was done—would sail away and never bother me again." Roux scowled. "It didn't work out as planned."

"So you hired the Andrianou family to search for the ship and started looking?"

"Not at first," Garin interjected before Roux could reply. "We hired another boat at Pylos and went looking." He continued as he ate more of his omelet. "It was all terribly boring, but Roux became convinced he'd found the clockwork."

Roux nodded. "When I was in those waters, I knew it was there."

"How?" Annja asked.

"I just knew."

Garin made air quotes. "His 'Spidey senses' tingled."

Annja couldn't help herself. She laughed, then caught the look on Roux's face. She cleared her throat. "Sorry."

"Anyway," he said, "after I sensed…became convinced the clockwork was there, I hired Pavlos Andrianou and his ship. To my everlasting regret, it seems."

"It's not everlasting," Garin said. "Either they will kill you or we'll kill them." He smiled. "I vote for killing them."

"Really?" Annja protested. "Over breakfast? You couldn't have saved that?"

Garin shrugged. "Thinking about killing someone only sharpens my appetite." As if to prove that, he made a show of enjoying his meal.

Frowning at the thought—she did not condone the taking of life, even though on occasion she'd been forced to do exactly that—she reached down into her backpack for her tablet PC. She powered it up, brought up a map of Europe, then selected an area that covered the Aegean and Mediterranean seas. "That's a lot of region to cover."

"People traveled everywhere in the known world. Trade was flourishing. It's not any different these days. People have always been desperate to find and develop new markets."

"I was talking about the clockworks. They were scattered, it seems."

"They are. I found one in Shanghai."

Garin looked at Roux in surprise. "I don't remember that."

"You weren't with me."

"How long ago was that?" Annja asked.

Roux turned his attention to his plate and bit into one of the "heavy" biscuits. He seemed to have no problem eating it. "Before Garin's time. Before Joan."

The mystery of how old Roux was boggled the imagination. "But—"

Roux leveled his fork at her. "That particular clockwork has been dealt with. It is of no concern."

"What happened to it?"

"It's gone. As it should be. Let's concentrate on what we're looking for out here."

"Did the Shanghai clockwork offer any clues?"

"If it did, would we be here today?"

Annja was prepared to ignore his biting sarcasm because that was Roux's tone under normal circumstances, and the present circumstances were far from normal.

It was Roux who sighed. "I apologize. I didn't mean to sound—"

"Like an ingrate?" Garin finished. "A thankless jerk, an ass?"

Roux and Annja looked at him.

"What? I've had time to think about this behavior."

"Apology accepted," she told Roux. "Was there anything significant about the clockwork in Shanghai?"

"Annja, these clockworks have been in existence for over two thousand years, that I know of. They're all evil, all immensely destructive—imagine what might have happened if one had come into the hands of the Andrianou family. However, none of them before this butterfly have offered any real clue as to their origins."

"You're talking about the inscription."

"Precisely. Do you have a translation for it yet?"

Annja had already checked her email and there hadn't been a message from Papassavas. "Not yet."

"We need one soon if we're going to get anywhere."

"Tell me about the ship you found the snail on."

"It was an Ottoman vessel," Roux said. "It was sent to the bottom of the sea in 1827 in the Greek War of Independence."

"What was a Greek artifact doing on a Turkish ship?"

"I don't know."

"What was the name of the ship?"

Roux shook his head, then stopped himself. *"Timur's Blade."*

"Timur was supposed to have been the first man to forge an iron sword."

"From a meteorite, as I recall," Garin put in.

"The captain wasn't modest, was he? Did you do any research on the ship?"

Roux shook his head. "It was obvious that someone aboard had picked up the snail as a keepsake. Since it went down in 1827, I knew they couldn't have more knowledge of the clockworks than I did."

Annja pushed her plate away. "Okay, I'm going to get to work."

"You're sure you won't have anything else?" Roux asked.

"I'm sure."

Garin cleared her plate and replenished her wine. Roux put the dishes into the sink and ran the water. Annja watched in amazement.

"Why is it the two of you aren't married?"

Roux answered without looking up at her. "Who says we haven't been?"

Garin smiled. "And why settle for one woman when you can have so many."

"Ew. You're a pig." Annja turned her attention to her computer as she accessed the Wi-Fi aboard the ship.

26

Hi, Annja,
I don't have any information about automatons. I wondered if I could get your autograph. I'm a big fan.
Becky

Annja filed the request under PR and kept moving through the feed on the alt sites.

Hi, Annja,
Just caught the episode with the ghost shark. You ask me, that thing looked fake. Worse than the shark in *Jaws*. Can't believe you did that. Not up to your usual standards.
Gator Crider

Thanks, Gator. I agree, and the "ghost shark" was so not my idea.

Annja,
What happened with the witch story? Now that you're out of jail, am waiting to hear how you plan to proceed.
Also, your attorney just called me. Said you missed your court date and there's now a bench warrant out for you in the state of Massachusetts. I thought you were going to take care of this. The last thing we need is more legal troubles.
Doug

P.S. I got a lead on a story you're gonna love! A haunted
doll factory in Germany that burned down in 1853! Supposed to be the inspiration for *Chucky!* We can't pass
this one up. Call me.

Annja groaned. Germany sounded good. Archaeolog-
ically rich. And dolls could be interesting. The Russian
nesting dolls, the *matryoshka,* were fascinating. The Indian *tanjore* dolls had a lot of history. The *kachina* dolls
made by the Hopi Indians were wrapped in tradition and
a hint of mysticism.

The subject was tantalizing, almost enough to warrant
a call to Doug. But she knew she'd have a hard time getting off the phone with him.

Roux and Garin needed her full attention at the moment.

Hi, Annja,
The butterfly you found is pretty cool. Reminds me of the
mechanism discovered in that ancient Greek ship off the
coast of Antikythera Island in the Aegean Sea in 1900.
Looks like it should be a Transformer, but it also looks
like you can flip it around and make something else out
of it. Tried that yet?
Shockyoudead

Trying to move the pieces of the clockwork butterfly
around hadn't occurred to Annja. She'd have to try that.
Once she got her hands on it.

Hey, Shock,
I don't know much about the Antikythera Mechanism.
Would you be willing to talk about it?
Annja

She added her satphone number and logged the reply,

then went on to the next entry. Her phone rang almost immediately but she didn't recognize the number.

"Hello?"

"Is this Annja Creed?" The voice was male, quiet, and the guy sounded young.

"It is. Who is this?"

"You said you wanted to talk about the Antikythera Mechanism." Gunshots and screams could be heard in the background, mixed in with what sounded like zombie growls.

"You're Shockyoudead?"

"Yeah."

"What kind of name is Shockyoudead?"

"That's my gamer tag. My name is Chandler. Do you Skype?"

"I do."

"Let's Skype. Talking on the phone is difficult when you're fighting zombies."

He rolled off his Skype address and hung up.

Annja entered the Skype address and was answered almost immediately.

"Hey." The kid on the other end of the video connection was blond haired and blue eyed. He wore a Batman T-shirt and shorts.

He sat in front of a television with an Xbox controller in his hands. His fingers and thumbs flew over the buttons and joysticks. On the television screen, a zombie horde came after a POV character wielding a shotgun.

"Maybe you could pause your game," Annja suggested.

"No can do. I'm on a timer and there's no save point here. You want to talk about the Antikythera Mechanism, right?"

"Yes. What do you know about it?" Annja settled back on the bar stool.

Garin walked around behind her and stared at the tablet PC. "You're talking to a *boy?*"

Chandler looked at the screen and waved. "Hello."

Garin waved back. Then he realized what he was doing and stopped. Chandler had gone back to fighting zombies.

"Yes," Annja said. "He knows about the Antikythera Mechanism."

"I don't know what that is." Garin folded his hands over his chest.

"It's a clockwork," Chandler said. "Kinda like an early version of a Transformer."

Garin frowned. "A transformer? As in a device used for distributing electrical power?"

"No, as in a robot in disguise."

Garin just stared at the screen.

"Why don't you bring me the butterfly so I can have a look at it?" Annja said, turning to Garin.

"I really like the butterfly," Chandler added. "The way it's constructed is what made me think it was a Transformer."

"Because it could be in disguise.... Tell me about the mechanism."

"The guys who found it in 1900 didn't know what it was and didn't know what to do with it, so they filed it away in a warehouse and forgot about it. Kinda like Indiana Jones did with the Ark of the Covenant. Spyridon Stais, one of the archaeologists who tried to figure out what the mechanism was, thought maybe it was part of something bigger. Just a piece of a contraption." Chandler smiled. "It would be neat if that was just one piece of a giant robot lost on the ocean floor, wouldn't it?"

The boy's wonder won over Annja's heart. "Yeah, it would be neat."

"Anyway, nobody knew what to make of the mechanism, but in 1951 a British physicist named Derek Price dug it out of the warehouse and took another look at it. You know, to see if he could figure out what it was. He thought the Greeks used it as an astronomical calculator."

"I remember."

"Yeah, so the Greeks could figure out where the stars and planets were. Want to know something equally rad as the giant robot under the sea?"

"What?"

"If the Antikythera Mechanism is part of some outer space communications array. You know, E.T. phone home."

Annja grinned. "I don't think it's going to turn out to be that, either."

"Me neither, but the Greeks were really into clockpunk."

"Clockpunk?" Roux repeated at Annja's shoulder.

Chandler looked over on the screen and waved. "Hello."

Roux waved back. Then he grimaced and dropped his hand.

"Clockpunk is a type of science fiction where everything is powered by springs being wound up," Annja explained. "Like steampunk, which is centered around steam power, clockpunk is about gears and springs."

"Yeah," Chandler said. "Maybe we can get away from the internal combustion engine and go to windup cars. Except, who's going to have to do all the winding? That job would suck."

"It would."

"Inventing solar-powered robots first would be best. Then they could do the winding." Chandler frowned. "Except then you'd have to worry about the Singularity."

"What is the Singularity?" Roux asked.

"It's when artificial intelligences come to life and start thinking for themselves. Maybe they'll decide they don't like humans so much. They'll either eradicate us or assimilate us." Chandler shivered. "Scary stuff."

Roux looked at Annja. "What is wrong with this child?"

"Nothing's wrong with me," Chandler said. "I've got Asperger's." He studied Roux, who seemed puzzled. "You don't know what that means, either?"

"No."

"Seems like there's a lot you don't know. It means I stink at social situations, but it doesn't mean I'm stupid. A lot of high-functioning Asperger's kids are autodidacts." Chandler thought for a moment. "That means we self-educate based on personal interest."

Roux scowled. "I know what an autodidact is."

Chandler turned his attention back to his game as the zombie swarm doubled in size again.

"And one of the things you self-educated yourself on was the Antikythera Mechanism," Roux said.

"Exactly. Since there wasn't too much on that, I went on to automatons, specifically the Greek ones. Because that's where the Antikythera Mechanism came from."

"What do you think of the butterfly?" Annja asked.

"Other than maybe it's disguised? And that I wonder if it was a caterpillar before it was a butterfly?"

That hadn't occurred to Annja.

Roux stroked his beard.

"The early Greeks built automata that were toys, religious idols and models that showcased scientific principles. One of the biggest early builders was Hero of Alexandria, a mathematician and engineer. In Egypt at the time, the Romans were bossing everybody, and this guy, he created the *aeolipile,* the Hero Engine, powered by steam. It was a precursor to jet engines, but I consider him to be the true

father of steampunk." Chandler smiled. "My friend An-
drew insists steampunk was invented in Victorian England. It's one of those ongoing arguments."

Annja grinned.

"Hero also invented the windwheel," Roux said.

"Yeah." Chandler smiled in encouragement. "You *do*
know some stuff."

"I happen to know a lot."

"Sure you do. That's why I'm having to explain the Antikythera Mechanism."

Roux started to say something but Annja touched his
wrist. He kept his mouth shut with some effort.

"You can add siphon, fire engine and water organ to
Hero's list of accomplishments." Chandler shifted in his
seat to focus more intently on the game. "Originally, people
thought the Antikythera Mechanism came from Rhodes.
You know, where the Colossus was supposed to be? The
Colossus of Rhodes?"

"We know about the Colossus," Annja said.

"Kinda weird how something that big just disappeared,
isn't it?"

"Yes. Some people no longer think it was ever real."

"Whatever. It's too awesome not to have been real.
Something happened to it." Chandler shrugged. "Maybe
it was a Transformer. Maybe it just jetted out of there one
night. Anyway, those first archaeologists thought it was
from Rhodes because they had a history of mechanical
engineering there. But most of the recent archaeologists
believe the Antikythera Mechanism was probably from
Corinth in Greece."

"Why?"

"They have better equipment now to look more closely

at the mechanism. Archimedes—you know who that is, right?"

Roux answered quickly. "He was a mathematician, astronomer and inventor. Came up with the principle of the lever."

"Sure, but he also invented siege engines. You know, battering rams to knock down city walls." Chandler's eyes seemed to glaze over as if he'd gone back in time to Archimedes. "They also said he designed machines to lift enemy ships out of the water, and he was supposed to be able to set ships on fire out at sea with a mirror weapon, but *Mythbusters* pretty much busted that one. Oh, I found a website—I'll send you a link—that mentions this guy Michalis."

Annja shook her head. She looked at Roux, who also shook his head.

"Yeah, not much is known about him. They think he lived in 350 or 400 BC. He had a reputation as a fantastic toymaker. Lots of clockworks. Supposedly made creations based on the myths, and stuff nobody had ever seen before." Chandler sat up a little more. "Anyway, that's what I've got. Hope it helps."

"It does," Annja said. "It gives me some new directions to think in."

"I gotta go. The zombies are about to take this to a whole new level. Bye."

The screen blanked before Annja could reply.

Garin reentered the room carrying a protective briefcase. He glanced at the tablet PC. "You're through talking to the brat?"

"Yes," Annja said. "He's not a brat."

"He's annoying."

"He's also clever," Roux said.

"Whatever." Garin placed the briefcase on the counter, worked the locks and opened it.

The clockwork butterfly lay secured in a formfit section of foam. Gently, Annja took the device out of the container, already consumed with possibilities.

27

Hours later, her back stiff from sitting at the counter working on the butterfly mechanism, Annja leaned back and stretched. At one time, the butterfly might have moved and taken on new shapes. Those days were over. The parts were all crusted over and immovable.

At least, at present.

The site Chandler had given her on Michalis was tantalizing but not that helpful. The man, if he existed, was more myth than flesh and blood.

She repacked her computer in her backpack and slung it over a shoulder, then went up on deck to the pilothouse.

One of Garin's security people nodded at her. "You're looking for Mr. Braden and the older gentleman?"

"I am."

"They are forward. Taking in the sea, they said."

Annja thanked him. *Taking in the sea?*

She strode across the rolling deck, having already easily acclimated to her sea legs. However, the lack of sleep was catching up to her. She knew she was going to have to rest soon or fall down.

Roux and Garin stood at the front of the vessel, staring out as the waves crashed over the bow. Terns glided on the breeze, and Roux flicked pieces of bread onto the wind, which the birds caught, jockeying like fighter pilots. They talked quietly between themselves, and occasionally even laughed. Annja didn't know if the unaccustomed civility was the product of good memories or the bottle of wine they passed back and forth.

Evidently they shared some preternatural sense, as well, because they turned around at the same time.

"Spying?" Garin demanded.

"Light-headed. Stopped to get my footing." Annja walked over to join them, disappointed to have broken up the moment. And she was also a little sad. No matter how much they shared with her, she'd never experience the camaraderie they had after so many years. Of course, periodically Garin still tried to kill Roux. That she could do without.

"You need to sleep," Roux said.

"I will. Soon. What are you two doing out here?"

"Admiring the sea." Roux handed her the bottle and she drank. "It's the only thing in the world that hasn't really changed as long as we've been around. People are born and die. Cities are built and razed. Empires and nations rise and fall." He shook his head. "But the sea? That's eternal."

"You've had too much wine," Garin growled. He snatched the bottle from Annja and took a pull. "Have you found out anything?"

"Thodoros Papassavas called me regarding the translation on the butterfly."

"Ah." Roux waited in anticipation.

"Not much information, I'm afraid. The inscription was put there by a Roman centurion named Gabinius, who logged the artifact in the name of Julius Caesar. So there's no information."

"The inscription doesn't say where the clockwork was found or why Caesar wanted it?" Roux asked.

Annja shook her head. Standing there in the wind, feeling the ocean all around her and the rolling deck of the ship beneath her, she could understand why Roux and Garin were so drawn to the ocean. It was exhilarating.

"Michalis the Toymaker is incredibly interesting, though. According to my research, Michalis was thought to be a demigod."

"A child of the gods?" Roux asked.

"Yes. The son of Hephaestus, the god of fire and blacksmiths, craftsmen, sculptors, metals and volcanoes. In Greek legend, Hephaestus was also known as the lame god because he had a clubfoot. He was the only god to be thrown out of Olympus and return."

"The gods are not real," Garin said.

"Neither are people who live hundreds of years, or swords you can pull out of the air." Annja reached into the otherwhere and pulled out the sword. "Yet here we are." She allowed the sword to vanish.

"You don't truly think Michalis was a demigod."

"No, but why is Roux so interested in him and the clockworks he made?" Annja shifted her attention to Roux.

He pursed his lips.

Garin cursed. "He's not going to tell you. So Michalis was thought to be a demigod. Do you know where he lived?"

"No, but Dr. Papassavas believes the inscription on the butterfly was in a language native to Mycenaean Greece."

"Why would a Roman soldier write in that language?" Roux asked.

"The inscription was written in code. That makes me think Gabinius was working on the down low. Used a local dialect so it wouldn't be as noticeable when he illegally 'exported' the clockwork he had found for Caesar."

Roux pulled at his beard. "It's also possible Gabinius was hiding what he'd found from other Romans who were looking to sabotage Caesar. I understand Caesar had many enemies in his final days. All throughout his career, actually, but they were more active at the end."

"Using a local language is something I would do," Garin agreed. "Do you know who Gabinius was?"

Annja shook her head. "That's another mystery."

"Then let us hope Troiai's lucky strike leads us to answers we can use," he said.

"How long till we reach the site?" Annja asked.

"Probably after dark this evening. So we won't be able to go into the water until morning."

"Then I'm going to sleep while I can." Annja adjusted her backpack over her shoulder.

"Would you like us to wake you for dinner?"

"Please."

KESTREL DROPPED ANCHOR off the west coast of Elba. Annja stood at the railing and surveyed the island. The Greeks had named it Aethalia because they'd mined iron there and the furnaces had filled the air with powerful fumes. Those mines had led the Etruscans and the Romans to invade. Jason and his Argonauts were supposed to have visited there.

But the most famous resident to have lived there was Napoleon Bonaparte after his exile in 1814. And despite his connection to the place, he'd only stayed a year.

"You're up early," Garin said from behind her, startling her.

Annja wiped away the coffee she'd spilled as she watched the sun rising out over the Mediterranean with him. "I barely remember stumbling back to my cabin after dinner. I assumed you weren't up this early."

"I've been up a few hours."

"What about Roux?"

Garin frowned. "Still sleeping. He didn't appear to be resting well when I checked on him. I think he's haunted by nightmares he hasn't had in a long time. I believe Melina Andrianou's presence in his life again has brought back unpleasantness."

Memory of the burning warehouse and the dead bodies and destruction had haunted Annja's sleep, as well. "She leaves quite an impression."

"Until that moment six years ago when I found him in such bad shape, I'd never truly believed Roux could die. Even when I'd tried to kill him."

"I know. I've never seen the—" there was nothing else to call it "—*fear* I saw in him yesterday."

"While he was fevered, he talked about the torture, raving. Even after everything I've seen during my long life, it was horrible to listen to. And if he didn't heal the way we all seem to now, he would be a broken man."

During the time she'd spent with Roux and Garin, Annja had seen both men recover from wounds and injuries that would have killed lesser men. As Garin mentioned, her recovery rate also seemed…much more efficient than it had been. Whatever had extended the two men's lives had also seen to it that they healed faster and better than ordinary flesh and blood. That made her wonder if her lifespan would also be affected by her being the bearer of Joan of Arc's sword. Only time would tell.

"Let's discuss what's waiting for us down there. I've been busy while you and Roux have been napping." Garin headed for the wheelhouse. "Come with me."

"I BROUGHT REMOTE operated vehicles to do the preliminary work. Diving time is limited, so I wanted to ensure we could make the most of it." Garin nodded toward the workstation where a young man manipulated joysticks.

"This exploration has paid off quite well. It appears Sebastiano Troiai keeps a very accurate log of his salvage work."

The computer screen revealed an underwater view of the seafloor and gave her the sensation that they were slowly flying. On the screen, the world was a deep blue. Beautiful fish swam around coral reefs and through kelp beds. The ROV startled a squid into quickly jetting away, leaving a fog of dark ink behind.

Annja watched, mesmerized, as the submersible glided through the water and rendered the seafloor in sharp relief. "How deep is it here?"

"Eighty-seven feet to one hundred eleven. It's within scuba depth."

"Unless the shipwreck we're looking for lies in deeper water."

"The ocean floor here remains pretty consistent."

"Any sign of the Andrianous?"

Garin shook his head. "None so far. But we won't be able to stay hidden for long. It won't be long before they find one of Troiai's crewmen who can give them an approximate site location."

Annja sighed. She hated being this helpless when they were up against the clock.

"These people know what they're doing, Annja. Let's leave them to it and get something to eat."

"I want to be doing something."

"I know. But one of the first things Roux taught me when he took me under his wing all those years ago was to rest when I was able. After the action starts, there will be no time for it."

Reluctantly, Annja went with him.

Hours later, while sitting in the wheelhouse and taking a turn with the ROV, Annja found part of a ship's hull sticking up from the seafloor. Roux and Garin were out on the deck—how they weren't fixated on the ROV searches, Annja didn't understand.

Cautiously, she brought the ROV around and scanned again, more slowly now. As she continued the search, her excitement grew. She had one of the men get Roux and Garin.

"This is a Roman galley," Annja said when Roux and Garin joined her. "It looks like a *liburnian,* a small bireme that carried twenty-five pairs of oars. This was one of the most commonplace ships on the Mediterranean."

"That also means it was one of the most sunken ships in these waters," Garin observed. "It might not be the ship Gabinius sailed on."

Annja panned the ROV around. "Troiai said he found a few artifacts. He didn't say he found the ship. When a ship gets sunk, it usually goes down in pieces. Sometimes a shipwreck can float for miles underwater, and it can lose cargo all along the way. Usually you can map a spread of that cargo." She piloted the ROV up and back, then zoomed the magnification out. "You can see a hint of a trail. See the amphoras here?" She pointed out the containers visible on and in the seafloor. "They're in a fairly straight line."

Roux tapped the screen. "What's that over there?"

Working the joysticks, Annja piloted the ROV toward what had caught Roux's eye. A few minutes later, she was looking down at a bronze statue of a Roman soldier that was missing his head.

"That's not a clockwork, is it?" Garin asked.

"I can't tell." Annja moved in closer, but still wasn't able to tell much about the figure other than it was a swordsman in what looked like leather armor.

Garin drummed his fingers on the workstation. "I don't

like the idea of getting into the water with a clockwork that might come to life at any moment."

"You're welcome to stay here and watch." Annja looked at Roux. "What about you? Are your Spidey senses tingling?"

Roux shook his head.

"Okay, so maybe a clockwork isn't down there." Annja tried not to give in to her disappointment. "But that doesn't mean there's nothing down there to find. Where is the dive gear?"

28

Annja flipped over *Kestrel*'s stern railing and hit the water cleanly. She stroked down, feeling the cold that was kept at bay by the dive suit. Inside the full-face scuba mask, she breathed easily. No matter how many times she dived, she knew she would never get used to the strange world that spread out around her.

Underwater lamp in hand, she followed the anchor line down to the shipwreck. Roux, Garin and four other divers from the ship trailed after her.

Reaching the ocean floor, Annja checked her dive watch and depth gauge. The deeper divers went, the less time they could remain under and the faster oxygen was consumed.

She kicked her fins toward the shipwreck, not able to see it yet, but knowing where it was. Her heart raced and she worked to calm herself to preserve oxygen. Fewer than fifty feet from *Kestrel*'s anchor rope, she swam over the shipwreck.

In its day, the ship had been eighty feet long and ten feet across, not nearly as big as Lord Nelson's ships-of-the-line that were one hundred and fifty feet long. And they were canoes compared to the container ships that plied the oceans these days.

But in first century BC, the biremes had been deadly ships. Now, fewer than thirty feet of the ship's prow remained intact. She had broken in half. The stern was two hundred yards away, indicating that she had gone down quickly and hadn't moved much. It was just luck she hadn't been found before.

She swam and dug and took pictures with the underwater camera she had brought. During her investigation, she turned up a few gold coins, more of the amphora, the missing head of the bronze statue—which wasn't a clockwork and didn't move when she swam near it—along with several pieces of pottery. She gathered and placed the finds in salvage bags Garin's crewmen transferred back to *Kestrel*.

"Annja." She heard excitement in Garin's voice. "I found something."

"What?"

"A box. A bronze box. And it looks like it's still watertight."

Annja swam back to join Garin in the stern section. Roux was slightly ahead of her, his fins moving in practiced flicks that propelled him steadily through the ocean.

Garin floated, gazing down at the bronze box he'd found. "Treasure, do you think?"

The box was almost two feet long by a foot and a half wide by six inches thick. The possibilities that it presented were staggering.

"I can't open it down here, in case it is watertight." Garin picked up one corner of the box. "And it's heavy."

Annja lifted, as well. "Very heavy."

"Do you want to go up now to see what's inside?"

"Of course I do, but we're going to stay down here our full dive."

"Still, it's going to be hard to wait," Roux said.

"Yes, it is."

JUST AS ANNJA'S watch was showing they'd reached the outer limits of their dive time, she spotted a corner of what looked like a book sticking up near an amphora she'd swum by earlier. She knew a book wouldn't last any time at all unburied in the open ocean. Thank God it had been covered by sand.

Hovering over it, she worked to free it from the ocean bed, quickly discovering that it had been made of copper sheets and bound by copper hoops. She didn't try to open it, afraid that she would damage it.

Securing it in a net bag she'd brought for artifacts, she swam back toward the anchor and prepared to surface.

THE BOOK WAS unreadable, but only because neither Garin, Roux nor Annja could decipher the small script that covered the copper pages. It did, however, look a lot like the inscription Papassavas had translated, so she set it aside to copy later and send to the professor.

The object that held everyone's interest was the box Garin had found. He worked on it carefully down in the workspace in the middle of the ship. In the end, when he had it open, it held a small fortune in gold coins and gems.

Garin smiled, pleased with himself. "Nothing like finding a fortune to start your day out right."

Roux was not impressed.

But on second look through the gold, they found a small clockwork cricket that was still in working order. When it was wound, the wings fluttered musically and it chirped.

"Not as impressive as the butterfly," Garin said. "And if this thing was so active, you have to wonder what the butterfly did."

Annja agreed as she took pictures of the copper book to send to Papassavas. "So we rest now, dive again later this afternoon?"

"Yes."

ALL DAY THE next day, Annja worked the shipwreck. They started bringing up the amphoras, which were going to be interesting finds all on their own. Ships' captains used to transport all kinds of goods in these because they were watertight. More importantly, the contents of the amphoras would help more accurately date the shipwreck. Annja also took a sample of the ship's timbers, as well. During the time period, most of the ships had been constructed of elm. The wood could also be carbon dated, like much of the contents of the amphoras.

During this retrieval dive, she discovered another item embedded in a timber. Only a glint from the underwater lamp she carried enabled her to see it. At first she thought the thing might have been part of the ship.

It was a red-gold pipe the length of her hand from middle fingertip to the base of her palm. Using her knife, she dug the pipe out of the timber. With the dark blue around her, she couldn't examine the pipe very well even with the lamp. She put it into her net bag for the time being and continued her search.

"WHAT DO YOU have there?" Roux asked, joining Annja at one of *Kestrel*'s workstations.

"A piece of pipe, I think, but it's not made of any metal that I can identify." She handed it to him.

One end was closed, embossed with the head of a bull with a ring in its nose. The other end was open and packed with some kind of wiring that she didn't understand.

"This isn't electrical?"

Annja shook her head. "This is old, Roux. I found it stuck in a ship's timber. It went down with that bireme. I don't know what the wires are. Maybe some kind of decoration."

Roux handed it back to her. "Curious."

Her phone rang and Thodoros Papassavas's phone

number and picture showed up on the viewscreen. Annja scooped up the phone and answered it.

"What is it exactly you're working on, Annja?"

"You tell me. Did you translate the book I sent you?"

"I did." Papassavas sighed. "But this is only the beginning of the story. I'm afraid I'll never hear the end of it."

"If I find out, I promise to tell you. What do you have?"

"The book is a journal by presumably the same Centurion Gabinius, whose inscription I translated earlier. The code was the same."

"Probably one he and Caesar created for this mission."

"Mission?"

"I don't know what else to call it."

"Well, the term certainly fits. According to the book, Caesar sent Gabinius in search of an island that supposedly housed, and I quote, 'the works of Michalis the Toymaker.' I have never heard of such a man."

Annja's excitement started to spike. "Why was Gabinius sent to find Michalis's island?"

"Because Michalis was supposed to have weapons there that Caesar planned to use in his conquests. Caesar learned information about Michalis, who lived nearly four hundred years before Caesar, and thought he had discovered where to look for the man. So he sent Gabinius to discover if the stories were true.

"Gabinius found the island, based on Caesar's direction, but they encountered several problems there. Gabinius promises a full report at a later date, but doesn't elaborate, other than to say there were many dangers and many traps. And that he had brought a key stamped with a bull's head on it."

Annja looked at the piece of pipe with even more curiosity. "Key?"

"Yes. It's supposed to be to one of the doors in Michalis's workshop. But there are other doors, Gabinius says. They barely got out with their lives, but he was planning to return after reporting to Caesar. He and his men had been away for a long time and he felt they didn't have enough warriors to deal with everything that was ahead of them."

That doesn't sound good.

"Does he mention the location of the workshop?"

"He does. There is an island 'not far from Lesbos that bares much in common with Lesbos,' including a lagoon in the center of it. Caesar had discovered that Michalis was of Mycenaean Greek heritage. Gabinius was from that area, too, which is why Caesar assigned him the job of tracking down Michalis's lair." He hesitated. "There's also a very disturbing passage. A warning, if you will."

"What does it say?"

"'*There, in the master's workshop, the shade of Michalis guards his creations. If you disturb the master, death will come to any who trespass and do not come in peace.*'"

"Okay, that's creepy." Annja pulled her tablet PC over to her and opened a webpage to a map of the Greek islands. There were a lot of islands. She would have to find some way to winnow down the list. "Can I get a copy of your translation?"

"Of course. It's already in your email."

"Let me read it and get back to you if I have any questions."

"Read it and get back to me because *I* have questions." Papassavas laughed. "Lots and lots of questions."

By THE NEXT morning, Annja thought she had the island picked out of the dozens in the Aegean Sea. To the best of her ability, she'd recreated Gabinius's voyage from his journal, using landmarks that still existed. She'd also gone through several topographical maps of the area, as well as nautical charts.

"You're sure this is it?" Garin asked after she'd made her case.

"It has to be."

They sat in the galley drinking wine.

"If it's not, we're wasting a lot of time getting there."

Roux shook his head. "I think she's right, Garin. I've read the journal translation."

"The translater she used could have been wrong."

"Either way, we can't stay here. If there were anything here to find, I would know it."

Garin grinned. "Spidey senses."

"As you will. The point being, this is a solid lead, and we can't continue to sit idle here. The Andrianous will find us eventually. I'm surprised they haven't already."

Cursing under his breath, Garin nodded. "All right. Whether we find this toymaker's hidden shop or not, I've already made a fortune off this."

Roux smiled at him. "With the Andrianou family after us, you still have to live long enough to spend it."

"I'll have the captain get us under way."

Annja flipped through the translation again on her tablet PC, hoping she was right...and at the same time fearing she *was* right.

"GRANDFATHER?" MELINA STOOD in the harbormaster's office next to the cooling corpses. She scanned the ship's manifest in the computer system.

It had taken her two days to find a young official susceptible to her charms, who was also married and too cheap to have an affair at a hotel. Melina had persuaded him to take her back to his office so they could have privacy. The instant he'd gotten her there, she'd put a knife to his throat and forced him to tell her the codes to the records.

Then she'd slit his throat, careful to not get any of his blood on her.

"Yes?" her grandfather answered through her earbud.

"I have found Garin Braden's ship, *Kestrel*. It has just left the isle of Elba." Melina watched the dot floating across the digital representation of the Mediterranean.

"Then they have found what they were looking for."

"Possibly." Melina didn't care about that. Roux would be on *Kestrel*. She seethed to kill the man. "We could take a plane and bomb them. Be done with all of it."

"No." Her grandfather's response was sharp and immediate. "I want to learn the secret of the clockworks, *kopela mou*. I've had *Titan* ready since they left Genoa. We can catch them when they get to their destination. There's no sense in picking them up early and missing out on the clockworks. Meet me at the pier. We'll get under way at once."

"All right." Melina sent Garin's ship's coordinates to her grandfather, then she stepped over the dead man and left the office. *Soon,* she promised herself. *Very soon now.*

29

The chill of the Aegean Sea nipped at Annja despite the protective swimsuit as she dove in. She powered up the Pegasus Thruster propulsion vehicle attached to her air tanks and headed toward the bottom where everything looked blue. With her dive belt rigged for neutral buoyancy, the DPV shot her smoothly through the water, pushed by the thruster's small but powerful fan blades. The DPV assist at one hundred and seventy feet a minute made it feel like she was flying and required nothing from her except occasional changes of direction.

Here in the lagoon, the ocean floor sank more quickly than she would have expected. Instead of a gentle slope from the island, the descent was a straight plunge to three hundred feet, like the land mass had been squeezed up from the bottom.

When the gathering gloom got so dark she could no longer see well, Annja pulled the portable lamp out of her belt and switched it on. The bright cone of light pierced the gloom and lit several of the schools of small fish that hugged to the safety of the island. A three-foot squid bolted out of Annja's path and retreated toward the coral reefs that stretched at least twenty feet up from the ocean floor.

Annja switched off the DPV and righted herself with her swim fins, hanging effortlessly a few feet above the reefs. She played her light around the area, searching for the cave mouth that had been described in the journal. The light and the darkness, combined with the distortion created by the depth, made it difficult to judge distances accurately or see surfaces clearly.

Roux and Garin joined her, followed by the five-man security team Garin had ordered to dive with them. Another security team had set up on the banks of the lagoon. *Kestrel* waited above just outside the lock a half mile away, lying at anchor and too far away to be of any immediate help. The security team took up positions around them, holding their spear guns at the ready.

Garin swam forward, adding his light to Annja's. "Are you sure this is the place?" His voice over the radio sounded thick inside the full-face scuba mask.

"I don't know. Maybe." Avoiding the sharp coral, Annja swam closer to the rocky base of the island. "You read that journal the same as I did. Papassavas could have missed something in the translation. And there have been a number of earthquakes in the Aegean Sea. More frequent because of continuing activity between the African and Eurasian tectonic plates. If that kind of friction can make the Pyrenee Mountains in Spain and the Zagros Mountains in Iran, it can also erase any sign of a cave mouth here." She floated above the reefs, then swam down behind them as much as she could.

Garin snorted. "You keep track of earthquake activity?"

"A little."

"That speaks ill of your personal life."

"Hey. Tracking artifacts and nearly getting killed *is* my personal life. It's also yours, I might add. Who got me into this?" Annja swam farther down, trailing a gloved hand over the slick walls of the island foundation. Several colorful fish exploded out of nearby nooks and crannies, seeking other shelter. "The Aegean Sea is a hotbed of earthquake activity because it's landlocked over the plates. Since the ocean levels have risen in the past few thousand years, several ancient cities are now underwater. Earthquakes and tsunamis turn over the ocean floor and bring remnants of those cities to the surface. That makes me very interested."

Reaching the craggy rock, Garin separated and swam in the opposite direction from Annja. Two of the security men swam after him. "There are remote operation vehicles aboard *Kestrel*. Perhaps, since the opening isn't ready to hand, we might withdraw and let my people search with those."

Annja wasn't ready to abandon the hunt yet, though. "We're down here now. We can search till we have to go up for air. A ROV isn't the same as being here."

Ignoring Garin's grumbled response, Annja pulled herself along the stone wall, hoping for some indication the cave existed—or had existed. They couldn't have traveled this far, risked this much, for nothing. She wouldn't accept that.

"Annja." Garin's voice was suddenly very quiet, very tense. "Stop moving and crowd in against the rock."

Annja did so immediately. "What do you—"

Abrupt movement cut through the water only a short distance out in front of the reefs. For a moment, Annja couldn't make out what the creature was, but just almost seeing it triggered an automatic flight response in her that she had to resist.

The shark twitched languorously, coming closer. The long body was unmistakable, as were the first and second dorsal fins that distinguished it from a dolphin. The head was an angled wedge with a slash of a mouth. The great white was close enough now that the gill slits on its side were visible. The lamplight caught the black eyes for just a moment.

Annja let go of her lamp and reached into the otherwhere to pull out her sword. Even having it there in the sea with her, she didn't feel safe. The great white was the apex predator, pure death in the sea.

With a casual flick of its tail, the shark changed direction and disappeared into the deep blue.

"Annja?" Garin said quietly.

"I'm okay. It's gone."

"Good. I've never been face-to-face with one of those, and I really don't want to entertain the opportunity. That thing was at least twenty feet long."

"From here, it looked bigger." Annja released the sword and let it vanish, but she remained still for a while longer. "Do you think it's really gone?"

"For the moment. It was only curious. Not hungry."

"Good thing." Annja took a deep breath, not sure she had been breathing through that near-encounter.

Then Roux said calmly over the radio, "The door is here."

The announcement chased the residual fear from Annja's mind. Catching hold of the rocky crevices and kicking her fins, she whirled around. The DPV scraped along the stone wall.

Roux floated ten feet away, hanging in the water with an outstretched hand. Below him, Annja looked up, seeing him as a shadow against the bright surface a hundred feet above. His hair floated in the water.

Garin swam over to Roux. "How do you know?"

Pulling back his hand, Roux swam toward the craggy surface. "I know."

"Spidey senses," Garin said.

Ignoring the jibe, Roux grabbed hold of the stones and

settled in against the wall. He searched the fissures with his right hand, then drew back. "Annja?"

Kicking her fins, Annja swam close to Roux and latched on to the rock, as well. She played her light over the surface, wondering how the old man had found anything in the darkness of the water.

The light glinted off a dull metallic surface almost hidden by the rocks. As she peered at the spot, though, she made out the small head of a bull that wasn't much larger than her fist. Once she'd seen it, she didn't know how she had missed it.

Intricately detailed, the bull's face glared out from the rocky surroundings. Annja couldn't tell the color of the device for certain, but she was willing to bet it was that same reddish gold composite as the one they'd found off the coast of Elba. A nose ring dangled beneath the bull's heavy chin.

"It looks like the translation was correct." The LED lights inside Roux's face mask lit his smile. "Now let's see if the mechanism still works."

Annja hesitated. "You think there's a door here?"

"I do."

Glancing around the surface, Annja tried to spot any definitions that broke up the natural rock. "I don't see a door."

"Cunning artifice—you wouldn't."

Annja shook her head. She could be wrong about the island. It might have been pushed up from the ocean floor in the beginning, but it had sunk down, as well. "Even if there is a door, it can't be airtight. When Michalis lived here, this part of the island was above the water level. Whatever's behind that door is probably flooded."

"We still need to go inside, Annja. The device that lies within must be found."

and drew out the curious pipe they had found in Elba. She affixed the open end to the bull's head.

Nothing happened.

The pipe slid over easily, then twisted just as easily around the bull's head.

Frustrated, Annja drew the pipe back and examined it in the lamplight. "It's not working. If this is even supposed to work." She ran her fingers along the pipe's surface, searching for any imperfection that might offer a clue as to how she was supposed to proceed.

She fitted the pipe back over the bull's head, twisting again with the same result. Then, remembering the coiled mass of wiring inside the pipe, inspiration struck her and she held the pipe steady and pushed the end of it with her hand.

Bright flares flew from the pipe at both ends and it vibrated within Annja's grip. She kept it pressed to the bull's head.

Almost immediately, a mechanism within the pipe slammed into motion and the shrill *whir* of gears spun through the water and reached Annja's ears. The pipe became rigid, sticking out from the wall. A little panicked, Annja tried to pull the pipe back only to discover she couldn't. It had latched on to the bull's head.

The pipe vibrated again, and this time part of the casing fell away as two lengths thrust out from the pipe at ninety-degree angles. She took hold of one of the lengths that had sprouted from the pipe.

Garin and Roux floated nearby, watching carefully.

Releasing the light, letting it float from her weight belt, Annja took hold of the other length and tried twisting it like a corkscrew because she didn't know what else to do with it. She tried turning the pipe to the right to no avail, then got the same results when she tried turning it to the left.

"It's stuck." Garin swam closer. "Let me."

Stubbornly, Annja set her feet against the stone wall and pulled.

Snik.

The sound carried well through water, and this was loud enough to be heard through their face masks…and it came from inside the stone. Garin waved his hands and kicked his feet, holding back. Behind his scuba mask, his eyes widened.

Roux held his position, watching intently.

A moment later, as more mechanic thumps and grinding sounded within the rock, the pipe fell free of the bull's head and a section four feet by three feet slowly swung open. Annja scooped up her lamp and flashed it inside the uncovered area. The door was operated by a mechanical arm powered by clockwork gears mounted on the smooth stone wall inside.

Roux swam forward, adding his light to theirs. "Well done, Annja."

"If we don't get killed inside, sure." Annja put the pipe back in the bag at her belt. "Want to bet that Michalis left his lair and all his toys unprotected?"

Garin gestured for Annja to go ahead. "Ladies first." He grinned. "Second mouse gets the cheese."

Annja didn't care. No one was going ahead of her. She intended to be a clever first mouse. She pushed the lamp ahead of her and followed the bright beam into the side of the island.

30

Aboard *Titan,* Melina stood with her grandfather and surveyed the images from the small drone they'd launched. The unmanned aerial vehicle sailed briskly above the island and looked down on the lagoon a half mile away.

On the computer screen, five members of Garin Braden's security force hid in the olive trees around the lagoon. They wore camous and would have been hard to see in the brush except that the UAV's thermal imaging picked them out of the surroundings easily enough.

One of the men looked up. On the screen, he'd been designated number two.

"Check number two." Her grandfather peered at the screen. "Normal vision. Magnify."

The designated guard immediately changed from the reds and yellows against the cooler colors of the forest to a man dressed in camou fatigues and sporting green face paint as the view zoomed in. He was raising a pair of binoculars to his eyes, following the drone's path.

"Get the drone out of there. That man is suspicious. You've been there too long."

Melina shifted, thinking that the old man and Garin Braden were somewhere nearby, though they had not seen them on the island. She was looking forward to meeting up with them again. This time there would be no escape.

They had made good time following *Kestrel* to her present location. "Roux is in the water."

The drone operator seated at the control station a few feet away complied with the order he'd been given. The on-screen view dipped suddenly and the leafy foliage blotted out most of the blue sky as the UAV sped across the upper branches.

"We can take them in the water." Melina pointed at the nautical map of the area spread across the desk in the control room. "It's a half mile across the island to reach the lagoon, but I can take a team through the water. The journey will be twice the distance, but we have DPVs that will get us there in minutes."

"Once Roux and Garin Braden see you, they will call for their men."

"They have five men on the bank of the lagoon. Send another team there to engage them. A surprise sniper attack will put most of them down before we have to risk a man."

"There are more men aboard their ship."

"Then take out the ship." Melina trailed her finger across the map to the position where Garin Braden's vessel lay in wait off the entrance to the lagoon. "You have enough firepower to easily accomplish that. If you leave at the same moment my team does, then you can intercept them by the time I reach Roux."

Georgios hesitated only a moment, then nodded. "Be careful. That old man hasn't lived this long without learning a trick or two."

The salty taste of her father's blood filled her thoughts. "My father made a mistake the last time we had him. I will make no such mistake. I will bring you Roux's head."

"Then get it done."

Turning on her heel, Melina radioed the twenty men she'd already selected for her team.

ON THE DECK less than five minutes later, her wrecking crew assembled around her, Melina strapped a serrated knife to her right calf, caught the APS underwater assault rifle one of her team tossed her, and made sure the waterproof holster for her pistol was properly sealed. The Avtomat Podvodnyy Spetsialnyy had been created in the early 1970s by the Soviet Union for their special-forces teams on underwater operations. The weapon was still manufactured and exported by the Tula Arms Plant in Russia.

Titan yawed slightly on the ocean waves and sunlight glinted into Melina's eyes. Her team quickly gathered around her, in yellow-and-black dive suits that matched hers. She pulled her hair back, spit into her mask and wiped it clean, then pulled it over her head. Then she shrugged into the air tanks and switched on the regulator, making sure the flow was good. Flicking on the underwater radio, she looked at her team. "Radio check."

All twenty men gave her a thumbs-up. Behind them, the overland team was already loading into one of the rigid hull boats they'd brought on the expedition. They bristled with automatic weapons.

At the ship's stern, Melina picked up one of the white Torpedo 3500 DPVs the ship's crew had brought up from belowdecks. With the battery, the device weighed fifty pounds and was manageable enough. In the water, it was nothing at all. Its top speed was three and a half miles an hour and it could maintain that speed for forty-five minutes. The trip around the island would take less than twenty.

At the stern, Melina looked back. Her grandfather stood on the deck behind the pilot's cabin and leaned on the railing under the rear boom arm. He grinned at her, looking more piratical than ever.

Melina pitched the Torpedo overboard and followed it down into the cool, blue water. Her team crashed into the sea around her. After orienting herself, she swam to the DPV, grabbed hold and powered it up. Angling her course to take her closer to the island, she accelerated to full speed, leaving a trail of bubbles in her wake.

SEVENTEEN MINUTES LATER, according to the GPS device on her wrist, Melina reached the lagoon inlet. She powered the Torpedo along the channel, cutting the speed only slightly. After checking the GPS again and learning she was only two hundred yards from the bank where the security team had set up camp, Melina cut the DPV's power completely and turned in the water to face her team.

"Send up the radio relay."

One of the men pulled a streamlined pack from his shoulders, opened it up and took out a portable marine radio. The depth gauge indicated they were forty feet down. The man filled the flotation device attached to the radio from his air tank till it swelled up slightly larger than Melina's fist. When he released it, the device rose steadily toward the surface, trailing an antenna array behind it.

Melina swam over and took the other end of the radio relay. She plugged it into her scuba helmet. *"Titan."*

Her grandfather answered at once. The salvage ship's four diesel engines labored in the background. "Yes."

"Give us one minute to close on them."

"Done. Do not fail me, *kopela mou.* Do not fail your family. Get revenge on our enemies for your father."

"It will be done." Melina unplugged the marine radio and handed it back.

The man reeled the antenna back in, bled the air from the flotation device and repacked it.

Melina took her APS underwater rifle from her shoulder and readied it. The weapon carried twenty-six rounds in the unwieldy flat magazine that hung underneath it. The maximum effective distance was sixty feet at a depth of seventy feet. That distance halved at a depth of a hundred and twenty feet. Still, it sprayed steel bolt darts almost five inches in length and was more deadly than a spear gun.

With the rifle ahead of her, Melina swam quickly, searching the water for her prey. A short distance ahead, farther down, a small cluster of lights drew her attention. She angled down, breathing deeply, her heart rate picking up. This time the old man would die, and everyone with him would die, too.

ANNJA PLAYED THE lamp around the water-filled space, realizing quickly that she was on a spiral staircase. Garin followed her as she went up, staying within arm's reach. The gloom in the small chamber was complete. Small steps carved into the stone walls cycled up.

"Evidently Michalis preferred a more scenic view." Annja kicked her fins again, moving up slowly. Lights bounced around her, coming from Garin's lamp as well as those of Roux and the two security men who had accompanied them in.

"This passageway was widened and the steps were cut into it," Roux said, "but I think it was already here. Perhaps the lagoon was part of a natural cistern on top of this area, which wore this chamber out of the rock. The uneven width in places makes me think this was part of a natural cave system within the island that engineers took advantage of."

Only a short distance ahead, a dark opening loomed

in the wall. Annja pointed her lamp at it and angled forward. Just as she reached it, a flurry of movement exploded from the shadows and came straight for her. The lamplight caught a momentary glimpse of short, thick tentacles streaking for her face.

She couldn't get a hand up in time to protect herself, so Annja twisted to one side, throwing her body with as much leverage as she could manage. The tentacles latched on to her scuba mask and yanked her head sideways. Light from Garin's lamp lit up the thing that had hold of her, but she still couldn't see it clearly enough to figure out what it was.

It was at least a foot long and seemed to shift colors, matching first the wall, then the water around it, even shifting to match the color of her dive suit. When the creature twisted, wrenching her head, she caught a glimpse of a strangely shaped eye, like a *W* in a bulb of flesh in what she assumed was its head. Then tentacles blotted out the eye as they slid across her faceplate.

The tentacles seemed to make up half its body, and the other half had lateral fins that undulated. Suckers along the tentacles pulsed against the face mask. *A cuttlefish!*

Getting an arm up between her and the creature, Annja pushed it away.

Knocked loose, the cuttlefish backed away and flattened against the wall on the other side of the stairway. Annja reached for her sword and pulled it into the water with her. With the blade in her hand, she calmed quickly.

On the wall, the cuttlefish suddenly disappeared. Or, at least, it seemed to. The thing mimicked the color of the stone behind it. If Annja hadn't known it was there, she wouldn't have seen it. One of the weird W-shaped eyes stared at her.

"Annja?" Garin swam up to within a few feet of her.

He held his spear gun before him, aiming in the general direction of the creature.

"I'm all right." Annja let the sword vanish and wiped at the thick goo that smeared her faceplate. Most of it slid off. The creature had tried to bite her. She remembered that distinctly, and some part of her knew that would have been bad.

"That was a—"

"Cuttlefish. I know. I've seen them before." Annja took a deep breath and relaxed. "Just never so close up, and never so unexpectedly."

"Were you bitten?"

"No."

"Good, because cuttlefish are toxic. They've got a strain in Australia that is quite deadly."

"Pfeffer's flamboyant cuttlefish, yes."

Evidently unnerved by the presence of so many invaders, the cuttlefish leaped from the stone wall and shot down the passageway.

Picking up her lamp at the end of its tether, Annja directed the beam into the opening the cuttlefish had come from. The cavity ran back about six feet, tapering to about two feet across at the back. Silt had gathered across the bottom and a few plants struggled to survive among the stones that had probably once formed a wall to close the hole off. It was a good hiding spot for a predator's ambush, but held nothing else of interest.

Annja finned upward again, conscious of the air she was using and the minutes ticking off her dive watch. Only a short distance ahead, she came to a door made of the same alloy as the clockworks they had found.

31

Shining her lamp over the door's surface, Annja couldn't discover any markings or any means of opening it. She looked for another bull's head, but there wasn't one.

"It's not a problem." Garin floated beside her. "This is why we brought explosives and cutting torches. Trockel."

One of the security men separated from the others and swam toward them, answering in German, "On my way." He was already busy rummaging in the backpack he carried.

"Wait. Do not damage the door." Roux swam up to join Annja and Garin. "Everything we've heard of Michalis suggests he was a careful man." He shone his light around. "This door will be safeguarded against attack. If we force it, there's no telling what might happen."

"The Greeks and the Romans didn't have explosives and cutting torches the way we do now," Garin argued. "We can get in."

"And if you're wrong? What then?"

For a moment, Garin returned Roux's stony stare. Then he raised a hand to Trockel. The man obediently held his position a few feet away. "Annja? You get to cast the deciding vote."

"Let's take a closer look."

"We're running out of air. If you wait too long, we'll

have to return to the surface and whatever is down here will go undiscovered."

"If we make a mistake we could lose what's behind this door forever."

Roux pounded on it with the hilt of his knife. The staccato rap sounded solid and immediate. He put his ear to the door and struck the door again. Inside his face mask, he was smiling. His blue eyes cut to Annja. "Do you hear that?"

"There's no void on the other side of this door." Annja realized what that meant. "This door is fake."

"Exactly." Roux pulled back from it. "Very clever, very tricky man we're dealing with here. There's no telling what would happen if you managed to rip the door off those fake hinges, but I'm willing to bet it wouldn't be good. Especially not in this confined space."

Annja played her flash beam around the passageway. "There has to be another door, and it has to be within reach of this landing. Michalis didn't have the benefit of swimming up like we do." She searched the wall of the landing at eye level. There had to be a lever or trigger of some kind.

"Here." Garin floated off the edge of the landing in front of the door and pointed to the side.

Swimming down to join him, Annja directed her light where he indicated. Another bull's head glinted on the wall. She took the pipe from the bag at her waist and attached it to the mechanism. When the sections sprung out again, she set herself and pulled.

Beside the door and the landing, several stones suddenly jutted out of the wall a couple of feet, making an impromptu staircase that went clockwise this time.

Kicking upward, Annja swam along the revealed steps fifteen feet till she reached a blank section of wall where the steps ended. She immediately searched for another bull's head and found it on the outside edge of the top step.

Attaching the pipe key again, she pulled and heard metal gears meshing on the other side of the wall. Only this time no door opened up.

"Something's wrong." Annja studied the wall, trying to find where the door might be.

Roux swam up beside her, playing his light over the wall, as well. "Perhaps you simply haven't pulled the locking mechanism out far enough." He took hold of the pipe key, set himself and pulled, then began twisting. "This one turns." He turned it to the left, twice.

The wall beside Annja yawned open, revealing darkness within. She anchored herself to peer into the new passageway. On the other side of the entrance, a smaller set of steps curved upward. The passageway here was only six feet across, making for some tight turns.

She pointed her light up the steps till they twisted around on themselves and she couldn't see any farther. Just as she started to push her head in and follow the steps, the wall to her left vibrated.

Hundreds of metal spikes no bigger around than her little finger shot through the mortise work, filling the passageway and up along the steps, reaching almost all the way across, leaving a safety margin of only three or four inches. The maze of spikes looked like a colony of sea urchins had exploded inside the passageway, filling the area with quills. Three small fish that had been inside the passage writhed on the rods.

Garin sighed in disgust. "It's a trap. There has to be another door."

"Wait." Roux set himself again and took hold of the pipe key. "If the lock turns one way, let's see if it turns the other." He twisted the key twice.

The spikes withdrew with thin, metallic shrieks, vanishing into the walls in seconds. That was impressive. Michalis had constructed everything to last. Including the lethal traps. As soon as the spikes vanished, though, the door swung closed again from the inside.

Annja briefly considered trying to block the door from closing, but given the weight and the mechanism powering it, she figured she would lose whatever she tried to do that with.

Roux kept turning the pipe key to the right this time. After two more turns, the door opened again to reveal the hidden stairway. Small holes in the mortar indicated where the spikes had come from.

"Wait, Annja," Garin said.

Annja wasn't about to go in yet, anyway. She wasn't about to ignore the possibility of the spikes exploding out of the wall while she was inside.

"Since Michalis likes his fiendish little surprises, he might also like them with a twist."

"You mean like with a timer on the passageway?"

Garin shrugged. "It's something I would do."

Annja checked her watch. They were getting close to having to abandon the exploration so they could return to the surface. "How long do you want to wait?"

"Depth gauge indicates we're thirty feet below sea level. The island elevation around the lagoon is forty feet maximum. How far away Michalis's workshop is depends on whether it's underwater right now."

"We'll wait two minutes, then." Annja marked the time and made herself breathe calmly to conserve her air.

As she swam closer to the cluster of lights on the lagoon floor, Melina made out three distinct human shapes in green-and-blue dive suits. She also made out the artificial lines of a door in the stone wall behind them. Excitement rushed through her. Not only was she going to get to kill Roux and his companions, but she was also going to get to plunder Michalis's workshop.

She pulled the APS underwater rifle to her shoulder and slid her finger over the trigger. She kicked her legs, swimming strongly toward the men. One of them was starting to raise his spear gun when she opened fire. The water muted the rapid tattoo beat of the rifle, but the weapon recoiled against her shoulder hard enough that her aim quickly slid off target. The last four or five spikes missed the man and thudded into the ocean floor, stirring up the silt.

Still, with at least a half dozen rounds in him, the man choked and gasped. A blood cloud formed around his midsection and he spat blood inside his full-face scuba mask.

One of the other two men floated lifelessly in the water, bleeding, as well. The surviving man, already wounded and partially obscured by the dark mist around him, leveled his spear gun and fired.

The spear whipped by Melina as she trained her weapon on him. She squeezed the trigger and the darts ripped into the man, joined by more rounds from other shooters among her team. The man shuddered and went still, then started drifting away on the slight current that swept around the reefs.

Melina paused to reload her rifle and unclip the light from her weight belt. Pausing at the door, she looked inside but saw only darkness. When she pushed her light inside, she spotted the spiral stairs leading up. Craning her head, she searched the passageway above, still not seeing any lights.

She turned back to her team. "Dennison," she said a little smugly—another name under her belt.

"Yes."

"Take three men. Two teams of two." Melina pointed to either side of the door. "Circle the island a hundred yards. Make sure that the old man and the others aren't still outside the cave. If you see them, radio me. If you don't, come back and set up guard here."

Dennison quickly called out the names of three other men and made the assignments.

Pointing her light ahead of her, Melina followed it up. She cradled the underwater rifle in her left arm awkwardly, but kept her finger near the trigger. Her head pointed in the direction she wanted to go, she let her fins do the work.

"BRING THE GUNS on deck," Georgios Andrianou said, staring at the small ship ahead of them.

The crew aboard *Kestral* had taken notice of *Titan* as she swung out around the island. The ship's captain hailed them over the radio, but Georgios maintained silence. Several of the other crew were on deck, now taking defensive positions with assault rifles. Roux's people had come well-armed.

On *Titan*'s decks, the crew bared the ship's fangs. When she had first seen service as a military rescue/salvage ship for the Greek navy, *Titan* had been outfitted with two Mk 38 chain guns that fired 25 mm rounds at two hundred rounds a minute. The belts loaded into the weapons at present were high explosive incendiary rounds with tracers.

Those weapons were usually hidden away in secret compartments aboard the ship. Since the arrival at the island, they'd been mounted on the prow. Topping out at a little beyond eight feet, they were highly visible when the crew stripped away the false cargo hulls.

Two other teams mounted M2 Browning heavy machine guns on gimbals on the upper deck, giving them two hundred and seventy degrees of movement. Another pair of the .50-caliber machine guns was being locked down in the stern.

"Sir," Captain Skarvelis called from the helm, "*Kestrel* has seen us."

"Are the weapons ready?"

"Yes."

"Then proceed, Captain." Georgios lifted a pair of high-power binoculars to his eyes.

Skarvelis stood in the center of the control center and held on to the desk. "Helmsman, make for *Kestrel*."

"Aye, Captain."

Georgios felt *Titan*'s deck sway slightly beneath his feet as the ship came about to starboard. If the crew aboard *Kestrel* had been suspicious about the other vessel's intentions before, the course adjustment erased those doubts.

"Chain guns, open fire."

Immediately, the 25 mm cannons burst into thunderous life, hammering the surrounding ocean with ear-splitting noise. Twisting spumes of white foam flew into the air, but the majority of the ammunition slammed into *Kestrel*. The incendiary rounds chewed through the unarmored salvage ship and knocked holes in her sides. The men firing assault rifles abandoned their attacks and retreated as the 25 mm rounds raked the deck.

"Ready torpedo."

"Torpedo ready, Captain."

In addition to the guns, *Titan* also carried a Yu-7 torpedo launch system that had been recovered from a Chinese smuggler's ship that had gone down four years ago. Georgios's son had found out about the shipwreck after rescuing the crew at sea. One of the young sailors had told them about the smuggler's ship in great detail. Xydias had the crew killed, threw them into the sea and returned for the plunder. The torpedo system had come in handy on a number of occasions.

"Fire torpedo."

"Firing torpedo."

On the deck, between the two chain guns emptying brass in catchers, the torpedo leaped from the launcher and took to the water. For a moment Georgios saw the white trail left by the torpedo as it streaked through the ocean.

"Ready torpedo," Skarvelis ordered.

"Readying torpedo, Captain."

"Fire torpedo when ready."

"Aye, Captain."

Some of the sailors aboard *Kestrel* returned fire, but only a few stray bullets hit *Titan* because they were still fifteen hundred yards away. One of Skarvelis's sailors went down, blood darkening his uniform. A few other rounds ricocheted from the bulletproof glass wrapping the wheelhouse.

Skarvelis remained calm. "Helmsman, stay on this course till that second torpedo is away."

"Aye, Captain."

Titan continued to bear down on the stricken ship. Thick, black smoke spiraled from *Kestrel*. Her wheelhouse was shot up and several bodies lay scattered across the deck.

"Firing torpedo."

Georgios still tracked the first torpedo, as he saw the second torpedo leap from *Titan*'s deck. *Kestrel* tried to take evasive action, but it was too little too late. She'd been at anchor and not expecting such an aggressive attack.

The ship shuddered as the first torpedo slammed into her amidships. A wave of water exploded upward and rained down across the deck in a deluge. She dropped in the water almost immediately and wallowed heavily, obviously beyond control. A short time later, *Kestrel* shivered again as the second torpedo took her astern.

"Helmsman, adjust course. Let's pass *Kestrel,* then come about on her port side."

"Aye, Captain."

In less than a minute, *Kestrel*'s fate was written and she was sinking into the Aegean Sea. Her crew threw lifeboats into the water and jumped in after them, no longer in a position to fight.

Satisfied, Georgios nodded to Skarvelis. "Good job, Captain."

"Thank you, Mr. Andrianou."

Turning his attention to the computer screen, Georgios watched as snipers brought down the last of the security team that had been left on the lagoon beach. He waited impatiently for Melina to contact him and let him know they'd made a clean sweep of the battlefield.

32

The darkness in the passageway remained complete, even after Annja broke through the surface of the water. Surprised to discover she was above water level, she shone her light around, searching the narrow passageway for other traps.

Roux and Garin surfaced beside her and added their lights to her own. Shortly after, Garin's two men also surfaced.

Overhead, the cavern roof was uneven and worn smooth enough to suggest that it, too, had at one time been underwater. The sleek surfaces added more evidence that water had formed the cave system a long time ago.

"Do you see any more of those bull's heads?" Garin swam over to the wall nearest the spiral stairs. The stairs ended eight feet above their present position, so getting into the larger cave chamber outside the passageway would require using them. He shone his light along the edge of the stairs carefully, touched the surface in a few areas to wipe away lichens.

"No." Annja swam to the stairs and began to climb. The heaviness of the air tanks and the Pegasus Thruster bit into her shoulders and weighed her down. She slipped off her fins and secured them to the harness across her chest. Once she was out of the water, she took a pair of joggers from the pack at her back and put them on to protect her bare feet.

Moving cautiously, Garin joined her. He secured his own fins and pulled on a pair of joggers, as well. He also opened the waterproof holster on the Smith & Wesson .500 Magnum secured across his chest so the weapon would be available.

At the landing, Annja paused and scrutinized the cave they were stepping into. A stone wall that reached the ceiling blocked the view, forcing her to choose one of two paths. In the center of the wall, a five-foot-tall bull's head carved in bas-relief stared out at them.

Garin growled in frustration. "A choice of two paths? Choose right or die."

Annja pointed her light at the floor, surprised to see that, under the thick layer of dust, it was covered in the shiny metallic alloy. She slid out of her air tanks and scuba mask, leaving them dripping on the floor. The swim fins joined them. Moving slowly, she walked to the right and peered around the corner of the wall. "There's a path here."

Garin divested himself of his gear, then walked to the other end of the wall and stopped in the corner. "There's a path here, as well. And more carving in the stone." He wiped away dust with a gloved hand. "It's an image of Michalis."

Annja brushed at the wall beside her. "Nothing here." She crossed back to Garin and took out a small 35 mm digital camera from the pack. She took three pictures of the image of Michalis in a vast cavern filled with clockwork figures in the shapes of animals and people.

"So does that mean this is the safe way?" Garin flicked his light back at the other corner. "Or is this just a trick?"

"It's a trick," Roux announced, stepping ahead of Garin's two men. "Both ways are a trick, and ones that will probably lead you to your deaths if you should follow them." He stood in front of the bull's head on the wall. "Think about it. Two ways. Choose right and you continue on without risk. Choose wrong, you lose a person, then make the right choice." He shook his head and smiled mirthlessly. "No, this man wouldn't give you easy access to his secrets. He would make you pay blood, then leave you defeated. Those paths are booby-trapped or they'll lead you on a wild-goose chase." He glanced at Garin. "It's the same thing you would do."

Garin didn't say anything. He walked back to the gear they'd dumped on the floor, then picked up a spear gun. Returning to the corner, he slammed the gun butt against the first tile around the corner, angling the spear gun so his hand was at something less than a hundred and eighty degree angle to it.

The gun butt thudded heavily against the tile. Nothing happened. Moving to the next tile, Garin repeated his effort. This time a small group of spears shot down from the ceiling, ripped the spear gun from Garin's hand and bent against the floor.

Cursing, Garin looked at the ruined spear gun.

Annja pocketed her camera, picked up another spear gun and duplicated Garin's efforts on the unmarked passage. Two tiles down, mechanisms whirred and the floor suddenly dropped away. Balanced at the edge of the drop, she directed her light down. Twenty feet below, metallic stakes gleamed.

The path continued on the other side of the four-foot opening.

"Easy jump," Garin said.

Annja smiled. "Want to go first this time?"

"No."

Catching hold of the wall, Annja leaned out over the

opening and struck the next tile with the spear gun. More whirring vibrated through the stone, but it was cut short by a glistening blade that thrust from the cavern wall horizontally and raced toward her. Even her reflexes were almost not enough to save her as the blade slid through the space where she'd been standing. The wind from its rapid passing cast a chill over her, or maybe that was from the soaked dive suit, the cold in the cave or the fact that she'd dodged death by inches.

Garin had likewise ducked for cover, but he'd moved back and around the corner, which was the only thing that had saved him. The sharp blade nicked his left cheek in passing. Blood wept from the inch-long cut between his goatee and his earlobe. He dabbed at the cut, then sucked the blood from his finger. Before he took his finger from his mouth, a heavy stone block dropped from the ceiling and sealed off the passageway.

"This is beginning to get annoying." Garin cursed. "If neither of those paths lead us where we want to go, what is the true path?"

Roux studied the bull's head. "Annja, did you notice that one of the bull's horns is larger than the other?"

She returned to Roux's side. She stared at the carved image and discovered that the right horn was indeed larger than the left. Gently, she brushed dust from the horn and discovered Greek letters trailing along the underside. "Alpha, beta, lamda, upsilon, chi, and to one side is another, larger chi. Then there are two horizontal lines."

Garin snorted. "So the bull's head is some kind of mascot to a fraternity?"

"Almost." Roux glanced around the room. "We're missing a clue. There should be another group of letters on something somewhere in this room." He checked the nearby walls. "Look for it, but be careful. It would have to be within easy reach."

Annja dusted the walls. "What does that word signify?"

"Spelled under the horn? *Abluo* means to wash or cleanse."

"We're supposed to wash or clean something?" Garin asked as he searched the carved image of Michalis.

"No. The two chis, one smaller than the other, are the clue. This is a math problem, a very clever puzzle. You replace the five letters with numbers, multiplying them by the value of the second chi."

"Don't. You're making my head hurt."

"The alpha becomes a two," Roux went on as he knelt and continued to search, "the beta becomes one, the lamda becomes seven and the upsilon becomes a four."

Annja calculated the problem quickly in her head. "That gives you a product of eight thousand, seven hundred and twelve."

"Precisely." Roux beamed at her as if she were a prize pupil. "State the problem aloud, saying just the numerals, not the value placement."

Picturing the problem in her head, Annja did. "Two, one, seven, eight times four equals eight, seven, one, two." Then she saw what Roux was getting at. "The product is represented by the same letters." Excitement pulsed through her. "Upsilon, lamda, beta and alpha. It's the mirror image of the first number."

"Yes."

"This isn't a time for algebra homework," Garin growled.

"Sure it is. Diophantus, in the third century AD, is credited as being the father of algebra."

"Third century AD would put him well after Michalis."

"True. But the Greeks had been solving problems in an algorithmic progression well before then using geometry. The ancient Babylonians developed the formulas the Greeks incorporated. But it stands to reason that Michalis would have known a lot about math to do the things he did."

"So was he Greek or Babylonian?"

"He could have been both. A Babylonian enslaved by Greeks who rose to a position of power. Or a Greek who was enslaved by the Babylonians. Or a Persian. Alexander the Great was busy conquering the world at the time Michalis was creating his clockworks."

At the wall beside the entrance, Annja called, "I found letters here, but they're not the right ones. And you can see there's a section that can be depressed."

"Go ahead, find out what happens," Garin said.

"If we do that blindly, we could all die," Roux stated. "Or Michalis's workshop could be forever closed to discovery."

"I could get some earthmovers in here," Garin replied. "Trust me, I could find whatever is buried in this hill, with a whole lot less personal risk."

"But how much would you lose if you pursued that course of action?" Roux shook his head. "No. Find the letters we're looking for."

A few minutes later, Garin said, "I've got them. They're here under the chin."

"Are you certain?" Roux asked.

Grinning, Garin pushed on the carved chin. "We'll see."

Gears ground away inside the stone wall. Abruptly, the bull's head withdrew, backing six feet and turning to the left on a tracked runway to reveal a doorway to another dark cavern.

After a careful examination of the doorway and the tiles on the other side, Annja led the way inside. Her light reflected off several metallic surfaces and ignited the euphoric sense of impending discovery. She stepped forward, then stopped at a railing. Peering down, she saw she was standing on the precipice of a ledge.

Garin stepped up beside her and snapped to life a glow stick he had been carrying in his equipment bag. He pitched the glow stick into the darkness. As the blue glow arced into the pit, it revealed Michalis's workshop in teasing glimpses.

The glow stick hit the metallic tiles of the floor, rolled briefly and came to a stop. Shadows, long and lean, stretched from the fantastical metallic creatures that surrounded the flare. The blue glow revealed a unicorn, a rearing Pegasus with wings spread and a merwoman. Several other smaller clockworks sat on elegant marble tables. There were insects, fish, lizards and…other things Annja couldn't identify at a distance.

"This way." Roux walked to the left, following the circular observation deck to a flight of steps that led down. Annja was hard-pressed to keep up to him. Garin and the two security men trailed behind, all of them speechless in astonishment and awe.

"You said you came here for a clockwork, Roux?" Annja played her light around the hundreds of clockworks.

Roux didn't break stride, marching unerringly through the darkness so fast he was almost catching up with the light he carried. "I did."

"How are you going to know which one you're looking for?"

"Because I will." Unease tightened Roux's expression. "This thing is very dangerous, Annja. I cannot express to you how dangerous it is."

"Like the thing in China?" Annja still sometimes dreamed of the jade ogre she had helped Roux find in the abandoned City of Thieves. Memory of Garin and Roux with their hands on it, speaking a language she didn't understand, then the huge explosion afterward that had never been explained to her.

"Even worse. The artifact in Loulan City represented power. A dark casting that could be used for so many bad things. Horrible things." Roux took a breath and let it out. "But this, it has the power to twist and weave, to make done and undone."

"To make *what* done and undone?"

Roux pursed his lips. "What is and what is not."

"You're speaking in riddles."

"This thing was never meant to see the light of day. And I must find it."

"Can you tell me what we're looking for?"

"Not precisely. This thing…it will be something that weaves."

"A loom?" Annja pitched her light at the clockworks.

A human-size metallic seahorse stood on its curled tail near a table that contained a replica of the Parthenon. The small figure of woman a foot tall stood in front of the structure. She wore a breastplate and a winged helmet, and carried a spear. Beside her, an owl perched on a horse and a Gorgon stood to one side, her snake hair poised to strike.

"Roux."

He stopped.

"That's Athena standing in front of the Parthenon."

"Yes."

"She's the goddess of weaving."

Roux shook his head. "That's not the clockwork we're looking for." He turned back the way he was going.

Reluctantly, Annja moved with him, wishing she could have stayed behind long enough to see what the clockwork Athena did. But it was just as possible that Michalis created a clockwork of Athena because she was also goddess of arithmetic.

Garin and his men tossed more flares on the floor. Together, they created a ruby pyre that lit up more of the workspace. Several plants Annja could identify created gardens with nymphs and dryads and satyrs cavorting in them. Only then did she remember her camera and start taking pictures.

She was so distracted she almost tripped over Roux, who had come to a stop in front of her. Stepping to one side of him, she aimed her beam ahead and peered at what had caught his attention.

Two metallic legs stood revealed in the light. Each leg was massive and ended standing on a foot that had to be eight feet long and four feet wide across the keg-size toes.

33

Annja trailed her light up the huge legs and took in the rest of the giant. The figure was that of a young male in a kilt. A belt encased his hips and supported a long knife. He held a massive spear in his right hand. A small, mocking smile curved the warrior's lips. He was handsome, his wild hair brushing his shoulders. He gazed out as if looking across the room.

"Is that the Colossus of Rhodes?" Annja asked. When Roux didn't answer, she looked for him, only to find that he had moved.

He stood over to the left, in front of a giant clamshell that was ten feet across. He put his hand on the shell. "The clockwork I'm looking for is here."

"The clamshell?"

"No. Within the shell. Help me." Roux knelt in front of the clockwork clam and pushed on it. He called out to Garin.

Garin came immediately, holding the MP5 in one hand. His tense expression was made more severe by the dried blood on his cheek, his eyes so black they looked like holes. "This is it?"

"What we want is within."

After a brief hesitation, Garin knelt and laid his weapon on the floor, then began helping. "Tell me what the clockworks are, Roux. After all that we have been through, after all that we have been to each other over the centuries, I deserve that."

Stubbornly, Roux kept his silence as he strained against the clamshell. Then he said softly, "These things—not all of Michalis's work, but some—were constructed with an ancient power. A force even stronger than Joan's sword because they recognize no rules, no balance. These clockworks were fashioned before the concepts of good and evil had been fleshed out."

"So they're neither one thing nor the other?"

"No. These things...they *are* riddles. Very dangerous riddles." Roux glanced at Garin. "They're aspects of power that are able to channel even more power."

Garin pursed his lips, then nodded. "Michalis made this thing?"

"Yes."

"How could he have wielded something so dark?"

Roux shook his head. "Michalis didn't wield that power. It wielded him. As it wielded so many others throughout the lives of men. That power, once it was done with Michalis, left a taint that he used to fashion other clockworks that held powers of their own. As he worked the metal, he forged some of that remaining energy into pieces. I'd found several of them, but not this one. *This* is the one he used to create."

"What are you going to do with this?"

"I'm going to destroy it, as I did the others we found. As I'll destroy any others I discover." Roux strained against the clamshell. "Michalis didn't know everything that he was doing. He didn't know the extent of the power he was working with. Power like this—" he shook his head "—it blinds those who use it. Usually it corrupts them, turns them into vessels that never again truly know their own wills. Only a few people have ever broken the shackles to that particular darkness and lived to tell about it."

"Did that happen to you?" Annja asked.

Roux ignored the question. He pushed against the clamshell again, then fell back and cursed.

Garin pulled his dive knife from the sheath on his calf and thrust it in the gap between the two halves of the shell. He prized with both hands, adding strength to the leverage he had.

The knife blade snapped.

Annja continued her examination of the device, still overwhelmed by the intricacy of the clamshell's detail.

"I can blow it open," Garin said, backing away. "Since you're going to destroy whatever is inside, anyway, it won't matter if we use explosives."

Roux nodded. "Go ahead."

Garin turned to the two security men. Trockel again rummaged in his pack.

"Wait." Annja ran her hand over the clamshell's hinge, pointing her light at the bull's head she'd found with her other hand. The lock was almost hidden in the darkness and by the filigreed edge of the shell. She took the pipe key from her pack and engaged it, then pulled outward more easily than she'd expected.

Almost immediately, the clamshell started slowly opening, the top half lifting hypnotically.

Garin and Roux stepped back, ducking behind nearby clockworks, a standing crocodile and a harpy, respectively. Staying crouched even though there was no immediate reaction from inside the shell, Annja made her way around the clockwork and peered inside.

Instead of a pearl, the clam held the mummified body of a dead man. The tissue had gone gray-white with age and sunk in tight against the bones, making him look anorexic. The skull stood revealed in the horrible face, the lips sunken in so that the teeth were prominent. He—and it was a he judging from the dress and the physical aspects—bore no signs of violence. He looked like he'd simply climbed into the clam, laid down and died. A thin mattress supported the body. He wore a toga, and a leather satchel at his side held tools. His wispy gray hair fanned out around his head. A thin beard looked too big on the sunken face.

There, in the master's workshop, the shade of Michalis guards his creations. If you disturb the master, death will come to any who trespass and do not come in peace.

"Wait," Annja called out, freezing the others in place. "There was a warning, remember?"

Garin lifted his machine pistol and gazed around warily. "I don't see any shades. And this thing isn't getting up from that giant clam."

"That doesn't mean there isn't a trap."

"If there was a trap," Roux said, "this would never have opened. We're safe, Annja." He paused, then reconsidered. "Safe enough for the moment, at any rate."

"Is that Michalis?" Trusting that there were no more nasty surprises in store, Garin joined Roux at the foot of the giant clam.

"It would appear so. Although I had understood he was murdered by Romans. How he ended up preserved like this is anyone's guess. I sincerely doubt they took the time to lay him out and secure him in one of his own creations." Roux knelt respectfully and played his light over the corpse. The interior of the shell, like natural ones, glowed with an iridescence in the light. Roux gently removed the large, ornate ring on the dead man's right forefinger. He held it up to display the bull's head. "His seal." He glanced at Annja, then tossed her the ring. "A keepsake."

Annja caught it, but her attention was on the parchment scroll under the corpse's left sleeve. She pocketed the sigil ring, then leaned down and picked up the scroll. Trapping her light under her arm, she carefully opened the scroll just enough to make out the Greek writing. She couldn't read it, but Thodoros Papassavas or one of his cronies could.

Wrapping the parchment around the rod again, she reached into her pack and pulled out a plastic Baggie. She sealed the scroll inside and returned it to her pack.

"Annja, might I borrow the key?" Roux had taken a small metallic box from beside Michalis's body. The box held one of the bull's head keyholes.

Annja gave him the key, then watched curiously as Roux operated the lock. The box unfolded, laying out flat and revealing a crystal globe inside. Roux tossed the box aside.

"Ah. The weaver." Reverently, he held the globe up to examine it.

In the otherwhere, Annja felt her sword vibrating like a tuning fork. Without thinking, knowing only that she needed it, she pulled the blade into the workshop with them. The tingling along the sword continued. She tightened her grip on the leather-bound hilt.

The globe in Roux's hand might have been eight inches around, no larger than a baseball. It looked as if it was made of clear, flawless crystal, no trace of a bubble in it.

Yet inside the globe, a small golden spider no longer than the nail of her little finger, moved restlessly, spinning a strand of webbing that dropped it from the top to the bottom. Once at the bottom of the globe, the spider climbed back up the side, then it spun another single gossamer strand because the first one had mysteriously disappeared and it began its descent again.

"That's it?" Garin hunkered down beside them. "A clockwork spider trapped in a crystal globe?"

"Yes," Roux said reverently. "This is it."

"Doesn't look like much. Something that might capture a child's attention. For a time."

"Exactly. Sometimes the most dangerous things in this world are beautiful things, or innocuous." Roux rolled the globe over while the spider was descending again. The arachnid froze in place, then flipped over till it was moving down the strand again. "With children, all things are possible, and there are no moral boundaries. Only whim and imagination without restraint. No responsibility or consequences." He shuddered. "Picture the most dangerous weapon you know of, Garin. Those nuclear warheads the larger nations like to enter sabre-rattling contests with." He balanced the globe on his fingertips. "This is more dangerous than all of those things put together."

"The weaver." Recalling the model of the Parthenon and the Athena figure standing before it, Annja watched the spider slide back down the web strand. "Arachne was a mortal weaver who claimed she was better than Athena. Bad enough she didn't acknowledge that her skill was a gift from her goddess, but Arachne agreed to a weaving competition with Athena."

Roux nodded. "During the competition, Arachne not only won, but the tapestry she wove depicted embarrassing situations for the gods and goddesses. Arachne exposed the lives of the gods as if they were on some tawdry reality show."

"In the end, Athena turned Arachne into a spider." She couldn't take her eyes off the crystal globe. "Are you trying to tell me that is Arachne?"

"No." Roux shook his head. "This is a clockwork. A representation of Arachne, perhaps, but not Arachne. But it's been embued with that dark power. Loose in the world, this thing would spread like a disease, bearing death and discord."

Noticing for the first time how enraptured he was by the globe, Annja put down her light and dropped her hand on the old man's shoulder. "Roux."

As if shaking off a lethargy, Roux closed his hand over the globe, obscuring the spider from view. Then he stood, breaking the spell that had held them all at the dead man's final resting place. "It's something I need to destroy. It's too dangerous to exist in this world."

Annja stood, as well, feeling the fatigue from the last long days settling on her. Still, curiosity nagged at her. She was in a place *filled* with the stuff of legend. Turning, she directed her light out over the surrounding clockworks and suddenly felt a spray of warm fluid against the side of her face. She reached up to touch her face and drew her hand away.

Red stained her fingertips. The coppery smell of fresh blood filled her nostrils.

One of Garin's security men dropped in a heap without a word. When he flopped back bonelessly, the gaping gunshot wound in his temple drew her instant attention.

34

"Look out!" Annja reached forward and shoved Roux into motion, throwing herself after him as at least two bullets struck the open clamshell and ricocheted into the long-dead creator. The toga jumped from the impacts. Annja flattened Roux and rolled off as bullets cut the air over their heads, then they were both scrambling to find cover.

Garin rocked back on his heels and blood spurted from his right shoulder. If he hadn't been moving, the bullet would have struck him in a more terminal spot. He lost the MP5 for a moment, then kicked it ahead of him toward a clockwork apple tree. More bullets knocked one of the golden apples from the tree's branches as he sprinted for the protection the thick trunk offered. Garin scooped the machine pistol from the metallic tiles with his left hand, bringing it up before him as he settled in behind the apple tree.

The second security man fell midstride, the top of his head blown away as the staccato reports of automatic weapons thundered inside the workroom. The opening attack had been with a silenced weapon. Now there was no need for stealth.

Rolling behind a trio of dolphins standing on their tails on a wave, Annja gripped her sword and scanned the work-shop entrance. Whoever was firing at them had to have come from that way. The glow sticks Garin and his security people had thrown around the room were dying, allowing the darkness to gather, but she spotted movement along the observation deck. Men circled from either side, coming around to take them from two different directions.

"Annja," Garin called.

When Annja looked at him, he extended a leg and kicked the dead guard's dropped MP5 toward her. She caught the weapon as it spun across the tiles. Autofire thundered and muzzle flashes lit up a section of the observation deck. Bullets ricocheted off the metallic floor tiles in a spray of sparks, then ricocheted again off clockworks.

Whirling from behind the apple tree, Garin aimed at the area where the muzzle flashes had been and fired two quick three-round bursts. As he ducked behind the tree again, a man plummeted from the observation deck and smacked the floor.

Another gunner opened up from the left and his bullets chased Garin from hiding. Throwing himself forward, Garin slid across the floor toward a chariot harnessed to a pair of bulls with short, curved horns.

Roux raised his machine pistol and fired at where the muzzle flashes had been. Annja couldn't tell if he hit the gunman or not, but there was no immediate return fire.

That's because they're circling around. Adrenaline flooded Annja's senses as she scanned her immediate vicinity. The observation deck was going to be a problem. And the darkness hindered as much as it helped. She gathered herself, released the sword to the otherwhere and slung the MP5, then sprinted for the closest dead man. She grabbed the body's shirtfront with both hands and yanked the corpse across the floor. Bullets chased her to the apple tree Garin had abandoned. She slammed into the trunk almost hard enough to knock the wind out of her.

Garin fired again and the bright muzzle flashes carved his face out of the darkness in sharp relief.

Working quickly, Annja stripped extra ammunition and glow sticks from the dead guard's gear. She shoved them in the pack tied to the back of her weight belt. Carrying the extra magazines and glow sticks wasn't comfortable or convenient, but it worked. She kept one of the glow sticks in hand.

Two men were down. One of them remained in the glare of the dying light and wasn't moving. *Out of how many?*

Annja heard a curious sound and couldn't immediately place it, but she recognized the strident emotion in Roux's voice when he yelled, "Annja, move!"

Instantly, she dived toward the giant clam because it was the closest thing within easy reach that provided protection. Just as she started to slide behind the shell, an explosion lifted the clockwork apple tree from the floor and turned it into a vicious hailstorm of shrapnel that cascaded down in a discordant hail.

Deafened from the grenade, Annja snapped the glow stick she was holding, stood and hurled it up onto the observation deck at the back of the workshop. It spun end over end, growing brighter as the chemicals gained strength. A second later, the glow stick hit the back wall and dropped to the observation deck, illuminating it.

Caught in the blue illumination, two men aimed their assault weapons at the area where Annja had been. She'd already sprinted to her right and pulled the MP5 up in both hands.

Standing out like two specters, the men opened fire and the muzzle flashes flickered hot as acetylene torches, casting shadows over the men's faces. Annja squeezed the machine pistol's trigger in controlled bursts, aiming to kill because she couldn't risk letting the men get away. She had no idea how many had crept into the cavern after them.

One of the men went down immediately. The other tried to dodge back and track Annja. Her next burst stitched him across the chest and shoulder, causing him to stumble and spin. Unable to stop himself, he fell over the railing around the observation deck, yelling in fear till he smacked into the floor. He lay limp and broken, eyes staring upward and reflecting the blue glow on the observation deck.

That sound again.

Not knowing the target zone of this next grenade, Annja hunkered down beside a pair of mermaids sitting on a rock. The explosive landed at the feet of the colossus only a short distance away, then detonated. Shrapnel tore into the mermaids, decapitating one of them, knocking the arm off another and tearing chunks from the rock.

The colossus wobbled unsteadily, then its center of gravity gave way and it toppled backward like a boxer knocked out on his feet. The clockwork statue remained rigid and clanked when it struck the observation deck.

Seizing the moment, Annja ran toward the fallen colossus just ahead of a bullet storm over her position, then leaped onto the figure and continued running up the body. Some of the invaders saw her and targeted her. Bullets ripped sparks only inches behind her.

Garin and Roux picked out those gunners and blasted them. Annja was aware of at least one more shadow tumbling from near the front entrance as she leaped from the shoulder of the colossus onto the observation deck. Off balance, Annja threw herself forward and rolled, hitting the rear wall, and only then noticing that the man who had fallen to her bullets earlier wasn't dead.

Scalp wound bleeding furiously, the man scrabbled for his assault rifle and brought it up. The muzzle flash burned away the darkness that stretched across the ten feet separating him from Annja.

The bullets screamed over Annja's head by inches. Lying on her side, not daring to get to her feet, she squeezed the MP5's trigger and aimed for the center of the man's body. The machine pistol cycled dry and the harsh sound of gunshot died away, leaving her ears ringing even though her hearing had already been compromised within the enclosed space. For a moment she was afraid the man still wasn't dead, that he was only waiting to kill her when he opened fire again.

Then he toppled from his kneeling position, sprawling out loose-limbed.

Annja switched out the spent magazine with a fresh one. She rose to a crouch and gazed down at the battlefield. Several of the clockworks lay broken, scattered across the metallic tile floor, and the sight nearly broke her heart. So much history had been lost in seconds.

Muzzle flashes pinpointed Garin's and Roux's positions, but they were moving, too. Without speaking, they worked together, staying close and providing covering fields of fire for each other. Annja knew, though, that if she could pinpoint their positions, so could the invasion force. Even as she thought that, another grenade detonated near the last place she'd seen Roux by the giant clam.

Annja threw herself on the ground just ahead of the explosion that landed inside the open clamshell. On fire and in pieces from the detonation, Michalis's corpse flew through the air. Almost immediately, machinery ground to life inside the workspace. The sound of harsh clanking and snapping was even louder than the gunfire.

On the ground, Annja felt the observation deck lurch into clockwise motion as fast as a man could walk. Her stomach twisted with it. The gunfire halted for a moment.

Peering over the side, she saw that the floor below had started rotating counterclockwise at the same speed. The various clockwork pieces shivered and shook as the floor spun.

The rotation was nearly smooth, grinding now and again where debris had fallen into the gears or the grooves that had to have been cut into the wall. Dust and broken rock spilled out onto the observation deck around Annja as the observation deck tore through the facade. The amount of work that had gone into constructing the workshop astounded her. She wondered if it was all to protect the clockwork Roux had been after.

Several of the clockworks tumbled and spilled across the floor. A few of them lost pieces and gears rolled across the tiles.

The fallen colossus jerked and jumped along the railings, then finally broke into pieces and clattered to the floor.

Almost too late, Annja spotted the men rounding the railing toward her as they followed the observation deck. They looked almost ludicrous at first, running and barely managing to stay in place with the wall behind them, but closing quickly on Annja.

Before they reached her, though, panels along the wall crumbled and huge pipes thrust out. Sulfurous stink belched out of the one nearest Annja. Heat radiated from the thing, giving her scant warning before a glowing wave of heated liquid vomited out of the pipe. At least a dozen pipes had come out of the wall, but three of them weren't working.

Flamethrowers were used in 424 BC by Demosthenes, an Athenian general during the Peloponnesian War, to defeat the Boeotians during the Battle of Delium. The sulfur-based mixture wasn't the true Greek fire that had been developed a thousand years later in Constantinople.

Along with the flames, smoke and a sulfurous stench that burned Annja's eyes filled the workshop. Pools of fire formed on the spinning lower floor, ripping the shadows away and chasing men back. Garin and Roux were running, forced to abandon their last defensive position because of the stream of fire raining down on it.

Coughing, trying in vain to fill her lungs, Annya pushed herself up and retreated. Bullets spanged off the walls and the railing as her pursuers opened fire. She ran in front of one of the inert pipes and felt a blast of hot air wash over her. Stopping short of the next pipe that poured flaming sulfur over the lower floor, Annja turned to face her attackers, lifting the MP5 in her fist.

The first man made it under the pipe before the fiery sulfur mixture blasted out. Liquid flames splattered out of the pipe and poured down over the four. They screamed in agony as the fire ate into them. They seemed to melt as much as burn, and Annja knew it wasn't just the heat that was killing them. The mixture was caustic.

One of the men dropped to the observation deck clawing at his clothing, but his face was smoldering. As Annja watched, his flesh melted away and revealed his cheekbone, which then charred. Still screaming, his head engulfed now, the man fell face-first onto the tiled floor. His skull smashed apart on impact as if his head had been blown open.

Annja lowered her weapon. The men were dead; she didn't need to fire. Embers burned their flesh in different places, and the fire continued to consume them. It was a horrible way to die.

Glancing down, Annja tried to spot Roux and Garin, but couldn't. Everything was happening too fast. The flickering light, the glow of the strange liquid fire, sudden bursts of gunfire and the twisting shadows all contributed to the confusion.

She turned, preparing to continue down the observation deck, hoping to reach the stairs either by running there or waiting till they came around again.

A large man stepped out of the shadows and drove his rifle butt at her face.

35

Staying low, Melina raced back along the turning observation deck. She hadn't expected that to happen, and still didn't know how the feat had been accomplished. She thought the event was just as surprising to Roux because he'd looked startled in the mixed light of a blue glow stick and the liquid fire pouring down from the pipes thrust through the wall.

"What is going on?" Her grandfather's voice echoed inside her head. Since leaving the water, Melina had donned an earbud and radio hookup that reached the ship waiting out at sea. Some of her men carried cameras that provided video feeds to the ship.

"I don't know yet. The whole workshop has been turned into a trap."

"Have you found Roux?"

"He is still in here with me. We will have him soon." When she reached the railing in front of the stone steps leading down to the workshop floor, Melina vaulted the low railing and landed on the edge of the steps. One of pipes hung over her but hadn't yet started shooting fire. Their retreat was still intact.

But she wasn't leaving till Roux and his companions were dead. Not unless there was no other choice.

She turned to the two men she'd posted to guard the exit. "No one gets through that door but our people."

"Yes, ma'am." The guards hugged the sides of the steps, using them as cover.

Despite the danger inherent in the situation, Melina felt a smile on her lips as she closed in on the last spot she'd seen the two. There was no joy, only a savage hunger to see the old man dead. She lamented the fact that she wouldn't have time to make his death a long, painful one. Halfway to Roux's location, more gears began meshing and the tiled floor vibrated. Crouching, she took shelter behind a clockwork of Cerberus, the three-headed dog that guarded the Underworld in Greek myth.

Where the giant clam had been before one of the grenades had knocked it from its position, a hole opened up in the floor as the tiles irised back. For a moment Melina thought the opening might provide an escape route for Roux and his companions.

Instead, another clockwork rose from the cavity. This one was a man dressed in a toga. The liquid fire oozed across the now-uneven floor and down into the cavity from a half dozen directions and the light revealed that the statue wore a belt of tools at his waist.

Michalis. Seeing the clockwork standing there, Melina felt certain that was the person the thing was supposed to represent.

With imperial hauteur, the clockwork Michalis rotated to face the stairs, then remained locked into position, unmoving as the room spun around him. His right arm came up with an open hand. Then he froze, as if waiting.

She heard a gurgling chug blast from behind her. She turned and watched as the malfunctioning pipe above the stairs suddenly chugged to life. A cascade of liquid fire splashed out across her two guards below.

The burning fire coated both men and leached into their flesh as they turned to look up. Their skin cracked and popped and blackened as it burned, then melted from their bones. They were dead before they hit the ground and the impacts rattled their charred bones across the tiles, separating them like puzzle pieces.

More of the fire spilled across the steps, splitting the stone beneath the metallic tiles. The steps splintered, falling into chunks and leaving no retreat back up to the observation deck.

For a moment, Melina stared at the carnage, realizing she was trapped as death poured in. Then she recalled Roux. The old man would die before she did. She left Cerberus behind and headed forward.

THE MAN MOVED so quickly, was there so unexpectedly, that Annja barely had time to get a hand up to block the blow from the rifle butt. If it had connected, it would have broken her nose, her cheek or maybe an eye orbital or her temple. She would have been dazed or dead.

Her right forearm caught the rifle butt just enough to take some of the brunt. Her hand went numb for an instant and the MP5 slipped from her fingers. The impact drove her backward over the observation deck railing. Leaning out over the fiery floor below, feeling the heat almost hot enough to scorch, her feet no longer on the floor, Annja caught the railing with her left hand and hung on.

Towering above her, eager to press his advantage, the brute drew back the rifle again.

Annja reached into the otherwhere, clasped the hilt of her sword and brought it out. The blade caught the descending rifle, and she parried it to one side. Holding on to the railing with one hand and keeping her shoulders against it, Annja swung her legs up and wrapped her ankles around the man's neck as he drew back the rifle once more. Locking her feet behind his head, taking advantage of the fact that he was still using his weight to trap her in place, she yanked and twisted.

With no choice but to have his neck snapped or follow his head, the man stumbled, hit the low railing as Annja continued to pull on him and plummeted over the side. He screamed and flailed as he fell.

Unable to stop her own momentum, Annja rolled over the railing. She twisted, her back to the stairs, but she held on with her left hand. Below, her opponent sailed face-first into the pool of liquid fire. His screams came to a sudden stop.

When she hit the end of her arm, Annja felt like her shoulder had been pulled out of its socket. She held on through the pain, released the sword and watched it vanish, then reached up over her head to catch the railing with her right hand. Concentrating, she pulled and rolled herself back over the railing. She dropped to a knee because her head spun from the pain and the sudden movement, and bullets ricocheted from the spinning wall behind her.

Three men raced toward her, stepping awkwardly as they struggled to remain agile on the spinning observation deck.

Bullets beat a tattoo against the metal beneath their feet, then she saw Garin correct his aim from below and fire. One of the armed men spun away, caught by the flurry of rounds that sparked against the metallic walls.

The other two men pulled up short and turned their weapons toward Garin, discounting Annja because she was unarmed. They opened fire and Garin leaped from his cover behind the chariot to a clockwork horse.

Getting to her feet, ignoring the pain in her left shoulder, Annja drew her sword and charged the two men. Garin didn't stand a chance where he was. The man closest to her saw her bearing down and tried to wheel around. He fired a spray of bullets that burned the side of Annja's face. Then she brought the sword down, cleaving the man from his left shoulder to the middle of his chest.

Not breaking stride, she pushed the dead man into his companion, knocking him off balance. She stopped, kicked the dead man in the chest to force him back again and free her blade and stepped forward. As the surviving man took aim, she stepped to the side so that his bullets missed her, and spun, delivering a backhand horizontal sword swipe that took his head off. There was no time for regrets. It had to be done.

Staring out over the workshop floor, Annja took stock of how bad the situation had become. The liquid fire nearly covered the floor. Only islands of the metallic tiles remained, and those were buckling as the stone foundation beneath them began cracking from the heat.

She looked toward the entrance and saw that the stone steps leading up to the exit lay shattered and scattered in the liquid fire. Only a pile of rock half the distance to the observation deck remained. And that pile was useless because now it was in motion, as well.

Then she spotted the clockwork Michalis standing where the old inventor's body had been left in the giant clam. She saw the hand thrust out in front of him.

There, in the master's workshop, the shade of Michalis guards his creations. If you disturb the master, death will come to any who trespass and do not come in peace.

Only a few short paces away, a clockwork olive tree stood glistening in the rising heat.

Taking cover behind a Greek sailing vessel miniature, Roux exchanged shots with a gunman sheltering behind a Cyclops holding a club. The gunman didn't see the liquid fire sliding in behind him, didn't know it was there until it burned into his feet. When he tried to run from the new menace, Roux shot him and his corpse fell back into the creeping fire and was swiftly consumed.

"Roux!" Annja shouted above the noise of the conflagration and sporadic gun battles.

Reloading, Roux looked up at her.

Annja pointed at the statue of Michalis. "'Death will come to any who trespass and do not come in peace!' The olive tree. Use the—"

Bullets suddenly spanged off the railing and ricocheted off the wall behind Annja. She dove for cover, spotting Melina Andrianou closing in on Roux.

MELINA CURSED HER impulsiveness. She'd spoiled her shot at Annja Creed. The woman had been perfectly framed in the hellish light from the liquid fire that now filled the chamber. Melina reloaded her weapon as she stood behind what she believed was a model of the Parthenon. She didn't know what Annja Creed had been yelling, but the old man obviously figured it out.

Roux sprinted from the ship to the olive tree and shouted at his companion, "Garin!"

Swinging around the Parthenon, Melina steadied her weapon, then had to duck back as bullets from Garin Braden's machine pistol chopped into the building's columns, tearing some of them out and driving her farther into hiding.

Making her way back to the other end of the Parthenon, Melina felt the heat from the nearby trickle of liquid fire that was thickening even as she spotted it.

Roux grabbed branches on the clockwork olive tree and finally succeeded in pulling one off. He sprinted back toward the clockwork Michalis with the branch in hand.

Melina fired a short burst at the old man, but he dodged and weaved behind other clockworks, then Garin fired at her again, driving her back. Guessing what Roux planned to do, Melina popped out again, aiming this time at the clockwork Michalis's right hand and arm.

Her bullets hammered into the clockwork's limb and tore it away, scattering gears and pieces all around it, leaving a truncated frame at the shoulder. Her weapon cycled dry and she ducked back down as Garin targeted her again. She swapped out magazines as more bullets chopped into the Parthenon. The heat of the approaching liquid fire baked into her sweating face, but she didn't care.

You can't offer a laurel branch to a clockwork Michalis when he's got no limbs, old man. We're all going to die down here.

DESPAIR TORE THROUGH Annja as she surveyed the broken Michalis. She didn't know what would have happened if Roux had succeeded in placing the olive branch in the clockwork's hand, whether it would have stopped the destruction or merely opened an escape route. Now there was no way she'd ever know.

And Roux and Garin were trapped down there, waiting to die by liquid fire if Melina and her hired killers didn't get them first.

Annja shifted her gaze to the entrance coming up again. A door had locked down into place there. She hadn't seen it before because of the shadows, but she saw it now.

Releasing her sword, watching as the doorway cycled toward her, Annja stepped off onto the stone ledge in front of the metallic barrier. Bullets chopped into the stone wall beside her as she tried to examine the door. She hunkered down, studying it, then spotted the bull's head keyhole.

There's a way out. The knowledge gave her hope.

Taking the pack from her weight belt, she dug through the contents but couldn't find the key. Then she remembered that Roux had used it last when he'd opened the box that had contained the clockwork spider.

No!

In the middle of the extra magazines for the MP5 she no longer had, she found a block of C-4. The plastic explosive had the same overall shape as one of the extra magazines. It also had a half dozen timers already affixed to it.

Turning back to the metallic door, Annja pushed the plastic explosive into place along the bottom of it. Maybe Michalis had planned for rams and pry bars and maybe even sapper teams that would dig under the door, but he'd never seen anything like C-4.

Since there were six timers along the plastic explosive's length, Annja judged that the amount was considerable. Obviously Garin's men had intended to cut off chunks and use them as needed. She decided to use it all because there wouldn't be time to use it again later, and if she tried to parse it out, she might not have any effect on the stone and the door.

She pushed that thought out of her mind and set the timer for four seconds, to give her enough time to get away. After activating the timer, she stepped back onto the revolving observation deck and sprinted along it as bullets traced the stone wall and metal floor.

The explosion filled the cavern with thunder and a cloud of smoke that rolled out over the workshop floor like a massive wall of gray-white fog limned in gold by the liquid fire. Vibrations ran through the spinning observation deck, making it wobble and grate against the channels. It slowed and finally ground to a halt.

Reversing directions, Annja ran back toward the door, feeling the observation deck shiver beneath her. When she saw the door still in place, she wanted to yell her frustration. Only thoughts of Roux and Garin dying in the next few minutes prevented that.

Then she spotted the pile of rocks that had fallen from where the ledge had been. The door might not have been blown away, but it had been bowed upward and the stone beneath it had been blasted away.

There was a chance.

Not giving herself much time to think, Annja leaped for the broken area under the door. She knew that if she missed, she'd drop down to the stones below, but not have enough reach to scramble back up.

She slammed into the stone wall but couldn't find purchase. Sliding, she dug her toes into the side, stretched to feel a ledge above her, then leaped again.

36

Her fingers of one hand caught the ledge. She grabbed hold with her other hand, dug in with her joggers and leveraged herself up. There was enough room under the door to allow even Garin to pass.

Lying on her stomach, her head and shoulders thrust under the door, Annja yelled for Roux and Garin. "Over here!" Enough bare areas and rocks and clockwork remained that she thought they could make it. She waved to make sure they had seen her, but that attracted an instant hail of bullets.

Garin stood and shot the man who had fired at her, then turned and sprinted after Roux, who displayed the grace and speed of a mountain goat as he scrambled across the littered path.

Jamming her body against the door and using her left arm to brace herself, Annja reached her right arm down and hoped that Roux could make the leap when he reached the rocks.

He leaped, their fingertips brushed and he fell back down. Behind him, Garin caught Roux around the waist and hoisted him up. Annja grabbed his hand and pulled, yanking him up onto the ledge with her. Then she turned back to Garin and hoped she was strong enough to lift him.

He leaped and wrapped his large hand around her wrist.

He was solid, heavy, and the position was awkward. Annja's whole body shook with the effort of lifting him, and she saw bullets peppering the walls and pile of stones around him.

Then he was high enough to grab the ledge with his other hand and hold his own weight. Roux reached down and caught Garin under an arm and hauled. A few seconds later, Garin lay sprawled on the stone floor.

Annja forced herself up. "Get moving. Melina and her people are going to be after us."

Garin reloaded his MP5 and grinned. "You can go ahead. I'll stay here and make certain they don't get out."

A tremor shuddered through the island. Rock split off from the ceiling and tumbled around them. A few of the larger chunks thudded into Annja like hammer blows.

Roux balanced himself against the wall. "Apparently Michalis didn't just booby-trap his workshop. That liquid gushing into the cavern is feeding into something explosive through that hole in the floor."

The cavern shivered again, more explosively this time. Freed from its hidden hinges, the metallic door dropped with a hollow sound onto the rocks and fire below. A second later, a grenade slammed into the stone wall just a few feet from the ledge. Most of the explosion remained in the cavern, but some of the concussive blast washed over Annja, Roux and Garin.

Garin cursed as he fell back from the entrance. "I forgot they had those. Staying here isn't an option."

Annja led the way back to the ledge where they'd left their dive gear. Hurriedly, she pulled her tanks and swim fins and scuba helmet on, keeping an eye on the doorway in the wall, which had split. Once the regulator was switched on and air flooded her face mask, she headed toward the water.

The cavern rolled once more and she felt the power of the earthquake getting stronger. She tried not to think of everything that was being lost and concentrated instead on surviving. When she reached the water, she dove in and started swimming back the way they had come.

It wasn't until she was in the underwater passageway that she remembered the spikes that had shot out of the walls. She hoped that none of them blocked their way.

Or sprung free while they were swimming.

"COME ON. THEY'RE getting away." Melina waved on the five surviving members of her assault team. Her men were already in motion, streaking for the entrance because their lives depended on it.

The liquid fire covered the floor now and showed no indications of slowing down. Islands of rock, debris and clockwork provided an archipelago to safety. As she ran, the man in front of her slipped and fell from one of the overturned clockworks into the molten mixture. He died without a sound and melted into the fire as his clothing and hair caught on fire.

Choosing another path, Melina tried to estimate how far ahead Roux had gotten. His lead couldn't be much. She redoubled her efforts to catch him, sprinting up the metallic door canted at an angle to the ledge above, and throwing herself at it.

Her fingers clawed the ledge and she pulled herself up and over, not waiting to see if anyone behind her needed help. She ran through the passageway, bouncing off the sides as the island shook and thunder cannonaded around her.

She found where she'd done her best to hide the gear, pulling on air tanks, swim fins and scuba helmet quickly. Thank God the ones ahead hadn't had time to find and sabotage it. Then she picked up one of the APS underwater rifles, checked the magazine and dove into the water. With the rifle thrust before her, she swam hard, pushing herself, picturing how Roux's blood would look when she released it into the water.

ANOTHER QUAKE SHOOK the island, causing even the water in the passageway to vibrate. Annja slammed into one of the walls, halfway expected the spikes to spring free at that moment, then let out a breath when that didn't happen. She kicked her fins again, feeling her way through the darkness by trailing her right hand along the stone wall.

Keep the wall to your right. Just keep it to the right and you won't get turned around.

None of them had one of the underwater lamps they'd used the first time through. The thought had never crossed her mind and she regretted it now. That was going on the survival list: *If you carry a light to get where you're going, you have to carry one to get back out.*

Controlling her anxiety, Annja kept kicking her feet, concentrating on keeping her head clear of the wall. She didn't look back for Roux and Garin. She wouldn't have been able to see them, anyway.

A short distance ahead, she spotted the blue shimmer of the opening to the sea. She kicked harder, aiming for that tranquil blue, bursting through just in time to see the great white shark glide through and tear at one of the corpses hanging in the water at zero buoyancy. She backpedaled, staying near the opening, as the large predator took both legs off the dead man.

"MELINA! MELINA!" GEORGIOS Andrianou stared into the lagoon and held the radio handset tightly, willing his granddaughter to answer.

Black smoke rose from the center of the island and pooled against the low clouds. In several places, the island buckled and cracked open, leaving gaping craters in the forest and grasslands, as well as the beach.

Georgios had no idea what was happening. He'd lost radio contact, and he couldn't help but wonder if he'd lost Melina, too. More than that, though, he'd lost the opportunity to discover the power that had allowed the man Roux to hold back the years and live for so long. For the first time in a long time, Georgios Andrianou felt death dogging his heels.

He turned to Captain Skarvelis. "Put out the lifeboats. I will see my granddaughter rescued." And if she had the secret of the clockworks, Georgios would take that, as well.

"Sir." The captain stared at him. "We sank that other vessel, but she still has crew in the water. If you divide our crew, we're going to be shorthanded at both ends of the operation."

Georgios had heard the sporadic gunfire coming from *Kestrel*'s survivors. Skarvelis had moved *Titan* away from the encounter site and his men had used the heavy machine guns to dissuade pursuit. However, the lifeboats had proven surprisingly well equipped with machine guns and rocket launchers. Evidently Garin Braden was a man who believed in firepower.

"I gave you an order, Captain." Georgios drew his sidearm and pointed it at Skarvelis. "Get those boats in the water now."

Skarvelis closed his eyes. Sweat trickled down his brow. "Yes, sir." He gave the orders.

"I'm going with the rescue effort." Georgios holstered his weapon. "If you think about leaving while I'm not aboard, you cannot run far enough or fast enough to get away from me."

Skarvelis nodded, but he didn't look at Georgios.

Striding out of the wheelhouse, Georgios went to join the rescue effort. It couldn't be too late. Such an opportunity to find what his family had been looking for all these years couldn't just trickle through his fingers. He wouldn't allow it.

When Roux swam out of the opening, Annja grabbed his arm and pulled him to the side. She pointed up where the great white glided through the water with the dead man's legs clenched in that slash of a mouth.

"Shark."

"I see that." Roux caught Garin as he swam out of the passageway. In the distance, the great white rolled over and headed back in their direction.

Annja flattened herself against the wall and summoned her sword. Using it to slash was out of the question underwater, but it could still be used to thrust. And she felt more confident with the blade in her hand.

The shark was fifty feet or so from them and closing when Melina Andrianou arrived. Holding the rifle at the ready, she looked at them, then looked at the shark. Thirty feet away, she turned toward them and took aim. The shots sounded strange underwater, but there was no mistaking the effect.

A half dozen steel darts tore through the reef, knocking pieces loose, and embedded in the stone around them. Two of them pierced Garin's left leg. He howled in pain. Threads of blood streamed up from the wounds.

Sharks can smell a drop of blood in the water for two point five miles. In a sports bar on trivia night, that was a fun fact to know. Now it wasn't so fun. Annja moved her gaze from Melina Andrianou to the great white. The shark was the deadliest thing in the water at the moment.

Instantly, and despite the dead man's blood already clouding the water, the shark changed its course and headed for Garin. He pulled his dive knife and set himself, as if the shark didn't outweigh him by nearly two thousand pounds.

Annja pushed off the stone wall with the sword extended before her, following the blade through the water. The shark altered its course and came for her.

If you turn, you're dead. It will take you apart.

Staying behind the sword didn't seem advantageous, either, but Annja had no intentions of remaining helpless against the wall while it came back for her. Or feasted on Garin. Neither was acceptable.

Not fearing a creature less than half its size, the shark stayed on course. It was incredibly fast. At the last moment, Annja flicked the point of her sword, angling the blade so it sank into the shark's eye. Unbelievably, the shark kept coming, taking the sword up to the hilt. It shook its head, trying to bite Annja, but she used the sword as an anchor point to pull herself out of the way, avoiding the serrated teeth by inches.

She pulled herself against the shark as it kept swimming, hanging on because she was afraid that if she let go in the open water, the shark would turn on her and have her before she could escape. Holding on to the sword hilt with both hands, she threw a leg over the shark and felt the dorsal fin slide up against her calf. She used her leg for leverage and reversed her grip on the sword, turning her hands over one at a time.

Out of the corner of her eye, she spotted Garin kicking toward her as the shark swam in a circle to get rid of its unwanted rider. Garin caught hold of the right fin and angled his dive knife toward the top of the shark's head. He drove the knife deeply into the shark's brain at the same time Annja tore the sword along the great white's body.

The shark wasn't disemboweled, but it was turned nearly inside out from the massive wound, and it was dead meat floating in seconds. A massive cloud of blood surrounded Annja, Garin and the shark.

Annja tugged her sword free and looked back at Roux. He was on one knee in front of the passageway leading to Michalis's workshop. His other hand was raised as he stared at Melina Andrianou floating in the passageway.

Without a word, Roux engaged the trap. Almost immediately, the spikes shot out of the walls and pierced the woman's body. Behind her, the men who had survived the liquid fire in the cavern trap were also transfixed.

The weapon slowly dropped from Melina's hands as her blood filled the water.

Garin swam in front of Annja and looked at her wide-eyed. "Attacking a great white shark? That has to be the stupidest thing I've ever seen in my life."

Roux snorted. "I thought both of you were out of your minds." He glanced at the dead shark. "But it appears you succeeded."

Annja checked her watch. "We're almost out of air. We've got to go up."

Cursing, Garin pulled the metal darts out of his leg. Then he jerked a thumb upward. "We go slow and take a look around. If Melina and her people were here, you can bet her grandfather won't be far behind."

Together, they swam for the surface.

THE SHADOW OF a powerboat glided over the ocean above Annja when she was still twenty feet under. She angled for it, matching its speed easily because it was barely moving across the lagoon. A moment later, she popped up beside the boat and grabbed on to the side.

A man grabbed her wrist and brought his rifle around. He wasn't one of Garin's people.

Summoning the sword again, Annja ran the man through and let him fall, letting go of the sword and calling it back to her instantly. It didn't do much good, though, because the four other men aboard the rigid hull craft turned their weapons on her. She was just about to throw herself back in the water when Georgios Andrianou held up a hand and shouted, "Stop! Do not shoot her!"

The men held their fire, but they didn't like it.

Annja still thought she had a chance if she ducked behind the boat and swam as deep as she could as quickly as she could. She was holding her position when Garin squeezed her leg reassuringly as he swam under the boat.

Georgios pierced her with his gaze. "Where is my granddaughter? Where is Melina?"

"Down there." Annja held the sword out of sight, not knowing if anyone had seen how she'd killed the first man.

The island rumbled around them, slowly but surely disappearing beneath the waves. Black smoke hovered over the area, muting some of the sunlight.

"Where is the old man?"

Before Annja could answer that, Garin grabbed hold of the other side of the boat, announcing his presence. The mercenaries turned to face him, swinging their weapons. But it was too late. Garin had the big .500 Magnum in his fist and fired so quickly that the four shots sounded almost like one thunderous clap.

The heavy bullets knocked the men backward, dead almost instantly.

Georgios Andrianou held up his hands. "I surrender."

Garin held the massive revolver trained on the man. "I seem to be missing a ship. I trust you're to blame for that."

There was no response.

"Tell me, did you offer the men on that ship the chance to surrender?"

Georgios's lips tightened and he made no reply.

"And you turned your granddaughter into a killer."

"My granddaughter was a very brave woman."

"She tortured Roux for days."

"She did what she needed to do."

Garin nodded. Cold anger stirred in his black eyes. "I suppose, in the end, we all do."

"Garin," Annja said softly. "He's surrendered. There's no need to—"

The big Magnum roared and spat fire. The bullet caught Georgios in the face and reduced his head to scraps of flesh and splinters of bone. He toppled over into the Aegean Sea.

"There was a need." Garin shook the empty brass out of his pistol. He reloaded the weapon, then held the boat steady as Roux and Annja climbed aboard. Then he heaved himself aboard, as well. "Now let's see about getting a ride home."

Roux took the controls, bringing the boat around and powering it back toward the salvage ship.

They could hear gunshots out on the ship beyond the lagoon. Three lifeboats rode in the water next to *Titan,* and it was obvious that the survivors of *Kestrel* were boarding the ship and working their way through the enemy crew.

"It doesn't look as if we need to hurry," Roux observed. "Seems as if your people will have things well in hand by the time we get to them."

Annja was just as happy with that. She'd had enough bloodshed today. The sword vanished from her hand while

Garin was securing weapons and making sure they were loaded.

More explosions rolled over them from the island. As Annja watched, the tallest peaks of Michalis's island slid below the waves.

epilogue

Sitting under a festive umbrella at a small table outside a bar along the coast of Lesbos, Annja had to agree with Professor Thodoros Papassavas's assessment of the island. It was paradise. The beach was cool to the point that she needed a loose shirt over the yellow-and-orange bikini she wore. The wide-brimmed straw hat shaded her from the bright sun, and the big sunglasses allowed her to watch the fishing and tourist boats out in the harbor. A short distance away, a volleyball game was under way between college-age men and women.

Annja's tablet PC lay at her elbow, next to the sweating glass that held only the icy skeleton of the drink she'd had.

"Do you mind company? Or would you prefer to be alone?"

Glancing over, Annja saw Roux standing beside her in a Hawaiian shirt over a white tee, cargo shorts and sandals…with black socks that came up to midcalf. A straw hat hung over his back and wraparound sunglasses covered his eyes. He carried a drink in one hand.

"Company would be appreciated."

Roux nodded and sat across from her so he could also watch the sea.

Annja grinned at his drink. "If there was any more fruit in that, I think it would qualify as a salad."

Studying it, Roux smiled. "Perhaps, but it is a very *potent* salad." He sipped. "You've been busy the past two days."

"I've been calling everyone I can to raise interest in a salvage operation of the island."

"I take it from your expression you haven't met much success."

"Not yet, but I haven't given up."

"You realize not much may have survived, don't you? Michalis seems to have been adamant about that."

"I'd still like to see."

A young female server came by and Roux flagged her down, pointing to Annja's glass. Annja didn't protest.

"In fact, I was just thinking about calling my producer and telling him there's a legend of a ghostly minotaur haunting the island ruins."

He snorted.

"All I have to do is tweet a few times. By the time something gets picked up on the internet, it's the truth. Once it goes viral, it becomes legend."

Roux shook his head. "After all the years I've lived, I'm still amazed at the ways civilizations find to lie to themselves. I truly thought Orson Wells's October 1938 broadcast of *The War of the Worlds* would have taught people not to believe anything media put out there. And Richard Nixon and Bill Clinton should have taught them that leaders tell the biggest lies." He put up his hands in twin peace signs. "I cannot tell a lie."

"Nixon never said that. He said, 'I am not a crook.'"

"I know, and Bogie never said, 'Play it again, Sam.' He said, 'Play it, Sam. You played it for her, you can play it for me.' Wonderful film." Roux sighed. "People are so much better at creating fiction than they are at preserving the truth."

Annja laughed, then thanked the server for her refill. "Papassavas translated the scroll I brought out of the island."

"Oh?" Roux didn't really sound interested, but Annja didn't have anyone else to tell. Actually, she had told Doug Morrell that morning. Doug had been polite, then asked her when she planned on getting back to work. They were going to need material for *Chasing History's Monsters* soon. Especially after the witch fiasco.

"It was a warning to anyone who found Michalis to not take the spider crystal for granted, that it was the most dangerous thing he'd ever made."

"At least he knew that. Most of them don't." Roux adjusted his hat, then sipped at his drink.

"'Most of them'?"

"The people like Michalis who play with unfettered darkness."

"Are you ever going to explain what that is?"

Roux didn't answer. Instead, he said, "Joan's sword doesn't make you invincible, you know."

She did know that. Still, she wouldn't turn away from people who needed her help or things that made her curious. That just wasn't her way.

"Where is Garin?"

"Still asleep, it seems. Or maybe he found someone to spend the night with. He was hitting the bars when I saw him last."

The idea of Garin hooking up with someone bothered Annja, and then it bothered her even more that she was bothered.

Roux looked at her. "Isn't this your first time to the island?"

"Yes."

"Then why don't we go for a walk? We should make

some good memories while you are here." Roux sounded wistful. "In its day, Lesbos was said to be a wonderful place. Come with me and let me show you where Sappho and Alcaeus were purported to write their marvelous poetry." He held up his drink. "If we find more of these along the way, I may even be persuaded to recite some of it for you."

Annja didn't hesitate. She'd had nightmares about Michalis's workshop and the great white shark for two days. She put her tablet PC in her beach bag and stood.

Smiling, Roux got to his feet and looked out at the sea. Then he turned and began walking, sandals crunching in the sand.

Annja quickly caught up to him and linked her arm through his. Then Roux began to talk, telling her stories of heroes and heroines, of gods and goddesses, and willingly she let him sweep her away.

* * * * *

JAMES AXLER

DEATH LANDS®

Dark Fathoms

Between the devil and the deep blue sea...

Miles beneath the ocean's surface, a decaying redoubt barely protects Ryan and his companions from a watery death. Battling cyborgs programmed by artificial intelligence to kill them, they're desperate to escape. But above the waves a new threat awaits: a massive predark supership banished to the seas of Deathlands. Decades of madness have led to civil war between the citizens of the upper and lower decks. Now pawns in a bloody game, Ryan and the other survivors must destroy the ship or face their certain end at sea.

Available in September wherever books are sold.

GOLD EAGLE®

TAKE 'EM FREE
2 action-packed novels plus a mystery bonus

NO RISK
NO OBLIGATION TO BUY

James Axler
Outlanders®

COSMIC RIFT

Dominate and Avenge

Untapped riches are being mined on Earth—a treasure trove of alien superscience strewn across the planet. High above, hidden in a quantum rift, the scavenger citizens of Authentiville have built a paradise from the trawled detritus of the God wars. A coup is poised to dethrone Authentiville's benevolent ruler and doom Earth, once again, to an epic battle against impossible odds. Cerberus must rally against a twisted—but quite human—new enemy who has mastered the secrets of inhuman power....

Available in November wherever books are sold.